B.J. DANIELS

NEW YORK TIMES
BESTSELLING AUTHOR

HONOR BOUND

HQN™

HQN™

ISBN-13: 978-0-373-78932-0

Honor Bound

Copyright © 2016 by Barbara Heinlein

Recycling programs
for this product may
not exist in your area.

This edition published by arrangement with Harlequin Books S.A.

For questions and comments about the quality of this book,
please contact us at CustomerService@Harlequin.com.

® and TM are trademarks of Harlequin Enterprises Limited or its
corporate affiliates. Trademarks indicated with ® are registered in the
United States Patent and Trademark Office, the Canadian Intellectual
Property Office and in other countries.

www.HQNBooks.com

Printed in U.S.A.

With utmost appreciation I dedicate this last book
in the series to my agent, Lisa Erbach Vance.
Thank you so much for taking this journey with me.

CHAPTER ONE

Election night

IT WAS THE old priest's limp that caught Ainsley Hamilton's attention as the presidential election results were announced over the loudspeaker. A deafening roar rose from the bundled-up crowd gathered at the fairgrounds outside Beartooth, Montana, that cold November night.

Her father, Buckmaster Hamilton, had just been announced the new president. Music began to play loudly as the throng cheered. She watched the priest, hunched over his cane, edging ever closer to the platform where her father would be giving his acceptance speech. Ice crystals danced in the night air against the backdrop of the Crazy Mountains. Millions of stars twinkled in the velvet blue of Montana's big sky overhead. There was an excitement in the air as well, an electricity that had her feeling warm inside.

Ainsley's heart surged. She was so proud of her father, so happy for him. This was his night. He'd worked hard to get here. She told herself that nothing could spoil it for him, especially her sister Kat's concerns about security. The fairgrounds were crawling with Secret Service agents, sheriff's department deputies and National Guard; even the sheriff himself was here.

Her gaze went again to the priest as he limped forward. The crowd parted for him, seeing his physical disabilities as well as his determination to get closer. When he finally reached the elevated platform where she was standing with her family, he leaned heavily on the cane as if trying to catch his breath. Like her, he must have wanted to be part of this history-making night.

Another roar erupted from those gathered as her father strode out onto the stage. He smiled and nodded, then turned to motion to his wife and six daughters. They had been waiting in the wings out of the cold for this moment. Ainsley looked at her sisters.

Bo smiled at her, so pregnant with her twins that she appeared to be wearing a small tent. The grown twins, Harper and Cassidy, were holding hands, both crying. Olivia was dabbing at her eyes, as well. It was clear that they had all been moved to tears, all except sister Kat, who looked nervous as their mother led the way across the stretch of red carpet to her waiting husband.

Out of the corner of her eye, Ainsley noticed that the old priest was straining to see. His limp looked painful, she thought as she saw him clutch his cane with both hands. She knew her interest in him was because of his limp. It reminded her of another man, a man she'd trusted her heart to recently only to have it broken.

As if she needed a limp to remind her of Sawyer Nash and what a fool she'd been. Thoughts of him were never more than a heartbeat away. Unconsciously, she ran a fingertip over the burn scar on her wrist, another reminder of Sawyer.

The crowd was roaring again as Sarah joined her husband, followed by one daughter after another. Ainsley fell back, letting her sisters go ahead of her. Too many emotions had her feeling vulnerable. She wasn't ready to face all of these people right now.

As Kat started down the carpet to join their father, Ainsley had no choice but to join them. She took a deep breath, reminding herself that this night was for her father, the first Montanan to be elected president. The excitement of the crowd filled her heart to bursting.

Standing on the platform next to her family, she smiled at her father through her tears. Her pride in him closed her throat as she tried not to cry with this many people watching.

Fortunately, the cameras—just like the Secret Service agents—were trained on the future president as he hugged each of them and then stepped to the microphone to make his acceptance speech. She and her five sisters and mother moved back toward the warm room again as he took his place to the applause of the massive crowd.

Buckmaster Hamilton had won by a landslide, and no one within four hundred miles wanted to miss this, even on such a cold night.

Ainsley had been making her way back, willing herself not to cry, when the priest looked up and their eyes met. Recognition made her stumble. She would have fallen if her mother hadn't caught her arm.

But Ainsley hardly noticed. She was staring down into the priest's face. He wasn't as old as he had seemed when she'd first spotted him moving through the crowd, leaning so heavily on his cane. Even more shocking was that she *knew* him. A childhood memory surfaced in a wave of guilt because of the promise she'd been forced to keep all those years ago.

The man had been younger back then, but so had her mother. From her bedroom window, she'd watched the two of them out by the stables.

Ainsley, barely twelve, had seen at once that there was something wrong as the man had approached her mother. Her mother had taken a step back. Suddenly the man had grabbed her mother's arm. Her mother had been struggling to get free of him. Ainsley hadn't been able to hear them, but she could tell that they were arguing.

She'd rushed down the stairs and ran out to the cool shadows of the stables where they were standing. The man had seen her and quickly let go of her mother's arm. She'd been close enough that she heard what he said to her mother.

"This isn't over, Sarah." Then he'd disappeared

around the back of the building, but not before his gaze had bored into Ainsley. She'd known she would never forget those eyes. An electric blue that felt as if they had branded her.

"Who was that?" she'd demanded of her mother, recalling how he'd said her mother's first name.

"No one." Her mother had quickly wiped her eyes. "A stable hand. I had to fire him."

"He hurt you!" Ainsley had cried, seeing where the man's fingers had bit into her mother's arm.

"I'm fine," she'd said, pulling down her sleeve to hide it before she'd taken Ainsley's shoulders in her trembling hands. "You can't tell anyone about this, your sisters, especially your father. It will only upset him. I've taken care of it. The man won't be back. Do you hear me? Promise you won't ever tell."

"But he said—"

"Please."

It was the word *please* coming out almost as a sob that had made Ainsley make a promise she'd guiltily kept all these years. Weeks later her mother would drive her SUV into the Yellowstone River and be presumed dead when her body wasn't recovered from the iced-over river. For twenty-two years her mother would be dead—until recently when she'd returned from the grave with no memory of where she'd been.

Now those electric-blue eyes from her childhood burned into hers for one startling instant before they shifted to where her mother was standing next to her after steadying Ainsley when she'd stumbled.

It happened in a split second. But felt like slow motion. The man's hands twisted the top off the cane. Even when he raised what looked like a toy plastic pistol, she knew it was as real as her memory. Even as her mind argued that he would have had to go through security to get in here tonight, she knew he'd somehow avoided detection. Just as she knew he'd come here not to kill the new president—but the woman he'd argued with all those years ago.

As he raised the weapon, pointing it at her mother, Ainsley cried out. But her voice was lost in the roar of the crowd. All eyes, including those of the Secret Service agents, were on the president, not the old priest.

Ainsley didn't remember pushing her mother aside to launch herself at the man holding the gun. She didn't hear the weapon discharge. She hadn't even been sure he'd fired until she felt the burning heat an instant before she crashed into him, taking them both down. She hit hard, heard screams around her and a struggle.

The cold November night and the canopy of stars seemed to move in and out. Her chest burned while the rest of her felt as if she were freezing. Sounds were indistinguishable. Above her she caught glimpses of faces. They seemed to sway in the breeze.

Arms came around her, and a male voice was saying, "She's hit. Get an ambulance! Hurry! Ainsley, can you hear me? Stay with me, sweetheart."

"Sawyer?" She blinked, thinking she must be hal-

lucinating or dying, because then she heard Kitzie's voice. "Sawyer! You'd better see this!"

Fading in and out, Ainsley heard the commotion around her as she was lifted into strong arms. She fought to bring the man's face into focus, but the darkness closed in, and she dropped into it.

CHAPTER TWO

Days before

"HEY, COWBOY, I heard about that stunt you pulled. Chasing a killer on the top of a moving train? Who do you think you are? A modern-day John Wayne?"

Sawyer Nash chuckled into the phone, unconsciously rubbing his injured leg. "The chasing part wasn't bad. It was the getting shot and falling off the train that bruised my ego."

"Sounds like it bruised a lot more than that." Sheriff Frank Curry grew solemn on the other end of the telephone line. "Seriously, how are you?"

"Bored. The doc says I can't go back to work for a few months. They tried to saddle me with an office job, but you know me."

"I do. You like to be where the action is."

"Same could be said about you, Frank. How are you doing?"

A long silence filled the line, making Sawyer sit up straighter.

"I'm thinking about retiring after the election," the sheriff said.

"*Really?* Have anything to do with who gets elected?"

"Not exactly. But that's why I wanted to talk to you. As you know, our local rancher and senator, Buckmaster Hamilton, is the Republican candidate for president."

"If this is about canvassing for his vote, he's got it."

Frank laughed. "No, it's about his daughters. Well, one daughter in particular."

"Oh?"

"I hear she's in your part of the state. Her name is Ainsley Hamilton. She's the oldest of the senator's daughters. The other five are living around here now. Bottom line—I'm worried about her. Apparently there's been some man following her off and on for months now."

"A reporter?"

"I don't think so. She was home for a visit recently and happened to mention it. She thought maybe her father had hired him to keep an eye on her. Buckmaster swears he didn't, and I believe him. It just seems…odd."

"You think it has something to do with her father's run for president?"

"Seems likely."

"She get a good look at this guy?"

"Apparently not. He wears a cowboy hat, keeps his distance, but according to her, he's followed her from town to town."

"What does this Hamilton daughter do that takes her from town to town?" Sawyer asked.

"She's working as a scout for movie and television commercial locations in the state. I realize you're not a hundred percent—"

"More like seventy-five to eighty."

"So you wouldn't be up to seeing if you could find out what's going on?" Frank asked.

"As bored as I am? Are you kidding? Anyway, it sounds pretty cut-and-dried. I can check it out. If he's tailing her, he shouldn't be hard to spot. I could have a little talk with him."

"I'll email you everything you need to know to get started. Just send me the bill," the sheriff said.

"Not a chance. I owe you. You're the one who got me into law enforcement to begin with."

"And look how that turned out."

AINSLEY HAMILTON REINED in her horse to look back toward the mouth of the narrow canyon. Shielding her eyes from the glaring sun, she glanced past the walls of rock to the dark pine trees at the entrance.

The Montana sky was a cloudless blue overhead, the sun hot on her back, but there was a bite in the air reminding her it was almost November. Winter wouldn't be far behind. But fortunately, this was her last contract finding locations for productions. She hadn't even wanted to take this one, but Devon "Gun" Gunderson had made her an offer she'd felt she couldn't refuse. It had been fun for a while, but dealing with directors was getting her down.

Gunderson turned out to be worse than most because he was a perfectionist. He kept changing locations so it was no surprise that the commercial had run over schedule. She'd never imagined it would take this long to shoot. She'd already been here for two days, and as far as she could tell, she would be here another two or three days, maybe longer.

The canyon ahead of her would make a beautiful spot to shoot one of the last scenes before the commercial for a pharmaceutical drug company wrapped. But she wasn't sure she could convince Gunderson of it. While the others on his crew called him Gun, she couldn't bring herself to because he seemed to like his nickname too much.

At a noise nearby, Ainsley turned. A few moments ago she'd heard what sounded like someone behind her. Listening, she heard only the wind high above the canyon walls. Turning back, she studied the opening in the walls of rock. Nothing moved.

Had she been followed from the old mountain resort? Gunderson had gotten accommodations for them, even though the place had already closed for the season.

But that didn't mean that whoever had been following her for months wasn't behind one of the trees or rocks in this very Western-looking part of the state watching her. She'd sensed someone watching her for so long, that this time she could be only imagining it.

But her instincts told her it wasn't her imagination. Over the months, she'd often sensed the man's presence. As she did now. It gave her an eerie vulnerable feeling she didn't like. If only the man would show himself. She'd gladly confront him. But he was careful never to let her get a good look at him. All she'd gotten were glimpses of a shadowy figure wearing a dark-colored Western hat.

He also was careful never to appear when there were other people around. It was one reason she had mentioned it to only a few people. It made her sound unbalanced, since one moment he was there and the next he was gone as…as if he'd never existed.

It was enough to make a woman think she was losing her mind. Not Ainsley, though. She had too much common sense for that, she told herself and spurred her horse forward.

As she rode deeper in the canyon, she luxuriated in cool shadows that fell across her path. The day was getting warmer. But she knew from being born and raised in Montana that the weather could change in a heartbeat. That was one reason this commercial needed to be completed this week—before a storm blew in and snow began to fall and they all got stranded back in here.

The canyon was as lovely as she'd heard it was. One of the local girls hired to work in the kitchen had suggested it. With the sheer rock walls, a few scrub pines and the spring at the end of the canyon, it looked as Western as any part of Montana. Now all she had to do was talk Gunderson into taking a look.

Ainsley rolled her eyes thinking of the conversation she would have with him when she returned. Ahead, she could see where the box canyon ended in a wall of rock. Only one way out of here. Back the way she'd come.

She led her horse over to the rocks where a warm spring bubbled up. It was beautiful here, perfect. Gunderson would be a fool not to consider it. She groaned at even the thought of having to deal with him today. Just a few more days, she told herself. Then what?

The original company that hired her had another film crew wanting someone to scout locations for some winter scenes, but she'd declined the offer. She had to be home for election night. Her father wanted his family with him. She couldn't help being excited for him. Of course he would win.

Then maybe whoever had been following her from town to town would quit shadowing her every move. At first she'd thought the man had to be a reporter. And yet he'd never tried to talk to her. If only she'd gotten a good look at his face. With a shiver, she reminded herself that he could be anyone, and she wouldn't know it.

"Can you give me any kind of description?" the sheriff had asked after her father had insisted she talk to him.

"That's just it. I can't. If I didn't know better, I'd

think I was imagining him. I'll be somewhere, and I sense him watching me. I turn and catch movement as he drops back out of sight in a group of people or hidden in the darkness. One time I ran after him—"

"That's a bad idea," Frank had said.

Ainsley had laughed. "Tell me about it. I hadn't gotten very far, when I came to my senses. I don't think he's dangerous, though. I almost feel like he thinks he needs to keep an eye on me. I know that sounds crazy."

"No, it doesn't. Have you seen him recently?" the sheriff had asked.

"A few days ago when I was in town, but now I'm staying out in the mountains at this closed resort."

"At least there you should be safe."

But she didn't feel safe, she thought. Especially today when, unless she really was losing her mind, she sensed he had followed her into the canyon.

Her horse's ears went up at the sound of the clatter of rocks underfoot was carried on the wind. She rubbed her horse's neck as she looked back down the canyon. There were too many twists and turns for her to see very far.

"You heard it, too, didn't you?" she whispered to the horse. "I wasn't wrong. We aren't alone, are we?"

Another clatter of rocks echoed through the canyon. Her horse's head came up as the mare let out a whinny.

She'd definitely been followed. But this time, she was ready for him.

NEAR THE END of the mountain road, Sawyer rounded a curve, and the resort came into view. The huge old stone hotel looked abandoned, but behind it, he spotted a scattering of small equally old log cabins set against the mountainside. There were vehicles parked in front of all but one.

He'd stopped in town to get directions to the isolated resort. A woman at the general store had told him that the resort was closed, but some movie types were staying up there shooting commercials.

"At least that's what they said they were doing," she told him suspiciously. "I doubt any of theirs will be airing during the Super Bowl, from what I heard from the locals who got hired." She'd eyed him openly. "You looking for work?"

"I heard the place is for sale," he said noncommittally.

"It is. You thinking about buying it?"

He'd only smiled and thanked her for the directions.

Now, to the right of the hotel he saw a wide meadow where it appeared a carnival had been erected. None of the rides were moving, though, and he didn't see anyone around. The rides had taken on an almost ghostly look out in the meadow so far from civilization. Strange, he thought as he drove on in.

There was only one car parked in front of the hotel. As he pulled up, he saw the license plate read: MURPH. As he got out of his pickup, a nondescript dark-haired man came out of the hotel. He had on a tan uniform shirt that read Security. He eyed Sawyer but said nothing.

Sawyer tipped his Stetson and limped up the stairs to the wide porch. The view of the mountain peaks surrounding the place was incredible. He couldn't help taking in the breathtaking beauty of the area as he opened the huge, weathered wooden front door and stepped inside.

It was cool and dim in the old lobby. At one time, no expense had been spared to maintain this landmark hotel. But that was years ago. Times and tastes had changed. The carpet was as worn as the marble floors. He called out a tentative, "Hello?"

"In here," came a female voice from a room off the lobby.

As he headed in that direction, he debated how to handle this. The door was slightly ajar. He tapped on it.

"It's open," called the female voice from inside. "Don't be shy."

He stuck his head in the doorway to see a woman sitting at a desk, her head down as she scribbled something on a scratch pad. "I'm looking for—"

"You've found her," the woman said without glancing up. "Come on in."

As he stepped in, she looked up and gave him an appraising once-over. "Not bad. Not bad at *all*." She motioned in a circle with her hand. When he didn't move, she said, "Turn. Let's see your backside."

"Pardon me?"

"Don't pretend to be shy with me. I've seen more than my share. Turn around."

Sawyer did as ordered, chuckling to himself as he heard her let out a low whistle. What kind of commercials were they making up here anyway?

"Yep, you'll do," she said, getting to her feet. "Wait a minute. Are you *limping*?" Before he could speak, she said, "You can ride, though, right?"

"I assume you're referring to a horse?"

She smiled and jammed her hands down on her abundant hips. "Cowboys," she muttered under her breath as she sat back down. "You're the best I've seen today. Just tell me if you can ride for long shots." She was eyeing him as she talked. "You could also stand in for a carnie once they get the rides going. Yep, I'm betting they'll want you for a couple of days." She turned toward a board with keys on it. "You're in luck. We have one cabin left since the hotel is closed. So I'm assuming you wouldn't have driven all the way up here unless you could stick around for a few days?"

He started to correct her, to tell her that he hadn't come here looking for a part in whatever she was shooting. But instead, he heard himself say, "I can ride, and I can stay for a while."

"Great. Fill out this form and be back here by seven in the morning." When he didn't interrupt, she continued. "Here." She slid a cabin key across the desk at him. It was connected to a piece of wood with the number eleven burned into it. "There's food in the hotel kitchen 24/7 when we're shooting. You can dress just like you are. But if you feel you need wardrobe—"

"No." He'd play along but would draw the line at being duded out. "I didn't see any horses on the way in. Where do I—"

"Just go back out the front door and follow the smell. Ted will assign you a horse and saddle." With that she waved him out as her phone rang, and she quickly picked it up with a—

"Hey, that better be you calling to tell me you have what I need for tomorrow."

As he left, he hoped Ted would know where he could find Ainsley Hamilton.

AINSLEY TIED HER horse's reins to a tree limb and pulled the pistol from her saddlebag. She'd taken it from her father's gun safe before she'd left home the last time. She hadn't told him, not wanting to worry him. He wouldn't miss it, and she'd been afraid she might need it. He'd taught her and her five sisters to shoot at an early age, so a gun felt just fine in her hands.

"I don't want you to be afraid of guns, but also I want you to have respect for them," Buckmaster had said. She and her sisters had become quite adept at target practice since they were all fairly competitive.

The problem was the difference between a paper target—and a person. It was a person who'd followed her. Someone on horseback? If so, that would mean he'd gotten one of the horses being used for the commercial shoot.

And if she was right, he'd followed her, knowing that she was trapped in the box canyon with no way out if he decided to take this opportunity to finally confront her.

Show your face. The way he kept hidden added to her growing anxiety about the man. What did he want? Maybe she was about to find out.

She snapped off the safety, telling herself she wouldn't kill him—just wound him. Unless he was armed. That thought sent her heart pumping. He finally had her entirely alone. Was that what he'd been waiting for?

The sound of rock on rock. Gun raised, Ainsley moved through the narrowest part of the canyon and stopped to listen. She could almost hear him breathing; he felt that close.

TED WAS A young cowboy, skinny and tall with a shock of red hair and ever-present sunburn. He gave Sawyer a nice-looking roan and a saddle and told him he lived on a ranch not far away. It was clear that he was excited to be providing horses for a TV commercial.

"A friend of mine works up here. Ainsley Hamilton? Do you know where I might find her?" Sawyer asked.

Ted nodded and smiled, before pointing off to a wide open meadow and a stone cliff behind it. "She took off toward Box Canyon about twenty minutes ago. You could probably catch up to her. Wouldn't hurt to get some saddle time in before you have to go before the camera, I would imagine," he said.

"I'd appreciate that," Sawyer said and saddled up. Riding past the still and silent carnival, he headed for the canyon. The day was quite warm now for the end of October. The leaves on the aspen trees in the meadow hadn't fallen yet. Sun-dappled, they shimmered red, orange and gold in the breeze. Past them, the pines were a dark cool green at the mouth of the canyon.

The moment he rode into the ponderosa pines, the temperature dropped. The sheer rock walls cast the canyon in shadow. Sawyer noticed what appeared to be an old creek bed winding its way out of the canyon. He could see Ainsley's horse's tracks in the dirt.

Reining in, he swung out of the saddle. He'd decided to walk into the canyon, rather than ride, to give him time to consider how he would handle this. Normally he preferred the truth.

But he'd gotten the feeling from Frank that he was dealing with an independent woman who might resent him butting into her business. Also, she didn't know him from Adam. He figured it might make her less self-conscious if she thought he was just an extra hired on for the commercial. He might be able to find out who was following her, take care of the matter, and Ainsley would never have to be the wiser.

The commercial was supposed to wrap in a few

days, according to Ted. Sawyer figured he'd be able
to find the man tailing Ainsley long before that.

Tying up the horse at the opening of the canyon,
he ventured in. As he came around the corner between the two rock cliffs, he heard something and
drew up short. Standing just yards ahead was a
young blonde woman dressed in jeans, boots and a
blue-checked Western shirt, holding a gun on him.

CHAPTER THREE

"STAY WHERE YOU ARE!" Sawyer ordered as a stream of pebbles cascaded off the side of the cliff, clattering on the ground between them. Glancing up, he caught movement as someone stepped away from the edge of the canyon wall above them. He swore and held up his hands. Frank had faxed him a photo of the young woman, but it certainly hadn't done her justice. "Please, don't move!"

"I believe that's my line," Ainsley said and kept coming toward him, brandishing the gun. "Why are you following me?"

There wasn't time to explain. From the top of the canyon wall fist-sized rocks began to come down like a waterfall. She glanced up in surprise, the tumbling rocks distracting her enough to give him the edge.

Sawyer launched himself at her, wrenching the gun from her hand as he took her down, rolling them both back under the edge of the canyon wall. A moment later, an avalanche of larger rocks came crashing down just inches from them. Dust choked the canyon, and for a few moments neither could see anything.

The rocks continued to fall in a deafening roar. Neither of them moved until the trickle of rocks finally ended with several large boulders booming down in another cloud of dust.

Sawyer had covered her body with his own when the rock slide began. Now he lifted himself up on his arms to stare down at her. She was ghost-white and seemed to still be trying to catch her breath.

"Are you all right?" he asked, hating how close a call it had been.

She nodded, but he could see she was still shaken.

He moved to let her sit up in the small space under the rock face. She looked from the gun resting in his open palm to the huge pile of rocks next to them. From her shocked expression, she was just now realizing what had happened. If he hadn't come along when he had and thrown her under the ledge, she would have been under those rocks.

Ainsley stared at him, hugging her knees to her as she pressed her back to the canyon wall. Her blue eyes were wide, her bow-shaped mouth tremulous, lips slightly parted. He had the craziest desire to kiss her.

Those eyes focused on him, and he saw suspicion darken the blue. In a heartbeat, the two of them were back where they started. "Why did you follow me?" she demanded accusingly.

"I was out riding, getting used to the horse before my commercial shoot tomorrow, when I saw this canyon. If you were followed, it was by someone on top of the canyon wall—the one who I suspect started the landslide." She didn't look convinced. "I just got here. I'm guessing you were already armed and on foot when I entered the canyon."

She took a breath and let it out as she considered that. "That's assuming the slide didn't merely start on its own."

"It didn't. I saw a shadow up there as the first rocks began to come down. Someone was up there. If it makes you feel any better, I think you were right about being followed. It just wasn't me."

She seemed to hug herself tighter, but she was no longer looking at him with so much suspicion.

"Come on, let's get out of here. I think it's safe now." He had to move some of the rocks to make an opening for them to crawl out. The pile of rock had nearly blocked the narrow canyon.

Until he checked where the slide had started, he couldn't know for sure what or who had triggered the slide. But he was fairly certain of what he would find when he checked it out. Ainsley had been followed, and that person had set off the landslide.

"I would suggest getting out of the canyon in case whoever was up there is still around." He didn't think the person had stuck around, but he also didn't want to take any chances. "Let me go first—just in case." Sawyer eased out of the space he'd made, offering her a hand. She took it as she scuttled out and stopped. Her gaze widened at the sight of the huge boulders that had careened down. He could see that she was thinking the same thing he was. That had been a close call for both of them. She looked more afraid than even before.

Given that she'd suspected she'd been followed— not just this time—for months now, he could understand her fear. Had the man following her gotten tired of his game and decided to end it in this canyon? Or had he gotten too close to the edge and inadvertently set off the rock slide?

"The person up there probably didn't mean to set off the slide," he said, hoping to reassure her when he wasn't all that convinced himself.

Right after the slide had stopped, he'd wanted to hightail it out of the canyon in the hopes of catching the culprit. But one look at Ainsley and he knew he couldn't leave her. Also, he couldn't be sure that there wouldn't be more.

His guess was that whoever had set off the rock slide had to be somehow connected to the commercial, since they were so far from everything out here. Anyone could have gotten hired on; look how easy it had been for him.

He watched her glance up and, following her gaze, saw no one in the narrow strip of brilliant blue above them. He heard nothing. Nor did he see anyone. He was betting that whoever had set off the slide was long gone. But he couldn't count on that.

"Where is your horse?"

She pointed back up the canyon.

"I'll go with you to get it," he said. She didn't answer, just stood hugging herself as if reliving what had happened. "Here, you'll want this back." He handed her the gun, which he'd stuck in the waistband of his jeans. Her gaze lifted to his in surprise. She took the weapon, her fingers brushing his. She seemed startled as if she'd felt the same jolt he had.

She quickly pocketed the weapon, turned and started toward the boxed end of the canyon. He followed, limping and reminding himself that he wasn't up to much more of these kinds of antics.

Ahead of him, Ainsley had stopped next to a spring to retrieve her horse. He watched her swing up into the saddle. There was something both strong and determined about her, as well as vulnerable. He felt a pull stronger than gravity and cursed under his breath.

Just do this job and don't get involved. Whatever her story is, it ain't yours. Let's not forget what happened with the last woman you rescued.

AINSLEY HAD JUST retrieved her horse and put her gun away when she heard the roar of four-wheelers headed her way. As the sound came to a sudden stop, she caught voices coming from the mouth of the canyon. A few moments later, several of the crew appeared, including Devon "Gun" Gunderson.

"How did you think we were going to be able to shoot in this canyon?" Gunderson demanded. "We could barely get in past the fallen rocks."

Inwardly she groaned as she glanced around for

the cowboy who'd saved her from the rock slide. But he must have slipped out when the others arrived. She realized she hadn't even thanked him. Nor did she have any idea who he was, other than he was apparently an extra.

She was still shaken, but she did her best to hide it as she discussed possible scenes that could be shot near the entrance to the canyon and other locations she'd found for them. If anyone noticed that she wasn't herself, neither Gunderson nor the others commented on it.

Her mind kept reliving her near-death experience again and again. Everything had happened so fast. She'd heard what she'd thought was someone in the canyon, but now realized someone on the top of the canyon cliff had started the slide, just as the cowboy had said.

That made her shudder at the realization that she would have followed the sound of the rocks falling— right to her death—if it hadn't been for her mystery cowboy. She was still trembling from the near miss later when she rode back to the hotel.

SAWYER HADN'T WANTED to leave Ainsley alone, but once some of the people from the crew had shown up, he'd taken advantage of it. He found a way to get to the top of the canyon walls a few hundred feet past the entrance. A trail of sorts wound up for a spectacular view of the area.

But it wasn't the view he was interested in. Not

wanting to set off another rock slide with people in the canyon, he waited until they'd all left before he moved cautiously toward the rim. He knew exactly what he was looking for—a spot where the rocks had been displaced and any sign of recent footprints.

The wind was strong up here. It sang as it blew through the rocks and pines. He'd left his horse tied up in the pines below. As he walked, he found dozens of footprints. Clearly a lot of people had discovered this spot. He wondered how many people from the production company had known about the trail.

As he neared the edge of the rock cliff, he saw where rocks had recently been displaced. There were fresh tracks next to the spot. He bent down to inspect them. It appeared someone had been walking along the edge of the canyon and stopped at this spot to look down. The footprints ended where rock had broken away and dropped over the side.

Someone wearing man-sized cowboy boots had set off the rock slide. Had the man followed Ainsley? Had he known she was down there and purposely started the rock slide or had it been an accident?

Once he had ridden back and put his horse and saddle away, Sawyer headed for his cabin behind the hotel. He was deciding how to proceed when a female voice called, *"Sawyer?"*

He turned and swore under his breath as he recognized the last woman he'd rescued. Katherine "Kitzie" McCormick. She walked toward him, squinting in the sun as if she couldn't believe her eyes. He couldn't either. What was she doing here? His mind raced for an explanation as to his presence here, realizing he was going to have to tell her the truth, even though it could get him into trouble with his real job if his boss found out.

"Sawyer, what are you doing here?" she demanded in a whisper when she reached him. "I thought you were on medical leave? Tell me they didn't send you as my backup." Anger brought her words out in a spurt like machine gun fire. "If you think you are going to come in here like you have always done and save the day—"

"I'm not here…officially."

That stopped her cold. She took a step back, studying him openly. "What does that mean?"

It was clear that she thought their boss had sent him to check up on her—or save her again if the need arose. "I'm not on the clock officially or unofficially. It's…personal."

He caught the twinkle in her eye, the half grin, and cursed his bad luck along with his poor choice of words. Now she thought he was here because of her. He definitely was going to have to tell her the truth. "Is there somewhere we could talk?"

She smiled. "How about my cabin? Oh, hold on a minute," she said as an old pickup rattled past. "That's my delivery guy. I forgot he was coming today. I'll be right back."

Sawyer watched her take off at a run to intercept the driver of the truck. He couldn't believe his bad luck at finding Kitzie here, he thought as she stood talking to the driver, a guy wearing his baseball cap on backward.

"You're *working* here?" he asked when she joined him again.

Kitzie didn't answer as she led the way to a cabin on the other side of the wide expanse behind the hotel. As she pulled out the key for cabin No. 3, he worried. Given their history, he knew this could get ugly if he wasn't careful. She seemed to have it in her head that this was about the two of them. She wouldn't be happy when she learned the truth. But he couldn't see what choice he had. He certainly couldn't let her go on thinking what she was right now.

But what was *she* doing here? She pushed open the cabin door, and he followed her inside the small, cramped space. Glancing around, he took in the dated knotty pine interior. It was only large enough for a couch, fold-down kitchen table and one folding chair, a tiny kitchen with an old fridge, a miniature bathroom with a toilet and shower, and a bedroom with a bed that had seen better days. All the essentials of home, he thought, realizing his would be exactly like this.

Kitzie moved to the refrigerator, opened it and took out two beers. Without asking him, she handed him one, opened one for herself and curled up at the end of the couch.

He took the folding kitchen chair and pulled it up,

rather than joining her on the small couch. She didn't miss the gesture. A frown crossed her face before she checked it and took a sip of her beer.

"So, what are you doing here?" she asked.

"I'm doing a friend a favor." That didn't seem to relieve her curiosity. "So you're *working* here?"

"I'm undercover in charge of feeding everyone."

"You *cook*?" That would be more surprising than hearing she was undercover.

She rolled her eyes. "I oversee the kitchen. I grocery shop mostly and get two teens from town to do the real cooking."

"So you're…undercover?" he repeated, wondering if she was on the same case he was. Maybe Ainsley's father had made an official request for surveillance on his daughter.

"You first," Kitzie said. "If you aren't here… officially, then tell me about this…favor."

"I thought we might be here for the same reason. One of the other employees here has a stalker."

Her brow shot up, and he knew that wasn't her assignment. "A stalker? What employee?"

"Ainsley Hamilton."

"Ainsley?" She laughed and took a big gulp of her beer. The rich honey-brown eyes he'd once found beautiful had turned dark with instant jealousy at even the mention of another woman. Even one involved in a case. Anger pinched her features. She shook her head with both disappointment and fury. "And I thought you might be here because of me."

"I'm sorry you thought that. I think it was pretty clear when we broke up that things were over between us."

"Did you?" She wiped a hand across her mouth. "So you're going to save prim and proper Miss Ainsley. That is what you do, isn't it? Save them and leave them."

He ignored that, wondering why she had referred to Ainsley as prim and proper. "She doesn't know who I am. Or, as you said, what I really do. So I'd appreciate it if this stayed just between us. I'm still on medical leave."

"I noticed you were limping. Another heroic rescue on your part?"

He didn't answer that. "I'd appreciate it if Ainsley continues to think I'm nothing more than an extra." He waited for her to agree.

Kitzie took a deep breath and let it out slowly. "So someone is really stalking her?"

"Apparently. Have you noticed anyone on the commercial paying extra attention to her?"

The laugh had barbs in it. "Are you kidding? Every man here has paid her extra attention—not that it's gotten them anywhere. She's not…sociable."

He hated how quickly jealousy had reared its ugly head. He was sure Kitzie had been jealous of Ainsley before this, but now it would be worse. "I'm not interested in her, if that's what you're thinking. I've never even laid eyes on her before today."

Her smile was snide. "I'm sure you found her... refreshingly charming."

He took a sip of his beer and glanced around the cabin. This was one of the reasons their "relationship" hadn't lasted long. "So, how many people are up here on a daily basis since the commercial began?" he asked, changing the subject.

"It's a small video production crew, bare bones and, no doubt, low budget. They're still in preproduction right now and haven't starting shooting much yet. I can give you a list of the players. Ainsley is still scouting locations. Gun is hard to please."

"Gun?"

"Devon Gunderson, the producer-director. The rest of his crew he brought up from California with him. He's only been in town a few weeks."

If Ainsley's stalker had been following her for months, then it couldn't be any of the main crew or Gunderson, Sawyer thought. "I understand some locals have been hired?"

"You mean other than the teenagers I got to cook?" She nodded. "There's Ted Carter, the wrangler, and Lance Roderick, security."

"I've met Ted. I passed Roderick on the way in. That's it?"

She nodded. "A few people come and go. As for security, you don't really need more than someone to keep everyone out of the carnival equipment."

He glanced toward the window. "I saw the Ferris wheel all the way from the bottom of the mountain," he said as he watched the deliveryman wander over to talk to some older man working on the Tilt-A-Whirl. "I would imagine it attracts attention. Is it for the commercial?"

Kitzie nodded. "Gun wanted a carnival, so he hired some guy by the name of Ken Hale to haul it up here and get it going. From what I've heard, it's the final shot of the commercial. It will be up and running in the next couple of days. But I doubt you'll be here that long, once you save Ainsley from her...stalker."

He could tell that she didn't believe Ainsley was being stalked. What did she think—that the young woman had made it up to get attention? Probably. It was something Kitzie might have done herself. But she hadn't seen how afraid Ainsley had been earlier.

Kitzie was letting her unreasonable jealousy get the better of her judgment. He felt a deep sense of regret at the way things had turned out between them as he put down his half-empty beer on the table and rose. "I'd ask about your undercover assignment—"

"It has nothing to do with Ainsley Hamilton or her stalker. Nor am I about to let you in on it. We both know how...involved you get in a case. I don't want you in mine."

He nodded. "I cared about you, Katherine. I still do."

Tears welled in her eyes. "Just not enough, though."

He couldn't argue that. "Thanks for keeping it quiet about my real reason for being here," he said,

even though she hadn't promised. "I'm afraid whoever's been stalking Ainsley is getting more…
aggressive. Just between you and me, Ainsley had
a near accident today while out scouting locations."

"Let me guess," she said with a laugh. "You saved
her."

Sawyer could see that there was nothing more to
be said, so he did something he hated doing. He lied.
"It's good to see you again."

"Sure it is," she said.

"If you need my help—"

"I won't."

CHAPTER FOUR

AINSLEY SPENT A busy afternoon with the director and the cameraman discussing the logistics of the next few locations. Gunderson was upset about not being able to use Box Canyon. His cameraman, a long-haired thirtysomething named T.K. Clark, suggested some ideas, while "Gun" made more demands of Ainsley to find something perfect. Fortunately, she hadn't had time to think about earlier and how close she'd come to dying.

She was studying a local map for more ideas, when the woman who ran the cafeteria stopped next to her.

"You're certainly burning the midnight oil," Kitzie said. "Did you even have dinner?"

Ainsley was surprised, first, that Kitzie would even notice that she'd been missing at mealtime and, secondly, that the woman was talking to her at all. Since the project had begun, the attractive redhead had been anything but friendly.

"There's a group getting together around a bonfire," Kitzie said. "Come on. I heard there would be something to drink. You look like you could use one."

"Thanks, but I'm not much of a drinker."

"Well, I am," the woman said, taking her arm. "And I need the company, so come on."

For days Ainsley had wished for some female company since all of the crew she worked with were male. Growing up with five sisters, she missed girl talk. Not that she expected that with Kitzie. But she went along because of the woman's insistence and, also, because she didn't want to be alone tonight after what had happened in the canyon.

"So, where are you from?" the cafeteria manager asked as they walked toward the glow of a blaze some distance away.

"Beartooth, Montana," she said and told her about growing up on the ranch with her five sisters and her father. She didn't mention that she was the daughter of Republican presidential candidate Buckmaster Hamilton. Either Kitzie already knew that or didn't put it together.

"Huh" was all the woman said when Ainsley finished. By then they had reached the bonfire where the crew had gathered. Even Gunderson had joined them. He stood on the other side of the blaze talking to Ken Hale, the owner of the carnival that would be the last shot before the commercial wrapped.

Hale was a big man with a round red face and a hearty laugh. He and Gunderson seemed to be in deep conversation before Gun, as everyone called him, moved away from the fire.

"I'll get us something to drink," Kitzie said, heading for the cooler someone had brought. "Don't worry. I'm sure there is something nonalcoholic in there."

DEVON GUNDERSON TOOK his drink and walked toward the meadow until he reached the Ferris wheel. He turned to look back at the old hotel and the cabins tucked in the pines on the mountainside behind it.

He wished Hale would get some of the rides going. Tonight he'd love to be sitting on the top of the Ferris wheel when the lights came on in the small town in the distance. He did his best thinking far and away from other people.

A splattering of laughter rose beyond the pines where the crew had gathered beside the creek. He could smell the smoke of the campfire drifting on the breeze as he sat down on the Ferris wheel seat. It rocked, creaking under his weight.

From the first time his father had taken him to a carnival he had been enchanted. The lights, the noise, the brittle cheapness of it. He even liked the carnies calling to him, determined to steal his last dime on some game he couldn't possibly win. And then there had been the rides.

Just thinking about it made him smile. That's why he had to use a carnival in this commercial, his last. He had to return to that childhood place where he'd first began to dream that he could do whatever he wanted with his life. He'd known at a young age that he wasn't going to fulfill any of his parents' fantasies of success. He was cut out for better things. Like the carnival, he liked the sleight of hand, the lure of riches in a game of chance, the promise of something beyond imagination.

"I thought I'd find you here," Hale said, coming out of the darkness.

He grimaced to himself, having not wanted company. But even if he'd told the old carnie this, it wouldn't have kept him away. Not a man like Hale.

"Turn this thing on," Gun said. "I want to go for a ride."

The older man shook his head. "Even if I could see to crank it up, I'm not going to. Hell, I'd get you up on top and the thing would stop. I don't think you want to spend the night up there while I'm down here working on it in the dark."

"You might be surprised."

Hale shoved him over where he could sit next to him. He was breathing hard after the walk all the way out here in the meadow. "You sure picked an out-of-the-way place for this little…get-together."

"I like it out here." When he'd first seen the hotel, he'd been tempted to buy it when this was all over. He had thoughts of restoring it, making the place earn its keep, but had quickly realized that he wouldn't have liked it once it was full of noisy tourists.

"Aren't you going to miss it?" Hale asked.

Gun knew he wasn't referring to this place. "It's time. As that old gambling song goes, you've got to know when to hold 'em and know when to fold 'em."

"And know when to walk away or when to run?" Hale looked over at him. "Is that what you're doing, Gun? Running? I heard about your divorce. Another man, I heard."

He stood, this conversation over as far as he was concerned. Stepping off the ride, he started toward the hotel.

"I'm not sure I like where your head is at right now."

At those words, Gun stopped and turned to look back at him. It was too dark to make out Hale's features. The Ferris wheel seat rocked and creaked under the big man's weight. The breeze whispered through the nearby pines and rustled the dry grass of the meadow. A chain on one of the rides clinked softly.

"You don't want to go there," Gun said.

"Come on, I know you. You and I go way back. I know how you felt about her."

"Don't mistake a business partnership for friendship," Gun said carefully. "You're overstepping, Hale. Don't do it again. And I want that Ferris wheel running tomorrow." With that he turned and took the back way to his cabin, so he could avoid those around the campfire by the creek. He wasn't in a mood to talk to anyone.

AFTER MOVING HIS few belongings into his cabin, Sawyer had spent the remainder of the day learning everything he could about Spotlight Images, Inc., and its current employees. He'd had Sheriff Curry run all the license plates from the vehicles parked around the cabins and hotel, as well as the names of the crew. Kitzie had slipped a list of the names and jobs under his cabin door earlier.

It was definitely a bare-bones crew for a video production company. He'd been glad when Frank had called him with information on the main players.

Devon "Gun" Gunderson was the director as well as producer. Sawyer had seen him earlier in the canyon with Ainsley. Divorced three times, he was fifty-four, blond, blue-eyed and stocky. He had an air about him that told Sawyer he ran the show with an iron fist.

His camera and boom operator was a long-haired thirty-four-year-old named T.K. Clark. He'd been with Spotlight Images, Inc., since it began five years before. He wore his long, dishwater blond hair in a ponytail and sported a half dozen tattoos.

With the company since its inception, Nathan Grant was thirty-eight, divorced twice, and employed as a lighting technician and carpenter. He looked like the dark-haired moody type behind his horn-rimmed glasses.

Twenty-eight-year-old Bobby LeRoy was a handyman. He'd been with the company only a month.

None had any priors. The one man here with an

arrest record was the founder of Goodtimes Entertainment, the fifty-year-old who owned the carnival now set up in the meadow. Ken Hale was a big brawler of a man who apparently liked to fight, according to his several arrest records.

"He's all carnie. Born and raised traveling with his parents who worked the show," Frank had told him. "The only other one you asked about, the security guard, Lance Roderick? He's a former lawyer. Filed bankruptcy a year ago after being disbarred. Pulled some legal shenanigan."

From lawyer to security guard on a fly-by-night video production company. That definitely sent up a red flag.

Sawyer had thanked Frank and headed for the hotel. He managed to grab a bite to eat in the kitchen just before it closed without crossing paths with Kitzie or Ainsley. This time of year, it got dark by six. As he walked around, he noticed that Ainsley's cabin was unlit.

Voices and laughter carried on the breeze. He followed the sound to find the crew around a big campfire in the pines next to the spring creek. He helped himself to a beer from one of the coolers someone had dragged up and, staying in the shadows, simply watched. Of the group around the fire, he gathered most of them were the crew. The man he'd seen earlier, Lance Roderick, was still wearing his uniform shirt.

It was hard to tell if any of the men were more interested in Ainsley than was warranted. She was a beautiful woman. They all flirted with her and Kitzie, except for the man Sawyer took for the carnie, Ken Hale. Hale had left the fire for a while but had only recently returned. Hale had noticed Ainsley. His gaze kept straying to her. But his wasn't the only one.

Lance Roderick secretly watched her as if not wanting anyone to know. Bobby LeRoy wasn't as sneaky about it. Neither was T.K. Clark.

Not that he could blame them. Ainsley's face glowed in the firelight, making her even more striking.

The only person missing was Gunderson. Kitzie hung around for a while, joking with the men before saying she was turning in for the night. As the fire burned down and the night cooled, he watched people wander off. LeRoy, Clark, Grant and Hale headed into town, after trying to get Ainsley to go with them and failing.

Roderick stayed only for a little bit before he trundled off, saying he had to take a look around to make sure everything was locked down for the night.

Sawyer waited until the guard left before he moved up to the dying fire—and Ainsley. As he joined her, she didn't look up. All night she'd seemed lost in the flames, avoiding conversation with the others and keeping to herself.

That's why he was surprised when she asked, "Have you ever had your life flash in front of your eyes?"

She sounded tipsy, and he wondered what she'd been drinking. He'd noticed that her glass hadn't been empty while Kitzie was there. Kitzie had been keeping them both in refreshments.

At her question, Sawyer chuckled to himself given his near-death experience from the train— not to mention the rock slide earlier. "I take it yours passed before your eyes?"

She nodded, still not looking at him, her blue eyes wide in the firelight, her attention locked on the flames. "Today I realized I've never done *anything*. I'm the oldest of my sisters, the good one, the one *everybody* in my family depends on. But guess what?"

He hated to guess. Nor did she give him a chance.

"I've never *lived*. I've never…*cut loose*. The most irresponsible thing I've ever done is quit law school."

"Then why did you quit?"

Ainsley shook her head. "I don't know. Maybe it was my one act of rebellion."

"So, do you still want to be a lawyer?"

"Actually, I do." She laughed, losing balance and stumbling a little. He caught her arm. She wasn't just a little tipsy. She was *drunk*.

"What is that you're drinking?" he asked.

She frowned as she looked down at the liquid in her large plastic cup. "Tea. *Strong* tea. Kitzie made it for me."

He'd just bet she had. He took the paper cup from Ainsley and sniffed, wrinkling his nose. "I'd *say* it was strong. Hundred proof. Have you ever been drunk before?"

"I told you, I've never done *anything* before." She took it back from him and, draining it with a grimace, tossed the cup into the fire. The paper cup flamed up, sending sparks into the air. Smiling, she turned to him for the first time since he'd joined her.

She blinked. "I know *you*. You're that cowboy who saved my life and took off without even giving me a chance to say thank you."

"Sawyer Nash," he said, extending his hand.

Her hand was warm and small in his. "The new Ainsley Hamilton," she announced with a flourish. "I'm sick of being the old me. I feel like a snake that's about to shed its skin." Her eyes sparkled in the firelight. "I feel like doing something completely not like the old me." She looked around, her gaze lighting on the dark silhouettes of the carnival in the meadow. "I'm going to climb that Ferris wheel and bay at the moon."

He couldn't let her do that. Not in her condition. "Why don't I walk you back to your cabin?"

She shook her head. "I've had enough of men trying to protect me. Putting me on a pedestal. I'm like the princess who's been locked in her tower. I'm suddenly free, and I want to do something wild and completely irresponsible." Her big blue eyes locked with his. "Don't you want to do it with me?"

Damned if he didn't. She wasn't just beautiful with her long blond hair and moon-like blue eyes;

there was something endearing about her—even drunk. He also knew what it was like to be the good son, the one his parents had depended on.

She sighed. "There is so much I haven't done, I don't even know where to begin. What should we do first?" she asked, slurring her words. Her gaze went to the spring creek nearby in the pines. "I've never been skinny-dipping. Let's go skinny-dipping!" She began unbuttoning her Western shirt as she moved away from the campfire toward the creek.

Hell, that water would be freezing cold this time of year. But he couldn't very well let her go in alone. She'd drown for sure. He followed her trail of discarded clothing through the darkness of the pines to find her standing naked at the edge of a deep dark pool in the crook of the stream. Silhouetted there against the moonlight, she was a sight for sore eyes.

"You coming in?" she asked over her shoulder and then fell face forward into the water.

CHAPTER FIVE

AINSLEY WOKE WITH the worst headache of her life. She groaned as she opened her eyes and quickly closed them.

"Here, this might help."

Her eyes flew open, sending a dagger of pain straight to her brain. She grabbed the sheet and pulled it up to her neck as she stared at the strange man not only in her cabin, but also sitting on the edge of her bed.

"What are you doing here?" she cried and quickly peeked under the sheet. She was naked as a jaybird. *"Oh no, I didn't!"*

"You didn't," he said in a deep, sultry voice she remembered. This was the cowboy who'd saved her in the canyon—but at what cost? "Your virtue is safe."

"How long have you been here?" She spotted his boots by the door. *"You stayed all night?"*

"I didn't trust you not to do something even more…wild, given your condition."

"More wild than what?" she asked, her voice breaking.

"Skinny-dipping."

She groaned and, sliding back down in the bed, covered her head with the sheet. "Please tell me I was alone," she said in a tremulous voice from under the sheet. "The rest of the movie crew—"

"Weren't there. It was just the two of us." He pulled the sheet down until their eyes met and gave her a big smile. Had she noticed last night how handsome he was? Is that why she'd decided to go skinny-dipping with a complete stranger? Well, nearly a complete stranger.

"You were the only one naked," he said, as if trying to reassure her. "Actually, you were the only one who went in the water, except for when I had to wade in to fish you out."

She didn't think she could feel worse. "I might have had too much to drink."

"You think?"

"I don't drink but a glass of wine occasionally. Normally."

"So I gathered."

Ainsley realized she didn't remember any of this. Memory loss ran in her family, she mused, thinking of her mother's return from the dead and complete lack of memory of those missing twenty-two years. The stray thought might have made her laugh if she hadn't felt so awful.

"I don't remember…anything," she admitted.

"Don't worry. Nothing happened, other than you sobering up from the icy water enough that I could get you back to your cabin and to bed. *Alone.* I slept on the couch."

She glanced over and saw his black Stetson and his jean jacket on the couch.

"Now, drink this." He handed her the glass he'd been holding. As she peered suspiciously at the ugly thick brown sludge, he said, "Trust me. That is going to make you feel much better."

"It looks…awful."

"It's my own remedy for a hangover."

"I've never had a hangover before."

He laughed. "Apparently Kitzie was making your drinks? You might make your own in the future."

She was still staring at the glass of thick brown stuff.

"Best to chug it." He stood. "I don't know about you, but I have to get to work. I have to go before everyone in camp sees me leaving your cabin."

Ainsley felt her eyes widen in alarm.

"Don't worry. It's still early. Your reputation is safe."

She groaned. "I don't understand what happened last night, but it won't happen again."

"That's too bad. You were trying out the new Ainsley Hamilton. She was up for anything. I kind of liked her."

"I'll just bet you did." She tried to summon what dignity she could. "Well, I won't be needing your… assistance again because of intoxication."

"That's too bad, too." He gave her a wink before

he stepped to the couch. She sat up to watch him pull on his boots, hat and jacket.

"We won't be seeing that Ainsley Hamilton again," she said, more to herself than to him. "Back to the old, boring Ainsley Hamilton."

"Just between you and me, there is nothing wrong with the old Ainsley Hamilton either." With that, he left.

She took a whiff of the drink and her stomach roiled. Holding her nose with her free hand, she chugged the thick liquid and gagged. What had the man given her? She thought for a moment that she was going to be sick. But then her stomach began to settle down. After a few minutes, she felt better.

By the time she came out of the shower and dressed, she had faith she could do what had to be done today without going back to bed—or worse, curling up and dying.

Her cell phone rang. Checking it, she saw that it was her mother calling. It still gave her an odd feeling when she saw the name Sarah Hamilton come up on the screen—after believing her mother dead for twenty-two years. Almost two years ago now, her mother had returned out of the blue with no memory of where she'd been. Her mother's last memory was giving birth to the twins, Cassidy and Harper, both now almost twenty-five.

Ainsley was surprised that Sarah was calling and instantly worried. Her mother never called. Then again, Ainsley hadn't really reached out to her mother. She felt a stab of guilt. She certainly hadn't tried to make her mother's transition back into their lives any easier.

If anyone should be reaching out to her mother, it was Ainsley since she was the oldest of Sarah's six daughters and one of the few who actually remembered her. She'd been twelve when her mother had supposedly died after crashing her car into the Yellowstone River in the middle of winter. Her body was never recovered, something not that unusual in the wilds of Montana.

"Mother? Is something wrong?" she said into the phone.

"No, that is, I'm just checking to make sure you'll be home before election night. Your father wants us all together."

"I only have a few more days here, and then I was planning to come to the ranch."

"Good," her mother said.

The conversation stalled as it always did. Ainsley never knew what to say. She glanced at her watch. She really needed to go. "I heard you moved back into the house after you and Dad got married again." They'd had an impromptu wedding by going to the justice of the peace.

While Bo, Olivia and the twins, Harper and Cassidy, had been upset that their parents hadn't waited and had a "real" wedding with all six daughters in attendance, Ainsley was glad they'd been spared the event. She knew Kat felt the same way.

"Yes. I forgot how beautiful it is here on the ranch," her mother was saying. "The view from the main house is wonderful."

Her mother had returned from the dead to find her former husband had remarried, and a woman named Angelina Broadwater Hamilton wasn't just living in her house, but sleeping in her bed.

For a while the media had played up the love triangle between the three. Ainsley had seen how conflicted her father had been during that time. He'd loved Sarah, had six daughters with her and had grieved years before remarrying.

Then Angelina had been killed in a car wreck, leaving the door open for Sarah and Buck to get back together. Because he was running for president, it had taken them some time, but they'd finally tied the knot again. Ainsley knew her father was hoping their remarriage would bring his family together once more.

"Well," her mother said into the long silence. "I look forward to seeing you when you get home. Your sister Olivia thinks we should have a family celebration. Your father and I got married so quickly…"

"That sounds like a wonderful idea," she said, rolling her eyes. It sounded…awkward. But maybe they would all accept their mother, and things would turn out just fine. "I would love to help with the… celebration," she heard the old Ainsley say politely. "I'm sure my other sisters would, as well." Probably not Kat, but she didn't say that. Kat refused to call their mother anything but Sarah. Who knew what her problem was? Ainsley hadn't been home enough to find out.

"It would make your father so happy." But Ainsley could hear a note of happiness in her mother's voice, too. Maybe it was possible to put this family back together again—before both of her parents headed off to Washington, DC. According to the polls, Republican hopeful Buckmaster Hamilton was going to win by a landslide.

Landslide. She shuddered at the memory of yesterday and how close she'd come to dying. Sawyer Nash had saved her then—and again last night. She thought about the cowboy and found herself smiling. So Sawyer Nash was partial to the new Ainsley Hamilton, was he?

A part of her still wanted to cut loose and have more fun. She was sick of being the good daughter, the good sister, the good girl. Wasn't it time? But maybe she wouldn't be quite as carefree as she'd apparently been last night.

That close call in the canyon had made her realize it was time. She would definitely have more fun—as soon as she felt better. She wondered what Sawyer would think about that.

KITZIE HAD LET out a curse as she'd watched Sawyer come out of Ainsley Hamilton's cabin earlier. She'd blamed herself. She shouldn't have spiked the woman's tea. It had been childish and reckless. She smiled to herself. It had been fun to see another side of the prim and proper Miss Hamilton.

She wondered what Sawyer had thought of it. Of course, he had seen Ainsley home to her cabin. She should have anticipated that, knowing the man. But also knowing Sawyer, he wouldn't have taken advantage of a woman in that condition. Still, she knew his protective side and could well imagine him holding Ainsley's head while she puked in the toilet—if it had come to that.

Moving away from her cabin window, she told herself she had bigger fish to fry. Whatever Sawyer was up to, it was no longer any of her business.

Still it rankled her that Ainsley was just the kind of woman he would jump at saving. Even still injured and on medical leave, that was Sawyer. She wondered what friend had talked Sawyer into playing hero for the no-doubt future president's daughter.

Right now, though, she needed to concentrate on her own job. And yet it nagged at her. Was Ainsley really being stalked, or was this about getting attention during her father's election? And if there was a stalker, why would Sawyer keep his true purpose from the woman?

Kitzie shook her head, trying to clear Sawyer from her thoughts. It was a losing battle and had been for some time. She'd fallen for the man. That thought made her chest ache just as it had for months. She loved him, and even though she'd known he didn't feel the same about her, she'd thought he would eventually.

Fool, she told herself now as she hurried to get dressed for her undercover job overseeing the kitchen for the crew. Sawyer being here was a distraction she didn't need. She was no closer to solving her case than she had been when she'd hired on. She could feel the clock ticking. The video production company was set to move on in a matter of days. If she was right, the company was a front for the jewel thieves. She just had to prove it.

While other agents were looking into other leads, her gut told her the answer was here. Of the thirty-six mall jewelry stores hit across the country, this production company had been in the area all but one time. The most recent heist had been in St. George, Utah, where Spotlight Images, Inc. had been shooting nearby.

The burglars took only those items that had no serial numbers so were nearly impossible to trace. One of their favorites was a man's watch known as "the poor man's Rolex," which could be resold for five-hundred dollars. The rest of the gold jewelry would be melted down, no doubt.

A security camera had captured three men, all clearly in disguises, before they'd disarmed it. This was another reason she suspected the production crew. They had access to makeup artists and costumes.

They also had access to tools. In one burglary, they had used a battery-powered saw to cut the gate at the jewelry store. So there was some know-how, as well. They knew how to cut power to the store, shutting down the surveillance cameras. From what she'd seen of the small crew, they all seemed pretty capable of doing a variety of jobs.

The thieves had worn gloves, since no fingerprints had been found or any other evidence she could use to pin the heists on these men. So far they had eluded both the police and the FBI.

"Just because they're handy with tools doesn't mean they're jewel thieves," her partner, Pete Corran, had argued.

"They were in the area for all the heists but one," she'd argued back.

"Proof, Kitzie. And soon, or we're going to be pulled off onto something else. I am doing my best to keep an eye on the people who are capable of fencing that much loot. But nothing so far."

"This shoot will be over in a few days. They're talking about taking some time off, maybe going south for the winter," Kitzie had told him. "I'm telling you, they are going to fence the goods here in Montana in a few days. I can…feel it."

"I'm a believer in your gut instincts, partner, so give me something I can work with."

She wished she could. She'd been watching the bunch of them, but she hadn't turned up anything.

What if her instincts were off? Her boss thought they were. Since she'd screwed up, and Sawyer had had to save her months ago, she'd felt that her boss didn't trust her instincts anymore. She had to prove herself.

She needed this arrest because, without Sawyer, all she had was her career, and her boss was getting antsy. No mall jewelry stores had been hit for weeks now. Also, there were no close towns with mall jewelry stores. Either they were taking a break before the holidays or... Or they were here to fence the goods.

So was there a fence in Montana who could handle a major deal? Pete was busy on that end of things. In the meantime, she'd already scoped out the men on the crew who she believed were involved based on the one surveillance video, her experience with men and criminals. She even had a good idea who the leader was. She was putting her money on Gunderson. But she had no proof. Yet.

Now it was just a matter of waiting for the burglars to make a move. The one thing she couldn't do was let Sawyer distract her. Or worse, blow her cover trying to protect the Hamilton woman.

SAWYER DIDN'T OPEN the plastic bag in his pocket until he reached his own cabin. He gingerly removed the note he'd found the night before taped to Ainsley's door.

The handwriting looked hurried, a scrawl of letters that he feared said too much about the writer.

I'm so sorry. I never meant to hurt you today in the canyon. Please forgive me. I would never hurt you. You are the most precious thing to me.

Sawyer felt a chill as he pulled out his cell phone. He'd seen notes like this before from "fans" who could turn ugly in an instant.

"Any chance of getting some fingerprints run?" he said in the phone when Sheriff Frank Curry answered.

"You've already found Ainsley's stalker?" Frank asked, sounding surprised, before he laughed. "I knew you were the man for the job."

"We'll see about that." He related what had happened the day before. "I do think it was an accident, but she still could have been killed."

"Maybe he'll leave her alone now," Frank said.

"I don't think so. He's upset about yesterday, but I don't think it will deter him, especially if he's been following her for months. At least now I know that he is out here. He taped the note to her cabin door. That means he isn't worried about anyone seeing him around the cabins. Also, he had access to paper from a scratch pad like the ones I saw in the main office."

"You sound more worried," the sheriff said.

"I was hoping the reason he was following her had something to do with her father and the presidential race."

"You've ruled that out?"

"Not entirely. But I'd rather have a political fanatic than a romantic one. This guy seems a little too desperate that she might not like him after what happened yesterday. I'm anxious to find him and put a stop to this. The commercial will be over in a few days. He'll be easier to find here than when Ainsley leaves. At least I hope that is the case."

"Be careful."

Sawyer laughed. "You know me."

"That's what is starting to worry me. You've already been injured. I don't want to see you get killed because of me. What do you think of Ainsley?"

Sawyer thought of her naked in the moonlight. "She's quite the woman." He chuckled. "I'll send the note he left her. I'm betting he was upset enough that he didn't think to be careful about leaving his prints."

CHAPTER SIX

"HOW'S YOUR GIRLFRIEND?" Kitzie asked as she sat down next to Sawyer in the kitchen at breakfast. Everyone had already finished and gone back to work, so they had one of the tables to themselves.

He didn't take the bait. Kitzie knew that Ainsley wasn't his girlfriend—not that it stopped her from being jealous. "She isn't feeling so hot today."

"*Really?* Must be something going around."

"Yup," he said, knowing that Kitzie had purposely gotten Ainsley drunk last night. But he wasn't about to get into it with her. "Must be."

She chuckled.

"Thanks for the information you slipped under my door."

Kitzie glanced toward the back part of the kitchen where both teenagers were supposed to be cleaning up. Instead they were texting on their cell phones. "I did remember something that might help you." She lowered her voice. "Bobby LeRoy. I've seen him watching her. I didn't think anything about it until you told me what you're doing here. What caught my attention was that he wasn't looking at her like a man looks at a woman. He seemed…protective, you know what I mean?"

He considered that. "The security guard, Roderick? He seems a bit odd. Has anyone else been hanging around?"

"Not really. We're isolated here, so we don't get many visitors. The hotel owner comes up occasionally. The delivery guy brings up supplies every day or so." She shrugged. "He's been trying to butter up to Gunderson, thinks he can get into the movies. Don't we all?"

He was taking this all in as he finished his breakfast. Bobby LeRoy was young and foolish, from what he'd seen. Roderick? He was something else altogether. So was the wannabe movie star.

"I'm surprised you got a cabin," Kitzie said, studying him openly. "Murph must have liked the looks of you. I heard she turned down all the other cowboys who came up to audition."

"Murph?"

"Murphy Hillinger, the woman who hired you."

"Who has access to the four-wheelers and the horses?"

Kitzie shrugged. "Anyone who needs them."

"Including security?"

"I believe Roderick patrols the area every night on horseback. If that's all, I have to get my crew lined out on the lunch menu." She got to her feet.

He turned to look at her. "Thanks for your help."

"Anything for an old…friend." She left, having hardly touched her breakfast. "Good luck."

As LUCK WOULD have it, the first person Ainsley had to deal with this morning was Gunderson.

"The canyon scene isn't going to work out. I need you to find some other locations we can use, and I need them by noon," he ordered. "By the way, you look terrible."

"Thanks." Her cell phone rang as she was heading for the stables. It was her sister Kat. "Good morning," she said by way of greeting. "I can't talk. I need to get saddled up and off to work."

"You call that work?" Kat said but quickly got to her reason for phoning. "Dad asked me to call and make sure you were going to be home for election night."

"Mother already called me early this morning to confirm that I would be there. Did she mention to you that there is going to be a party, kind of a celebration of their marriage? Apparently we're putting it on for them. I said we would help."

Kat groaned. Besides refusing to call her mother, she still acted suspicious of everything Sarah did. "Whatever," she said of the party. "Election night we're all going to be at the Beartooth Fairgrounds, along with a thousand well-wishers and who knows how many crazies who might want the family dead."

"What are you talking about?" Ainsley asked. "This isn't about The Prophecy, that anarchist group from the 1970s that you're convinced our mother was a part of, is it?"

"She was the *leader*."

Ainsley rolled her eyes as she entered the stables. Ted was already saddling her horse. He grinned at her and mouthed, "Knew you'd need it this morning."

She mouthed *thank you* back.

"Security will be a nightmare, but you know Dad," Kat was saying. "We've all done our best to talk him out of it. The Republican Committee wanted it in the capital in Helena, but Dad wants it here. We should all wear bulletproof vests, not that it would probably do any good since Sarah's MO is bombs."

Kat had always been the doomsday negative sister, so it was hard to tell if there really was a security problem or if this was just Kat being Kat. Except since she'd met Max and fallen in love, she'd been more upbeat.

"I'm sure there will be dozens of Secret Service to protect him," Ainsley said, trying to lighten the conversation. "Let's just be happy for Dad."

"There will be a lot of Secret Service, but only because Sheriff Curry insisted on it. You know Dad. He thinks he's invincible. Frank is calling in local law enforcement as well as the National Guard."

"So it should be fine."

"Yep, one big happy family on parade."

Ainsley knew her sister's sarcasm stemmed from her problems with their mother and this crazy idea of hers that their mother was some kind of terrorist. "Now that Dad and Mom are married again—"

"I'm not worried about putting on a party for the two of them. There's a lot you don't know. Let's just hope Dad survives election night. Let's hope we all do. I have to go."

Ainsley disconnected, her headache pounding. Kat couldn't forgive their mother for disappearing for twenty-two years from their lives. Since it had only been months after the twins were born, Ainsley had speculated that maybe their mother had been suffering from postpartum depression. Why else would she leave six children and a husband she professed to love to try to kill herself that night in the river?

She sighed. Kat's problems with their mother aside, what was that about Dad surviving election night? Why did Kat always have to be so dramatic? And what was this about Mother being the leader of The Prophecy? She wondered where Kat got this kind of stuff. As far as Ainsley knew, some of the members had tried to throw their mother under suspicion to hurt their father's presidential campaign, but it hadn't worked.

Ainsley wasn't looking forward to election night either for her own personal reasons. She hated being in the spotlight. But this wasn't about her. It would be their father's night. He'd worked hard for this and deserved to have his family by his side when he won the election, which according to the polls, was in the bag.

She felt goose bumps along with a surge of pride. Her father would make a wonderful president. She just hoped it was everything he thought it would be. As for their mother... Just a few more days and she would be home. Then she could decide if Kat's concerns were valid.

"Good, I'm not too late to catch you."

She turned to find Kitzie standing in the stables doorway, silhouetting her against the bright October day. "A peace offering," Kitzie said and held out what looked like a small breakfast burrito wrapped in plastic. "I just ran into Gun, so I know you missed breakfast. Sorry about spiking your tea last night."

Ainsley took the burrito. "Thank you. Actually, you might have done me a favor last night. Now I'll never drink again." They both laughed.

"Well, I'd better get to work," Kitzie said and turned to leave.

She looked down at the burrito. Just the smell was enough to make her want to barf. "Hungry?" she asked Ted.

His blue eyes lit up. "Always."

"I thought that might be the case," she said, and thanked him again for saddling her horse before riding out.

Buck stood at the window of another nondescript room in yet another city. He was tired, but he could see the end just days away. Except there was a bone-weariness about him this morning that he couldn't seem to shake off. He knew it well. It was a feeling of impending disaster. It had been with him now for almost two years—not long before Sarah dropped back into their lives.

He told himself that he was too busy finishing up his campaign to worry. But late at night he would suddenly come out of a deep sleep and sit straight up in bed, terrified for apparently no good reason.

Of course there *was* a reason. Not that he let himself go down that particular perilous trail during his waking hours.

"This is it, Buck," Sheriff Curry had said to him the last time he was home. The sheriff had stopped by the ranch and said they should take a walk.

Buck hadn't wanted to hear whatever it was that Frank wanted to tell him. For more than two years since Sarah had returned, the sheriff had been warning him about Sarah and what Frank feared she was capable of doing.

"The election is only days away," he'd argued. "Whatever it is you have to tell me—"

"Let's walk," Frank had insisted.

When they were out of hearing distance of the house, the sheriff had stopped and turned to him. "We only have a few more days. I'm just concerned about the venue—"

"Sarah isn't going to do anything." He'd wished that he'd sounded more convincing. The woman he'd married hadn't come back. Instead, this different

Sarah had returned. Not a bad different necessarily. But definitely an unsettling different.

She was…stronger in some ways. Maybe scarier because of it. Add to that what had been happening since her return from the dead. People had been dying around them and all because of an anarchist group from the 1970s called The Prophecy.

He thought of the pendulum tattoo on Sarah's buttock. She swore she had no idea how it had gotten there or that she had nothing to do with the group— even though she'd known the members back in college. And it did appear that they had tried to implicate her—and failed.

So why was he so worried during those dark pre-dawn hours?

His campaign manager, Jerrod Williston, came into the room. A bright young man in his mid-thirties with blond hair and blue eyes, Jerrod had proven that he was the best at what he did.

He was on his cell, talking rapidly, but stopped when he saw Buck standing by the window.

"I'll get back to you," he said into the phone. Pocketing the cell, he asked, "What's wrong?"

"Nothing." Buck tried to shake off the premonition of disaster. "Just a little tired."

"It's Sarah," Jerrod said with a groan.

"Why do you say that every time?" Buck demanded, instantly annoyed. He'd spent the past two years defending Sarah to not just Jerrod, but also his daughters and everyone else, including the sheriff.

"Because every time it *is* Sarah. What has she done now? I thought all was well. Married, living in the main house on the ranch, none of the six daughters causing trouble. What could be wrong with Sarah now?" Jerrod sounded as testy as Buck felt.

"Nothing is wrong with her. I was just resting for a minute." He'd never been a good liar. "Okay, maybe since the sheriff is worried about election night," he sighed, "well, then, I guess maybe I should be, too."

Jerrod shook his head. "Your sheriff has called in the National Guard as well as local law enforcement and Secret Service agents. The only way to make you safer is to move the venue. You want to do that?"

His campaign manager knew he didn't. "No. Like I said, everything is fine." He worked up a smile. "If anything, it's the realization that this is almost over, and a whole other lifetime of dramas is about to begin."

The younger man laughed. "That's more like it, Mr. President."

"Not yet. Don't jinx it."

Jerrod made a mocking face. "You got this one. It isn't even going to be a close race. So relax. A few more days. You up to it?"

Buck straightened, fixed his tie and nodded as Jerrod began to go over his schedule for the last hours up until the election. He half listened, the rest of his mind back on Sarah.

The sheriff was convinced that something was going to happen election night. Buck tried to reassure himself. At least he didn't have to wonder much longer if his wife would try to kill him.

SARAH JOHNSON HAMILTON found herself wandering around the huge rambling two-story house feeling empty. Her phone call to her daughter Ainsley had left her feeling a little better. But ultimately her children didn't know her. She'd lost them, just as she'd lost those missing twenty-two years from her memory.

Since her return from the dead, she had wanted desperately to be back here in this home that she'd shared with Buck and her children. But it felt… strange after all the years she'd been gone. It also felt…temporary since after Buck won the election, they would be living in the White House.

But she knew that wasn't the only reason she felt out of sorts. During the twenty-two years she'd been presumed dead, her children had all grown up. Now they were all busy with their own lives—lives that had little to do with her. She couldn't blame them. The younger ones had no memory of her. Her six beautiful daughters had turned out fine without her. Probably better than if she had been here, she thought miserably.

Worse, her secret would be coming out soon—unless she did something. Exhausted and anxious after being on the campaign trail for months, she had begged off Buck's one last swing through the worrisome states, and returned home.

Buck had been disappointed, but his campaign manager, Jerrod Williston, had said it was exactly what she should do.

"I think it would be smart for you to do some charity events back in Montana these last few weeks before the election," Jerrod had said. "In fact, I've already scheduled one for you."

She'd started to argue that she didn't want to do any more of them right now since she knew they had nothing to do with Buck being elected. She suspected that Jerrod just wanted to keep her busy and out of trouble.

"Just one, I promise," he said. "You need to rest up. Things will get crazy by election night."

She had laughed at that, fearing how crazy it could get. That and her secret were what kept her awake in the wee hours of the morning. For so long she'd felt trapped, unable to change what she feared was coming until she got all of her memory back. She'd been waiting now for weeks to hear from the one man who could give her the final piece of her memory, Dr. Ralph Venable.

As she moved restlessly through the huge house, she was terrified. Terrified he wouldn't call. Terrified he would. Dr. Venable had been experimenting with brain-wiping for years. Until recently, she wasn't sure she believed he had wiped her mind of Buck and the kids all those years ago.

But then she'd seen what he could do. Now she lived in fear of the day he would show up and give her back the rest of her memories—including the one she didn't want.

After disappearing for twenty-two years and not being able to remember any of it, she'd been petrified of what she'd done those missing years. But as it turned out, it wasn't those years that she had to worry about. It was her college ones and what she'd done that had now come back to haunt her. How had she gotten involved with an anarchist group that thought they could change the world by bombing buildings and killing innocent people? The answer was love. Or was it lust?

A charismatic handsome young man named Joe Landon must have seen how vulnerable the bright-eyed, innocent Sarah Johnson had been. She'd fallen for him—and his cause, becoming a co-leader of the group for a while. Worse, she'd been told that she had been the true leader of the group, The Prophecy. Since then, though, Joe had taken back over, and, as her scorned former lover, he was determined to pull Sarah in again or die trying.

Sarah stopped in front of a mirror and stared at her reflection. Often she didn't recognize herself. When you thought you were twenty-two years younger than you were, it messed with your mind.

In the mirror, a blonde, blue-eyed fifty-nine-year-old woman stared back at her. She was still in good shape, still felt no more than thirty-seven, still believed she could do anything. Just as she had in college, she reminded herself with a tremor.

Her fear was that Joe Landon had something big planned for election night. She imagined a huge explosion that would kill them all once the polls were in and Buck had won.

She'd once believed that killing herself would save her family from ever knowing about The Prophecy and her part in it. Failing that, she'd disappeared for twenty-two years only to return with no memory of The Prophecy or the missing years.

But slowly, it was all coming back, thanks to Dr. Venable and Joe's determination that she would be the woman she'd once been—an anarchist who went by the name of Red. She'd even dyed her hair red, according to the photographs Dr. Venable, or Doc as he was known back then, had shown her of the group.

When she'd realized that Joe and The Prophecy were using her to get to Buck and the presidency, she'd decided to stop them by confessing all to Buck and the sheriff. But Joe, knowing her…intimately, had seen that coming and threatened her daughters to stop her.

Joe had also put a man she loved in the hospital in a coma. Russell Murdock had befriended her when she'd returned to find the life she'd left gone. Buck had remarried, her children didn't know her, and she didn't even know this older version of herself.

Russell had been the only one she could trust, the only one she could lean on. He'd also been the one who'd found out the truth about her memory loss and its tie-in to the anarchist group pulling her strings like a puppeteer.

And look what The Prophecy had done to him. Even if he came out of his coma after he'd been attacked, the doctor didn't have much hope that Russell would ever recover.

No wonder she was terrified. Election night loomed. Her six daughters would be coming home, so they could all be together when their father gave his acceptance speech. When she'd called Ainsley, she'd hoped she would say she couldn't make it home for election night. But of course all six of Buck's daughters planned to be there.

Sarah felt as if she was on a runaway train, and ahead there was nothing but an open abyss. She desperately needed to stop The Prophecy. Stop her former lover Joe Landon. But how, without Joe finding out and retaliating against one of her daughters or her grandchildren?

Her cell phone rang, startling her out of her thoughts. She checked caller ID. The hospital was calling. Her heart dropped like a stone. *No! Please God, don't let it be bad news about Russell.*

"Hello?"

"Mrs. Hamilton, you asked to be called if there was any change in Russell Murdock's condition..."

Tears burned her eyes. "Yes?"

"He has come out of his coma. The doctor is with him now."

Sarah hardly remembered thanking the nurse for phoning. She disconnected and burst into tears.

For months since Russell had been attacked she'd prayed for him to come out of the coma. But as more time went on, she knew that his chances worsened. She'd almost given up hope.

Now hope flared. If Russell could testify against the men who'd attacked him, then maybe it would all come out about The Prophecy. She didn't care if she went to prison as long as Joe was stopped. Russell would know what to do. He had loved her, asked her to marry him, stayed around because he was worried about her. Together they could stop Joe. She prayed The Prophecy was like a house of cards. Once you began removing a few of the cards… Grabbing her purse, she headed for the door.

AINSLEY KNEW SHE was bound to cross paths with Sawyer at some point. This was a small video production company. Somehow, she'd avoided him almost all morning. But as she was leading her horse out of the stables, her luck ran out.

He walked up leading his horse, and she remembered belatedly that he'd had an early shoot. "I was just thinking about you," Sawyer said.

"Yes, me, too." The words were out before she could call them back. She'd been thinking how embarrassed she was, how lucky she'd been to avoid him and half hoping that he'd already done his scene and had left for good. "I mean…I…"

He laughed. "You don't need to explain."

She looked away for a moment before turning to face him with a sigh. "About last night—"

"No explanation needed for that either." He grinned at her, and she was struck by how completely charming he was. "I heard that the landslide yesterday ruined plans to film there. Are you riding out to look for another location?"

She nodded.

"Would you mind if I rode with you? I haven't seen much of this country around here. I'd love to tag along." His gaze met hers. "That's if you don't mind."

Ainsley actually felt tongue-tied. She'd known her share of handsome cowboys, but there was something about this one. Not to mention he'd saved her life yesterday, but then she'd embarrassed herself in front of him last night.

"If you're thinking I'm a walking disaster who needs looking after—"

"I would never think that about you. Anyway, you said you were putting the new Ainsley Hamilton to rest, so there shouldn't be much saving to be done, darn it."

She couldn't help but weaken. He was doing his best to joke away last night and make her less self-conscious. She appreciated that more than he could know. Sawyer Nash was one of only a few people in the world who'd seen her at her worst. And naked, too, she reminded herself with a silent groan.

"Sure, tag along, if you want to." She ducked her

head, hating how juvenile she sounded. It reminded her of the first boy who'd ever asked her out, a high school freshman when she'd been an eighth-grader.

"Great," Sawyer said. "I'll get my horse some water before we go," he said and left her in the cool shadow of the barn as he led his horse over to the water trough.

Ainsley stopped to watch him go. For a moment, he was silhouetted against the daylight. His broad shoulders sculpted in relief. She shook her head at her wayward thoughts and tugged on her horse's reins to get the mare moving again, telling herself she hadn't noticed Sawyer's slim hips or his long legs or how he filled out his Wranglers. It was just like eighth grade all over again, except…except that more daring, care-free Ainsley Hamilton was fighting to get out again.

CHAPTER SEVEN

SAWYER RODE NEXT to Ainsley, debating telling her who he was and why he'd shown up the way he had. But just minutes ago she'd made it clear that she didn't like the idea of him riding along because he thought she needed saving.

But damn if she didn't need saving. That note he'd found on her door had been nagging at him all morning. Her secret admirer was more than a little obsessed with her. Following her from town to town meant he had some means of support rather than a regular job. It also showed how determined he was. A sane man didn't follow a woman around like that unless…

He looked over at Ainsley. He could see that she was at home in a saddle. There was something so strong and self-assured about her, not to mention beautiful and smart and funny, he thought, remembering this morning when she'd been hiding under the covers. He smiled to himself. He could see where a man might become infatuated with Ainsley Hamilton.

She glanced over at him and smiled as if content with the silence between them. He felt the same way. It was another remarkable fall day. A clear brilliant blue sky hung over the pine-covered mountains. Patches of golden-leafed aspens rustled in the breeze, and an occasional hawk would sweep past overhead, casting a winged shadow over them before disappearing behind a rocky bluff.

"It's beautiful, isn't it?" she said, looking out at the Western landscape as they rode along.

"Beautiful," he said, his gaze on her.

She glanced over at him as if she'd felt his stare on her and knew he wasn't talking about the country. Her smile was warmer than the sun on his back.

They found several locations that Ainsley thought might suit Gunderson.

"I think that's enough options," she said.

"One of the kitchen girls told me about a hot spring up this way," Sawyer said, not wanting their time together to end just yet. "I'm not sure it would make a location for the commercial, but if you want to see it…"

Ainsley glanced at her watch. He could tell that she was torn. The old Ainsley who always did what was right and prudent needed to get back to Gunderson with her latest ideas. The new Ainsley?

"Are you trying to lead me astray, Mr. Nash?" she asked when she looked up and saw the way he was studying her.

He grinned. "Is it working?"

Again she hesitated. "I suppose we better check it out."

They rode in silence a short way up a narrow valley until they came to a rock formation set against the mountain. Sawyer could feel Ainsley's excitement. He assumed it was because this would be a beautiful place for the commercial shoot since the canyon had fallen through, so to speak.

He dismounted, tying his horse to a pine tree, and started to reach for Ainsley, when she swung a leg over her saddle horn and slid down next to him. Feeling like a kid, he took her hand, excited to see the spring.

It was better than he could have imagined. Steam rose from an oval pool of clear water surrounded by large boulders.

"Why didn't I know about this?" Ainsley demanded of herself.

"I overheard one of the girls who work in the kitchen talking about it. They are planning to ride up here tonight with some boys they know." He looked up at Montana's big blue sky overhead. "I bet it is beautiful at night."

Ainsley was still looking guilty that she hadn't been aware of it. As if being the location scout, she should know everything about the entire state. She finally looked over at him. *"What are you doing?"*

He removed his coat, then began unbuttoning his shirt. "Going skinny-dipping."

"You wouldn't."

He laughed as he stripped off his shirt. "You were all for it last night."

"That was different. I was—"

"The new Ainsley Hamilton, the adventurous, the woman who was bound and determined to do everything she'd missed out on."

She lifted her chin as he reached to unsnap his jeans. "If you think you can tempt me to—"

"I wouldn't dream of it. I don't mind going in alone."

She opened her mouth, then snapped it shut. "You think I won't do it."

Sawyer cocked his head at her. The buttons on his jeans popped out one after another. As he began to shrug out of the denim, she turned her back. He smiled to himself as he stopped to watch her toss aside her jacket, then slowly unbutton her shirt.

He stepped into the warm pool. It quickly became deep. He sank into it, relishing the heat. "It's perfect!" he called to her. She had taken off everything but her bra and panties. He could see she was about to chicken out. "You won't want to ride back in wet underwear. I've already seen you naked, but I'll turn around if you like. I can be a perfect gentleman. If that's what you want." His words were apparently sufficient.

"I'm not as big a prude as everyone thinks I am," she called to him without turning in his direction.

He saw her unhook her bra, and he turned around as promised. He heard her enter the water a few moments later. He felt small ripples move against him. "Is it safe to turn around now?"

"I guess so," she said. She was neck deep in the water. Had the water been clearer he might have been able to see her below the surface. But he didn't need the view. He'd never forget what she looked like after last night in the moonlight.

He stayed where he was, sensing that's the way she wanted it. But he was smiling to himself. He was damned proud of whichever Ainsley Hamilton was sharing the pool with him. He admired a woman who accepted a challenge, especially for something out of her comfort zone.

"Have dinner with me tonight."

SARAH HURRIED DOWN the hospital hallway, reaching Russell's hospital room as the doctor came out. "How is he?"

He recognized her from all her other visits and like most people in the county, knew that she had been Russell's fiancé not all that long ago.

"It is nothing short of a miracle," the doctor said, closing the door behind him. "He's still a little confused. We'll need to run more tests, but it appears he will have a full recovery."

She breathed a sigh of relief that brought tears to her eyes again. "Thank you. Can I see him?"

"Just keep your visit short."

Sarah took a deep breath and pushed the door open. The first time she'd come to see Russell was right after his attack. He'd been so badly beaten that he hadn't been expected to live. The doctor had worried that he would have brain damage. So it really was a miracle.

As she entered the room, she let the door close behind her. Russell lay on the bed on his back, his eyes closed.

She moved quietly to his side and took his hand. His eyes opened at her touch, and he turned his head toward her, a smile coming to his lips.

"I am so glad to see you're awake," she said, unable to hold back the tears.

His smile wavered. "I'm sorry, I thought for a minute you were my daughter, Destry."

"I'm sure the doctor has called her."

He nodded and looked toward the door. "I thought the two of them would be here by now."

She stared at him. Now she was the one confused. "Destry and her husband?"

"Destry and Judy, my wife."

Judy? His deceased wife?

She stared at him. The doctor had said there was some confusion after such major injuries. "Russell, I'm so sorry. This is all my fault. I know you were just trying to help me. If I could take any of it back—"

He pulled his hand free, his frown deepening. "I don't mean to be rude, but do I know you?"

She was momentarily stunned. "Russell, it's me, *Sarah*." He still looked puzzled. *"Sarah Hamilton."*

His eyes widened as he finally seemed to recognize her. "I'm sorry, but I thought you were… That is…" He looked around the room as if now not sure where he was. When his gaze came back to her, he looked more frightened than confused. "I'm sure I recall going to your funeral." He fumbled for his call button to alert the nurse, all the while he just kept frowning at her.

Sarah stared at him, almost too shocked to speak. "You don't remember finding me on the road outside Beartooth months ago?" she asked, her voice breaking.

"*Finding* you?"

"You don't remember…" She couldn't bear to say the words. *You don't remember falling in love with me, asking me to marry you? You don't remember promising to help me?* The door opened behind them. Sarah turned as a nurse came in.

"I'm sorry, but you'll have to leave," the nurse said, glancing from Sarah to Russell and back again. Russell was visibly upset.

Sarah nodded. Russell was still frowning at her, looking scared since his last memory was going to her funeral all those years ago.

"I was just leaving." She forced a smile. *He didn't remember her.* She'd heard about head injuries where there was memory loss. His had apparently wiped out everything they had been to each other since she'd returned.

She thought of her own loss of memories due to

Dr. Venable eradicating them. At least for Russell, forgetting her was a blessing. "I'm so glad you're better," she said, her heart breaking.

AINSLEY PLAYED THE conversation over in her head, mentally kicking herself. She still couldn't believe that she'd actually gone skinny-dipping—again! It was so not like her and yet… She smiled to herself. She'd felt a sense of freedom like none she'd ever experienced. And Sawyer had been a man of his word. He'd behaved like a perfect gentleman.

So what had made her say she would have dinner with this cowboy? He'd caught her at a weak moment, she told herself.

"I thought you might enjoy getting away from here for a while," he'd said. "I feel like I'm in a fishbowl up here, you know what I mean?"

She knew that feeling only too well. But then she'd felt like that for months. "Not much goes on out here that someone doesn't witness. That's why there is so much gossip." Fortunately, she hadn't heard anything about her and Sawyer, given his early-morning exit from her cabin.

Ainsley had been ready to leave it at that. Going into town with him would only get tongues wagging. She had opened her mouth hoping a good excuse would come out.

"Unless you've gone back to being the old Ainsley Hamilton, the one who isn't allowed to have fun…"

She had groaned. Did he really think he could

dare her into having dinner with him? "Last night I was—"

"Drunk?"

"A little overdramatic."

"So you don't think going into town with me to the local café would be living too dangerous for you?"

Right then she couldn't imagine anything more dangerous. There was something about this man beyond his good looks, his obvious charm, his way of making her feel safe.

"You're making fun of me."

"Not at all. Like I told you, I like both the old and the new Ainsley. It will be interesting to see which one comes out with me tonight."

She'd laughed. It had felt good. It also felt good to be asked out by this handsome cowboy. She couldn't remember the last time she'd taken a man up on an offer for dinner. No way was she going to let that Ainsley Hamilton from last night out, but what would it hurt to let down her hair just a little?

"Okay, cowboy," she'd said. Only later back in her cabin did she worry. Sawyer brought out a woman in her she didn't know. It scared her, but it also excited her. Something told her that she should keep her distance from the man.

SAWYER HAD MADE up his mind that he would tell Ainsley the truth at dinner tonight—if she went out with him. He feared she might change her mind.

He didn't like keeping the truth from her, now that he'd met her.

But at the same time, she'd made it clear that she prided herself on her independence. As she'd said, she could take care of herself. The rock slide yesterday, though, had shaken that solid foundation she'd built her life on. She seemed to think she'd contained that urge she'd had to do things she'd never done. He wasn't so sure about that, given that he'd talked her into going into the spring with him.

Truthfully, he'd love to see the new Ainsley come back. Had she been sober, he would have gone skinny-dipping with her last night. But then again, had she been sober, it would probably have never crossed her mind.

On the ride back to the stables, Ainsley had asked, "I'm curious. What do you do when you aren't playing a cowboy extra?"

He'd avoided the truth. "I was raised on a ranch, so me and horses are a given. But I promise to tell you anything you want at dinner." He made an *x* over his heart with one finger. "Scout's honor."

Ainsley had seemed to relax a little. He knew she was still suffering from a bad hangover. He had no idea how much alcohol Kitzie had put in the drinks, but enough to down an elephant, he was betting. Kitzie. He pushed all thoughts of her away.

He wished he wouldn't have to tell Ainsley the truth until he'd found her stalker. That was why as soon as they got back to the stables, he'd set out to find the person who'd left the note on her cabin door last night. He had it narrowed down to the security guard, Lance Roderick. He fit the profile.

The rest of the crew seemed okay, since, according to Kitzie, almost all of them were from California and had been on the road during the months that someone had been following Ainsley in Montana.

He wondered again what assignment Kitzie was on but told himself it apparently didn't have anything to do with Ainsley's stalker. That was all he had to concern himself with. If Kitzie needed help, she knew where to find him.

THE TRAMP! WHAT HAD happened to the woman he'd adored from afar? From the shadows, he watched Ainsley and the cowboy ride back from wherever they'd been for hours. She laughed at something the long, tall cowboy had said, her laughter coming to him on the breeze.

He felt bile rise in his throat. She was *flirting* with the man as if she had no morals at all. Look at how she threw her head back when she laughed. Look at how she touched her hair. Look at how she gazed at the cowboy shyly from under her lashes. How could she behave like this? Wasn't last night bad enough?

The thought of her standing naked by the creek filled him with a burning anger. To take off her clothes with a man she didn't even know? He'd been so disappointed in her, but last night he'd excused her behavior. While staying back in the blackness beyond the campfire, he'd heard her talking about her life passing before her eyes because of the rock slide. He had attributed her lack of decorum to her near accident—one *he* had caused.

So he had excused her even when the cowboy had bundled her up and taken her back to her cabin. He had waited outside, counting the minutes. But the cowboy hadn't come back out. He'd moved closer. Ainsley had been drunk. If that cowboy laid one finger on her...

But at the cabin window in the back where the bedroom was, he'd heard only Ainsley's faint snores. He'd stayed there, listening. He'd learned how to move around the place without anyone paying him any attention. No one had been able to see him in the trees behind the cabin, and if the cowboy had tried anything, he would hear it and wake up, should he doze off.

Nothing had happened. Not that he was happy about the cowboy spending the night in Ainsley's cabin. What if someone else had seen the cowboy come out of there this morning? Her reputation would be ruined. People would talk. He thought of his mother and shook his head. She would not have approved. She would have demanded that Ainsley be punished.

The thought made his heart beat faster.

This morning he'd asked the girls in the kitchen about him. Sawyer Nash was nothing but an extra, some dumb cowboy who had a couple of ride-on parts in this ridiculous commercial.

Still, he'd been willing to let last night be forgotten if Ainsley came to her senses today. She had seemed to be her old, proper self this morning when he'd watched her with the director. He'd been cheered by that, and forgiving. Whatever she'd done last night, it wasn't her fault, so he would overlook it.

But now, watching her with this cowboy… He felt sick to his stomach. She had always been the perfect lady. She didn't wear trashy clothing like other women and, until last night, she hadn't imbibed any alcohol with the others on the set—at least not when he was watching. And he was always watching.

He thought of his mother and wished she were still alive. Had she been, he would have taken Ainsley home to meet her long before this. He would have been proud to tell his mother that Ainsley was the woman he was going to marry.

But now all he felt was disgust. Nor could he understand the change in her. Had he *caused* this? If so, then he had to do something. If Ainsley kept behaving like this, she would have to be punished. It would be for her own good. He couldn't let her disgrace herself with this…cowboy. He would save her from herself. His mother always said that when she'd had to punish him. The pain and scars were reminders.

As for Sawyer Nash… His anger boiled just under his skin, a hot lava that roiled through his blood. He would deal with him, as well.

CHAPTER EIGHT

SARAH LEFT THE hospital in a daze. Russell didn't re-member her. The part of his past with her in it was gone. Maybe forever. She felt bereft, her heart shat-tered. She hadn't realized how much she was depend-ing on Russell to help her. Russell's love had been the one given. He was gone from her life as if he'd never been there. As if they had never shared anything.

She thought of how she'd hurt Russell when she'd broken off their engagement and gone back to Buck. He'd understood why she'd had to do it. Buck was the father of her children. She'd never denied that she'd still loved her husband. But Buck had remarried. She'd thought there was no place in his life for her.

Then right before Sarah and Russell were to be married, Angelina had died, and Buck had told her he was planning to leave Angelina for her. He was going to tell Angelina that night, but had gotten the phone call about her death first.

Russell had known the moment he'd heard about Angelina's death. He'd known she would go back to Buck—and she had.

But she'd never stopped loving Russell. She could admit that now.

Stumbling to her car, she climbed behind the wheel and broke into sobs. Russell had been there for her, time and time again over the almost two years since she'd returned. He was the one person she could count on, no matter what. Even if her past was as dark as they both suspected. Without him... She'd never felt so alone.

She wiped her eyes and tried to pull herself together. She thought of Buck and her love for him. But she had never been able to be honest with him about the person she'd been. Russell had seen Red in her, and yet he'd still loved her. She hadn't realized how much she'd loved him. And now he was damaged... and all because of who she'd been, what she'd done and whom she'd loved.

Joe Landon. He was the other man she had apparently loved just as desperately, she realized. He was why she'd bought into The Prophecy and its cause. And yet knowing she and Joe had been together back when they were still teenagers, she didn't "feel" what that desperate love had been like because that memory hadn't been completely restored yet.

Once Dr. Venable gives you back the rest of your memory...

Would that memory flip a switch so that she would not only feel love for Joe again, but she would also become the anarchist called Red? Would she again believe that bombing buildings and killing people was the way to change the world?

Any day now, Dr. Venable would contact her, ready to give her the final piece of her memory. But what if that key to her past released Red and united her with her former lover/terrorist Joe Landon? What if she became a woman she didn't recognize?

Sarah told herself that she wasn't that young, innocent girl who'd fallen for Joe Landon. She was strong and capable. She could fight whatever the memory might make her want to do.

Either way, she was on her own. All she knew was that Joe had something planned for election night. She prayed it wouldn't mirror other horrible acts of terrorism. Joe needed Buck to become president. That was the reason she'd been brought back to Montana. She'd played her part. But what would that part be election night?

Sarah started her vehicle. She had no one to turn to for help. Russell was gone from her life. Nor could she go to Buck. Joe had big plans for her, Doc had told her. That terrified her more than she could admit. He was a loose cannon with more than an agenda. He felt she'd betrayed not just The Prophecy—but him, all those years ago when she'd fallen in love with Buck and had six children with him. Worse, when he'd contacted her about The Prophecy and she'd told him she wanted nothing to do with it—or him. That's when she had realized all those years ago that she had to kill herself to save her family.

But miraculously she'd survived and had called the one person she thought she could trust, Dr. Ralph Venable. He'd wiped away the memory of her husband and her children and swore she'd be content.

Content until Joe Landon had found them and forced her return to Montana—and Buck. And all because Buck was about to run for president of the United States.

Since her return, Joe had been pulling her strings. He hadn't forgiven her for betraying him and The Prophecy. He would want her blood. Just the thought of coming face-to-face with him again made her shudder. Or maybe his plan was just to kill them all election night.

As she drove away from the hospital and Russell, Sarah knew she had only one choice. She had to stop her former lover and bring down The Prophecy, no matter the cost.

JERROD WILLISTON GLANCED at his watch. It was time to make the call. He felt a small thrill each time he keyed the number into the disposable phone he'd been given. That thrill increased at just the sound of the charismatic, beautiful man who'd changed his life all those years ago.

He'd been headed for prison or the morgue the night he'd run into a church to hide from the gang members chasing him. At the time, he'd hoped to find something he could steal. He desperately needed to get out of town. Or at least get enough money to buy a gun.

When he'd heard someone coming from deep inside the church, he'd sat down on a pew with his hood pulled up and head down. He'd been pretending to search for spiritual guidance when Joe had sat down next to him.

He'd liked Joe from the first time he'd met him. Not exactly a father figure, he thought now with a laugh. But the truth was, he really had been searching for something, some meaning in his life.

He and Joe had begun to talk, their talk continuing through the night. As the sun was coming up, Joe told him that he could save him.

"You're just the kind of man my organization needs," he'd said.

At first Jerrod had thought Joe had wanted him to join the church. But then he'd asked, "Have you ever considered politics?"

He'd laughed, thinking he was joking. Born to a single mother on meth, he'd never thought he had a future. "You mean like for president or something?"

Joe had laughed. "I was thinking more behind the scenes. Someone who controlled what was going to happen in the world."

He couldn't imagine being in control of anything. His life had been one carnival ride with him never knowing if he would find his mother dead or if one of her boyfriends would beat the crap out of him. Not to mention the rough neighborhood where they lived and the fear he felt every time he stepped out the door.

"I can make you somebody important," Joe had said. "Would you like that?"

He hadn't realized how much he'd yearned for normal, let alone what sounded to him like the promise of a rocket to the moon.

"Then you're perfect for what I have in mind," Joe had said. "All I ask is for your loyalty."

He had it in spades. That had been eighteen years ago. Through Joe's guidance and powerful friends, Jerrod was now the campaign manager of the next president of the United States. Joe had been like a father to him.

"Problems?" Joe asked now as he took the call.

"Not really, though Buck is still struggling with—"

"Sarah. What now?"

"I don't think Buck trusts Sarah. He's worried about security election night."

Joe chuckled. "Fool. Must be awful not being able to trust your wife."

He said nothing, knowing that Joe and Sarah had a history, and she was a touchy subject for Joe sometimes.

"Don't worry. I'll take care of Sarah. I've been looking forward to this for a long time. Just keep Buckmaster focused. We are almost to the finish line. I'm proud of you, Jerrod. You've done an excellent job at your end. I won't forget it."

He hung up, more than pleased. He'd pledged his life to The Prophecy because of Joe. He'd made the man proud. It was something he'd never been able to do with his own father, whoever the man had been who'd deserted him and his mother all those years ago.

WHEN THE SHERIFF got the note from Sawyer, he had the techs check it for prints hoping for the best.

"Looks like we have three separate sets of prints," he was told.

"Did we get a hit on any of them?"

"Only one. Katherine McCormick, since her prints were on file with the FBI because she's an agent."

Frank leaned back in his chair in surprise. "But none on the others?"

"Sorry, whoever they belong to, their prints must not be on file."

Frank called Sawyer to give him the news and ask how it was that a female FBI agent's prints turned up.

"Kitzie," the cowboy said.

"You know her?"

"Yep. She's on an undercover assignment. Small world."

Frank heard something in his friend's voice and guessed there was history between Sawyer and… Kitzie.

"Now I'm wondering if Kitzie touched the notepaper when it was still in the main office. Or later when the note was on Ainsley's door where I found it."

"If she's aware of why you're there, that wouldn't be very professional on her part," Frank commented.

"No, it wouldn't." Sawyer sounded upset about that.

"There were two other sets of prints, but we didn't get a hit."

"Anyone could have touched that notepad."

"So you don't have any suspects yet?" the sheriff asked.

"I'm especially interested in the security guard, Lance Roderick. I'm taking Ainsley out to dinner tonight in town. If I'm right, Roderick will follow us."

BUCK'S HEART DROPPED like a stone when he heard the news that Russell Murdock had regained consciousness. He felt instantly guilty for such thoughts. He'd never wished for the man to end up in the hospital in a coma.

But he also knew how his wife felt about the man she'd almost married. There was a connection between Russell and Sarah that worried him.

"I just heard about Russell," he said when Sarah answered the phone. "Have you seen him?" He silently cursed himself for sounding so jealous. But he knew before she answered that Sarah would have run right to the man's bedside the moment she heard.

"Yes, he's…confused, but the doctor is expecting a full recovery."

Buck closed his eyes and gripped the phone tighter. Sarah was going to put him in an early grave. If it wasn't Russell, it was that weird Dr. Venable his wife had been seeing behind his back. "That's good to hear." He could almost see her bristle at his luke-warm tone. A part of him actually admired the man.

"It *is* good news. I'm sure his daughter and grand-children are relieved."

The sheriff hadn't found Russell's attackers, but Dr. Venable was suspected of being behind it. The doctor had disappeared right after that, and no one had seen him since. At least Buck hoped Sarah wasn't seeing him behind his back again. She'd promised she would let him know if the doctor con-tacted her again.

He wished he believed her.

"You don't have to worry about Russell," Sarah said, sounding tired.

"We've all been worried about him."

"I mean about me and Russell. I'm married to you now. I broke my engagement to him to be with you. Russell and I are…over."

Buck couldn't speak around the lump in his throat. His wife sounded so sad about that, so…broken. He finally asked, "Are you all right?"

"Just tired. The campaigning was exhausting. I have this other event later this afternoon, then I'm not going to do anything else until after the election if that's all right with you."

"Of course," he said quickly. "Just take care of yourself. I'll be flying home tomorrow or the next day. I'll let you know. If Jerrod tries to schedule you for more, just let me know, and I'll take care of it."

"Thank you. How are you holding up?"

He pretended to laugh. "Exhausted, too. But election night is almost here. Then campaigning will be behind us." At least until the next election, he thought, but didn't voice. He was dragging Sarah into a life she hadn't wanted. He would try to make her life as easy as possible once he was president.

"I love you," he said, hating that he sounded pathetic. For so many years, believing that she was dead, that she'd driven in the river all those years ago to escape him and their children, he'd been bitter. Now he had her back. Their daughters had her back. They were a family. Nothing could destroy that. Certainly not Russell Murdock.

But as he hung up, Buck couldn't shake the feeling of dread that had been riding on his shoulders for months now. Did he really know the Sarah who had come back to him?

SAWYER HAD BEEN forced to cut short his talk with the sheriff when there was a knock on his cabin door telling him it was time.

He rode a horse in a half dozen takes before he was told it was a wrap, but that he should be ready for another shoot early the next morning. His leg was bothering him, and he wondered if he really was up to even this easy of an assignment. Well, it had sounded easy anyway.

The rest of the afternoon he spent trying to find Lance Roderick. He'd glimpsed him going between the cabins earlier after he and Ainsley had come back from their ride. But when he'd tried to catch up to him, Lance had been nowhere around. There had been no answer at his cabin, and when Sawyer had tried the door, he'd found it locked. He really would have liked a look inside.

He'd been headed back to his own cabin when he'd spotted the two teenage girls from the kitchen. He watched them break off their conversation and hurry back inside. That's when he saw Lance. The man was half hidden in the shadows. Sawyer wondered if he'd been watching him—or the teenagers. While apparently not working today, Lance was wearing his uniform shirt. Medium height with brown hair, he had the kind of face and body that would be considered average. The kind of man who could blend into the scenery. The kind of man who liked to watch others.

"I think I have my man," Sawyer said under his breath as Lance quickly disappeared around the edge of the cabin where he'd been hiding. But before he left, Sawyer noticed that, like him, Lance was limping. From yesterday up on the cliffs?

His cell phone rang. Sawyer stepped away from the cabins to take the call. "Hope you've got some information for me," he said when he saw the caller was the sheriff.

"I ran Lance Roderick through the system again. Nothing came up. I know you were hoping for at least a restraining order on him from the past, but I couldn't find even a speeding ticket."

Sawyer couldn't hide his disappointment.

"Sorry. You're sure he's the one?"

"That's just it, I'm *not* sure." Sawyer swore under his breath. The man stalking Ainsley either hadn't been caught before, or this was his first time. "The problem is that until he does something, I might not know for sure. By then it might be too late. Let's see if he follows us tonight."

AINSLEY COULDN'T REMEMBER the last time she'd gone on a date. The other night, fired up with alcohol, she'd been ready to do something audacious. While she didn't feel ready to cut loose quite as much as she had, she still felt as if she'd missed out on life by being the "responsible" one.

She thought about earlier today in the hot pool and felt herself flush at the memory. She'd never done anything like that. It had felt so…liberating.

But at the same time, her behavior scared her. She was starting to like Sawyer too much. With him egging her on to be more adventurous and her own desire to be more daring, she feared where this might lead.

She wasn't fool enough not to realize how easily

she could get her heart broken or worse. Her father was about to become president of the United States. The last thing she would ever want was to have her behavior reflect badly on him. What if someone had seen her earlier in that hot spring with Sawyer?

Going out with him tonight seemed a bad idea. But at the same time, she had every right to date. She'd said yes, because…well, because she wanted to. Also she'd remembered the way he'd grabbed her just before the rock slide had come down and almost closed the canyon. He'd rescued her not just once but later that night.

A man like that was dangerous because he made her feel safe while, at the same time, he made her want to do things she'd never done before. He was too handsome, too charming, and she was…to put it politely, too inexperienced.

There that was again. Something else she'd missed out on. Only this time it was because she hadn't met anyone she wanted to get that intimate with. Another reason that going out with Sawyer Nash was—at least for her—beyond daring. He stirred up desires in her that made her want to throw caution to the wind and have a wild fling with the cowboy.

And that was so not her. Another reason she should have turned down dinner. She was playing with a wildfire and bound to get burned.

She felt a prickle of fresh excitement at the thought of spending the evening with him, which proved how much trouble she was in. He excited her. She really never knew what he would do next. Or maybe worse, what he might challenge her to do.

But now, staring into her cabin closet, she realized she had nothing to wear. Well, it was too late to drive into town, even if there had been a clothing store that sold more than boots and jeans.

On impulse she did something also not like her. She left her cabin and walked over to Kitzie's. The woman had never spoken more than two words to her before last night when she'd invited her to the bonfire and supplied her with drinks.

Ainsley didn't blame her. She was sure that the woman thought she was doing her a favor. She'd heard whispers behind her back. Everyone thought she was a straitlaced prude and soon to be an old maid. She'd often thought the same herself since she'd never felt an overwhelming desire for a man—until Sawyer Nash.

Now she tapped on Kitzie's door and waited, almost chickening out. The door swung open, framing the kitchen manager in the light. "Ainsley?" Kitzie looked past her as if expecting her not to be alone.

"I have a favor to ask. You don't happen to have a dress I could borrow tonight, do you?"

"A *dress*?" Kitzie frowned. She was holding a half-empty glass of red wine. "Hot date?" When Ainsley just shrugged, Kitzie motioned her in. Her cabin, though like all the others, looked more homey. Probably because she'd added throw pillows and a few more personal items. Ainsley had come with a suitcase full of work clothes, so she only had jeans, boots, shirts and jackets.

"I might have something," Kitzie said, eyeing her up and down. "Let me take a look." She disappeared to the back of the cabin.

Ainsley stood in the center of the so-called living room and waited.

"How about this one?" the woman asked, returning with a bright red short dress.

Her eyes must have widened at how low-cut it was, because Kitzie laughed and said, "It's a date, right? I even have some heels that should fit you."

"Oh, I don't know. It isn't *that* kind of date."

Kitzie laughed. "Then you definitely need to wear this dress. Trust me," she added with a wink.

"I trusted you last night with the iced tea," Ainsley reminded her.

"So true," the woman said with a laugh. "Apparently it didn't hurt your night. I saw Sawyer Nash coming out of your cabin this morning."

"It wasn't like that. He only rescued me from myself."

"Then, don't let him do that tonight," she said and thrust the dress at her. "Let me get the heels."

SAWYER HADN'T KNOWN what to expect when he knocked at Ainsley's cabin. If anything, he thought she'd come up with an excuse why she couldn't go to dinner. Nothing prepared him for what he saw when the door opened.

Ainsley, as beautiful as ever, her blue eyes sparkling, her blond hair floating around her slim, suntanned shoulders, wearing a dress he had hoped to never see again.

"Is everything all right?" Ainsley's earlier excited expression had turned to one of concern.

He quickly checked his shocked, horrified look and shook his head. He would kill Kitzie. He unfisted his hands at his sides and tried to relax. "Everything is…amazing. *You're* amazing. I'm sorry. I'm stunned at how beautiful you look."

She looked embarrassed as she ran her palms down the length of the red fabric. "The dress isn't too much?"

The dress was *way* too much, but he wasn't about to tell her. "You look beautiful in it." That much at least was true.

"I borrowed it from Kitzie, the kitchen manager."

He nodded. Kitzie was the last person he wanted to talk about ever with Ainsley. Right now if he could have gotten hold of Kitzie, he would have strangled her. "Ready?"

Ainsley nodded, and he took her hand as she climbed down the cabin steps, a little unsteady in the high, high heels.

They took Sawyer's pickup and drove into the nearest town. Open Range was like a lot of small Montana towns. Once a bustling community, it had shrunk to a post office, a gas station, a bar and a café.

He ushered her into the café and asked to be

seated by the window. The sun had set, leaving Montana's big sky a silver gray. Lights came on across the small town, twinkling against the dark of the pines.

The café was warm. Ainsley pulled her long blond hair up, making him aware of her slim neck, as she fanned herself. She wore a necklace and dangly earrings of tiny silver stars that glittered in the evening light like real stars.

"You're sure the dress is all right?" she asked again, looking unsure as she let her hair fall like down feathers around her shoulders again.

"All I see is the woman in it," he said truthfully. He was doing his best to ignore the dress and Kitzie's blatant in-your-face cruel trick that she'd played on him. But Kitzie had made one fatal error. The dress fit Ainsley better than it had her. It clung perfectly to her curves, plunging at the neckline to hint at the full breasts. Everything about Ainsley in this dress made him ache with desire. He was sure that hadn't been Kitzie's plan.

He thought of Ainsley's naked silhouette against the moonlight and quickly ordered them both drinks.

"I'll take a beer," she said and flashed him a smile. "I'm a Montana girl."

He ordered the same, smiling across the table at her. The café was busy but not overly noisy. He tried to relax as they made polite conversation.

But his gaze kept going to the parking lot outside. All the way here, he'd surreptitiously been watching his rearview mirror. As the waitress brought their beers, he saw the car pull up and recognized it at once from the ones that had been parked in front of one of the cabins back at the production company site.

Just as he suspected, they'd been followed—and by his number-one suspect. The blue sedan that pulled up out of the lights from the café belonged to Lance Roderick.

CHAPTER NINE

KITZIE WAITED UNTIL Murph took a break in the kitchen before she hurried into the room the production company was using as an office.

It took her a few minutes to find the spare keys for the cabins. She'd just pocketed Gunderson's when she heard Murph returning. She slipped out and ducked behind a log beam just as the woman rounded the corner.

That had been too close for comfort. Murph hardly ever left the office, and when she did, she usually locked the door. She either took her job very seriously or there were papers in there that she didn't want anyone to see.

Kitzie hadn't decided if Murph was only part of the video production company or also involved with the burglaries. Refusing to worry about how she was going to be able to return the key without getting caught, she hurried around the back of the cabins.

Minutes ago, she'd heard Gunderson and the carnival owner talking. Hale had said he wanted to show the boss something, and the two had headed for the meadow and the carnival equipment.

She knew she wouldn't have much time. But at the moment, everyone seemed to be occupied. Staying in the shadows, she moved to the back of Gunderson's cabin. The structure was small enough that there was only one door. She stood at the back listening. When all seemed quiet, she moved along the side.

Seeing no one, she quickly used the key and stepped inside. The cabin was as neat as she had expected it to be. Gunderson looked like a man who kept his affairs in order. Which made her worry that she was wasting her time searching his cabin. Nor did she imagine there was anything incriminating in the office.

These thieves had been too smart to leave anything lying around that would call attention to what they did when not making commercials. While her boss seemed to think she was barking up the wrong tree, as her mother would have said, Kitzie had to follow her gut instinct. And it told her that Gunderson was the leader of this band of jewel thieves and that he would soon be fencing what they'd stolen.

He and his cohorts probably wouldn't have the loot with them, though. But there might be some clue as to where they'd stashed it. Or when they planned to fence the goods and to whom.

She quickly went to work systematically searching the small area. She'd just gotten to the bedroom and was on her hands and knees searching under the bed when she heard heavy boots on the porch. As the door banged open, she slipped all the way under the bed and held her breath.

SAWYER WATCHED THE blue sedan out of the corner of his eye, wondering if Roderick would come into the café. Or if he had just come to watch. From where Roderick had parked he would be able to see him and Ainsley. Because of the darkness beyond the café lights though, Sawyer couldn't see him behind the wheel. But he was still there. He hadn't gotten out. Sawyer could almost feel the man staring at them.

He told himself that Roderick could have just decided to come into town for dinner. There was only one café in town so it wasn't exactly a coincidence that he would show up here.

But the security guard still hadn't gotten out of his car. Sawyer knew he hadn't come in for dinner. The man had followed Ainsley and now wanted to sit out there and watch. And probably work himself up.

Sawyer couldn't let that happen. "Can you excuse me for a minute?" he asked Ainsley, who was preoccupied with her menu.

Getting up, he headed for the men's restroom. But when he reached the hallway, he kept going on out the back door. Circling the building, he came up on the passenger side of the blue sedan.

He could see a dark figure behind the wheel. He was counting on Roderick being distracted as he watched the café—and Ainsley. Sawyer was within yards of the sedan when he saw something flash and realized what the man was doing. He was taking cell phone photos.

Sawyer couldn't see what Roderick was shooting. Photos of Ainsley sitting inside the café? Or something else?

Suddenly the sedan's engine roared to life. The driver had either spotted him or something had spooked him. Roderick quickly reversed, wheeling out of the parking lot in a cloud of dust and gravel. All Sawyer could do was watch him drive away, thinking what a fool the man was. Didn't he realize his car had been recognized, and he couldn't get away that easily?

KITZIE FELT A gust of cold air rush across the floor to her hiding place under the bed as one after another of the men entered the cabin. She counted four.

"We have booze here," Gunderson was arguing as the door finally slammed closed. She couldn't see anything from her spot back under the bed, but she recognized his authoritative voice. "Going into town is dangerous. Especially for you," he said, apparently indicating one of the men. "You tend to talk too much when you drink."

"I don't need you babysitting me." She recognized Bobby LeRoy's whiny voice and listened to him curse and slam out of the cabin. The door banged closed with a sound like a gunshot. Kitzie felt another gust of cold air rush across the floor.

"He is going to be a problem," Gunderson said after LeRoy left.

"There isn't much we can do under the circumstances." Ken Hale, the owner of the carnival. She knew his gravelly deep voice only too well since he made a point of talking to her every chance he got.

"Go after him," Gunderson ordered. "Try to keep him out of trouble. We just need him for a few more days. Nathan, you go with him."

"Talk about babysitting," T.K. Clark, the hippie cameraman, complained, but Kitzie heard him and Nathan follow LeRoy out the door. Before the door slammed, though, she heard Hale say for him to calm down LeRoy and that he'd be along in a minute.

"I have a bad feeling that punk kid is going to blow everything," Hale said to Gunderson after the others had left.

"Don't start with that crap about your gypsy blood, Hale. I know what I'm doing. In the meantime, we get the commercial shot, collect our money and then go our separate ways. I've always wanted to go to Ireland or maybe Greenland."

Hale's laugh sounded like a truck engine with a bad starter. "Screw that. I'm going someplace warm and sunny. Mexico maybe. Or even South America. I'm done being a carnie. I'm giving all my carnival equipment to my nephew. It's all junk anyway."

"Just make sure it all runs for the commercial. Let's not turn our noses up at the money that's kept us fed."

"I might need help getting things rolling the last day, but there will be free rides for everyone. The grocery delivery guy said he'd test any ride I wasn't sure was working right." Hale laughed. "Everyone loves a carnival."

Gunderson said something under his breath she didn't catch.

Just when Kitzie was thinking she would be trapped under this bed all night—that's if Gunderson didn't find her—the two left. She huddled in the darkness until she was sure both of them weren't coming right back before she slipped out.

Creeping to the window, she looked into the darkness beyond the cabins. Over by one of the vehicles, she saw that LeRoy and Clark seemed to be having a heated discussion. Nathan Grant was standing off to the side, clearly wanting no part of it.

She saw that Gunderson had walked partway down the mountainside with Hale. He was pointing in the direction of the carnival equipment. He looked angry.

Kitzie slipped out of the cabin, moving deeper in the shadows as Clark appeared to be trying to calm down LeRoy. It was clear that LeRoy was the weak link in the jewelry thieves' chain.

She wondered why they would put up with the new hire. They must need LeRoy for something more than helping get the carnival rides going. Whatever the reason, Kitzie knew he was the one she had to get close to. If this group needed Bobby LeRoy, then he must have some value. She just hoped he knew enough about the burglaries that she could get the proof she needed to make the arrests.

Time was running out. Gunderson was clearly the leader of this motley crew, just as she had suspected. He was the one she'd caught watching the others, especially if LeRoy got too loud at one of the meals.

The problem would be getting LeRoy alone. But maybe that would solve itself tonight since she figured there was a good chance he would come back to his cabin drunk.

Tonight LeRoy was hers, Kitzie thought as she watched Hale join LeRoy and his two babysitters. The four of them left in T.K. Clark's van. Gunderson watched them leave before walking toward the silent, dark silhouette of the carnival rides.

Kitzie hurried toward the hotel. Murph was behind her desk still. Hoping she hadn't noticed that Gunderson's extra cabin key was missing, she entered the office, the key palmed in her hand.

"Don't hate me, but I can't find my key to my cabin."

"It will cost you twenty-five bucks if you don't find it." Murph rolled her eyes and let out a curse as she turned to the board behind her.

"Wait, maybe that's it," she said, pointing to the key she'd dropped and kicked under the desk. It now lay against the back wall, near enough to the board with all the other keys.

Murph bent to pick it up, frowning as she did.

"Nope, it's cabin one. The keys are always falling off the board." She put Gunderson's cabin key back where it should have been. "You're in seven. Right?" She pulled down the extra key and spun around in her swivel chair.

Kitzie reached for the key, but Murph kept it in her hand as she leaned forward, her expression dour. "You go open your door and you come right back with this. You lose this one—"

"I'll bring it right back. I promise."

Murph shook her head in disgust but handed over the key.

Kitzie walked to her cabin, opened the door and, leaving it ajar, trotted back to the hotel—just in case Murph was watching. She handed her the key.

Murph said, "Close the door on your way out."

On the way back to her cabin, Kitzie planned her attack. She would be waiting for LeRoy when he got home. Even if he didn't know anything, it would give her a chance to search his cabin later after he'd passed out. She just had to make sure Gunderson didn't catch her. The first time she'd seen him, she'd known that Gun was dangerous. She wouldn't have been surprised to learn that he'd killed before.

SLUT! THANK GOODNESS he hadn't taken her home to meet his mother. What if she'd worn that red dress? It was disgraceful.

From a table in the café, he'd watched Ainsley and the cowboy. It was difficult to even look at her

dressed in that horrible red scrap of fabric. He'd
wanted to rip it from her ivory flesh, envisioning
her trying to cover her nakedness.

What had happened to the woman he'd fallen in
love with the moment he'd seen her? She wouldn't
remember, but that day in Livingston, she'd stopped
to help him. He hadn't known who she was at the
time. He'd just been startled that when he'd dropped
some papers, she'd hurried to pick them up before
Livingston's famous wind had sent them airborne.

As she'd handed them to him, he'd looked into
her beautiful face. He'd never believed in love at
first sight. Not really. There'd been other women, of
course, but they'd all disappointed him before things
had gone very far.

"Thank you," he had said in surprise at both her
generosity at helping a man like him and at realizing he'd found The One.

She'd been distracted, so she'd hardly noticed him.
A man had called to her as she had knelt to gather
up the stray papers littering the sidewalk. So she
hadn't really looked at him. But her act of kindness
had touched him deeply.

He had turned and watched her hurry to the man
who'd called her name. What a beautiful name. Ainsley. How unusual. His heart had pounded as he'd
realized it was meant to be. There were no coinci-
dences in life. People appeared because they were
supposed to.

The man had led Ainsley to his van with the business logo on the side. It hadn't taken him long to find out that she'd been hired to scout movie locations for a producer working with the local company. After that, it had been a matter of following her from location to location as other film and television commercial producers hired her.

It had been fun watching her work when he got the chance. He'd found ways to be around her. He had to be careful. A couple of times, he'd been afraid she'd seen him. If she realized that she'd seen him on more than one of the productions, she would get suspicious. That wouldn't do at all. She'd think he was some kind of weirdo. No, he knew he had to learn as much about her as possible before he introduced himself. He wanted to make the right impression.

Now, though, as he watched her smiling across the table at the cowboy, he felt so hurt, so betrayed, so angry with her.

He'd been deciding what to do when the cowboy had risen from the table. He'd thought the man was probably going to the restroom. He had considered going over to Ainsley's table, grabbing her arm and dragging her out of the café.

The cowboy, he'd noticed, had headed for the restroom, but at the last minute had stepped outside. How strange. Getting up, he'd done the same thing. The night air had been chilly, since he hadn't taken the time to put on his coat. He'd stayed in the shadows, wondering where the cowboy was going. Surely he wouldn't be ditching Ainsley.

A surge of indignation had him reaching into his pocket for the switchblade knife he always carried. He could kill the cowboy out here in the parking lot, and no one would be the wiser.

But curiosity had held him back. What, he'd wondered, was so important out in the parking lot that Sawyer Nash would leave his date alone?

He'd watched, mesmerized as the cowboy had sneaked through the dark toward a blue sedan. What in the heck? From his vantage point, he hadn't been able to see the dark figure behind the wheel of the car. Then there had been a series of flashes of light from inside the car's interior that lit up the man's face for an instant. He'd recognized him as Lance Roderick, the security guard. Now there was a weirdo for you.

The light had flashed again in the sedan, and with a shock, he realized that Roderick had just taken his photo. What in the—

He'd taken a step toward the car when the engine suddenly roared. Roderick reversed the sedan and, throwing gravel, left. Sawyer, he saw, was headed back toward the café, coming in his direction.

He hurried around the side of the café and in the back door, ducking into the men's restroom. What had that been about? He stood in the stall, half-afraid Sawyer had seen him and would come in. If he did... He fingered the switchblade. Let him.

But when the restroom stayed quiet, he washed his hands just as his mother had taught him and went back to his spot at the counter. His dinner had come while he was gone. But as he watched Sawyer and Ainsley, he realized his appetite had been ruined. What was that stupid security guard doing shooting his photo?

Worse, Ainsley was smiling at Sawyer in a way that made his stomach roil. He ate what he could. All the while, he studied her and the cowboy. Whatever Sawyer Nash's story, he thought, fingering the knife in his pocket, it was time.

THE NIGHT HAD turned cold by the time Gun walked back to his cabin. He walked slowly with his head down, feeling the weight of the world on his shoulders.

Since his conversation with Hale last night, he felt tense. Hale had always been a pain in the ass. But they'd worked well together because Hale respected only one thing. Money. Was that the problem now? He didn't want their arrangement to stop?

That worried Gun. It was one thing if Hale had merely gotten used to having the influx of extra money. It was another if he was *desperate* for money. Now that he thought about it, Hale had been testy and more nervous than usual since he'd arrived here. He'd complained about bringing all the carnival equipment. He'd wanted a bigger cut for his trouble.

Gun groaned to himself as he reached his cabin. Of his crew, he hadn't expected Hale to be the problem. LeRoy was a given. He was young, drank too much and knew that they needed him. Gun had been prepared for that problem. But not Hale, not the man he'd trusted all these years.

He opened the door to his cabin, stepped in and was locking it behind him when he froze. Earlier he'd been distracted when the others were here. But now he was alone in the space he'd occupied for the past few days. He liked to keep his place neat and clean. He liked to know where everything was. He didn't like anyone touching his belongings.

Turning slowly, he surveyed the main room. Nothing looked out of place, and yet he knew the cabin had been searched. One of the drawers in the small kitchen hadn't been closed all the way.

He took a step, not sure which room to check first. His instincts led him to the bedroom. There was the slightest indentation on the edge of the bedspread. Almost as if someone had put a hand down to help himself up.

Gun bent down and looked under the bed. He'd borrowed a vacuum the first day he'd arrived and cleaned the cabin before he'd moved in. Still, the cabin was old, the windows weren't well insulated, so of course there would be dust with everyone coming and going on the road.

Most people wouldn't have been able to see where the dust under the bed had been disturbed, but Gun did. His gut clenched at the sight. Not only had someone searched his cabin, but they'd hidden under his bed.

He quickly thought back. When? With a curse, he realized it had to have been earlier. Otherwise he would have noticed the drawer. Whoever had been under his bed had heard everything that he and the others had discussed.

So who had it been? And what was he going to do about it?

CHAPTER TEN

KITZIE FIGURED LEROY and his cohorts wouldn't be back until after the bars closed. Still, she wanted to be ready. She was preparing for her encounter with LeRoy when she got the call.

"The fence is Harry Lester Brown," her partner with the FBI, Pete Corran, told her the moment she answered. "He is flying into Montana." He sounded excited, and she could understand why. Before, they'd been running on nothing but a theory. With Harry Lester flying in, she knew they'd been right.

"He's still alive?" The man had to be in his nineties. He'd gained renown for fencing some of the biggest hauls in history from famous heists, but had dropped out of sight years ago.

"He's flying up from Florida tomorrow," Pete said. "He just booked a flight. Guess where he's flying to." Butte was the closest town to where Kitzie and the crew were right now. "You guessed it," he said, even before she got the chance to answer. "He wouldn't fly into Butte unless he was here to see the goods."

She wanted to agree. "But isn't this small potatoes for a man like Harry Lester?" It didn't seem likely.

"Unless he's fallen on hard times and needs the money."

She supposed that was a possibility. "What time is his flight?"

"Arrives at 9:45 p.m. It's the last flight."

"So he'll have to spend the night."

Pete chuckled. "Which is probably why he booked a rental car for two days."

Kitzie couldn't believe their luck. Her instincts had been right. Harry Lester Brown was coming out of retirement for this? "He must be planning to come here. The hotel is isolated enough. If anyone saw him, they'd just think he was some old man stopping by to watch the commercial shoot on the last day." She chuckled to herself. "The carnival will be up and running. Maybe he'll take a ride. You realize, if we are right, we've got this one nailed." She thought of her boss and his lack of faith in her. This would show him.

There was one loose end, though. They could put the video production company in the area of the burglaries in all but one of the cities. "To tie this up in a nice big bow, find out for me if there was a carnival in town on the missing date."

"Will do, but I think we both already know the answer to that. So this is it," Pete said, sounding as excited as she felt. "But where are the goods? You're sure they're not stashed in one of their cabins?"

"I don't think so because they could have been seen packing it in. I doubt Gunderson would be that careless. But it must be close by."

"I think I should come down there."

"Not yet. I'm going to try to get close to one of them tonight. If he knows anything, I'll get it out of him."

"Are you sure that's a good idea? We don't want to alert them. Also, it sounds dangerous."

She wasn't worried. She could handle LeRoy. It was Gunderson she had to stay one step ahead of. But at least with the fence flying in, this undercover operation was about over.

"I think it would be better if you stayed on Harry Lester Brown. But be careful. He might be old, but I'm betting he can still spot a tail."

Kitzie disconnected, wanting to do a happy dance. She couldn't help being excited and darned proud of herself. She'd been right. If she could bust this ring and take down Harry Lester Brown in the process… She wished Sawyer was around, so she could tell someone who would understand how big this was. The thought of Sawyer reminded her that he was on a date tonight with Ainsley Hamilton, who was wearing her special red dress. She smiled to herself, betting his…operation wasn't going as smoothly.

SAWYER RETURNED TO the table, more relaxed than he'd been all night. He now knew who was following Ainsley. Tomorrow he would have a talk with

Lance Roderick. It would probably take more than that to get the man to go away but with the new stalking laws…

Also, he suspected he would find proof in Lance's cabin that would support the case against him. Stalkers usually collected souvenirs, such as photos, objects that the victim had owned or touched, newspaper articles that mentioned them.

He didn't want to think about that tonight, though, as he looked across the table at his beautiful date. Ainsley looked radiant. He picked up his menu, feeling a little sad. This assignment would be over by tomorrow. He kind of hoped he would be here at least until the end of the commercial shoot.

"So, what looks good?" he asked as the waitress appeared at their table.

Ainsley smiled at him over the top of her menu. "Like I said, I'm a Montana girl. I'm going to have the rib eye." She closed her menu and beamed at the waitress. "Make that rare."

Sawyer laughed and closed his menu, as well. "Make it two."

The rest of the evening passed so pleasantly that he hated it had to end. They talked about growing up on ranches, laughed at the crazy stuff they did and saw, and found that they liked a lot of the same things. Sawyer couldn't remember a night he'd enjoyed more.

On the drive back, the Northern Lights put on a spectacular show. Streaks of blue-and-green flashes shot up from the edge of the earth against the midnight blue of the sky.

He stopped on a hill that overlooked a small valley. There was only one thing that could make this night more magical. Even before he turned off the ignition, Sawyer was already thinking about kissing Ainsley.

AINSLEY FELT AS if she was in a fairy tale sitting here in Sawyer's pickup. She wanted to pinch herself. Maybe it was the red dress and the matching shoes. Or the wonderful meal. Or the light show nature was putting on.

Or maybe it was simply the man sitting next to her as they looked off into the fall night, but she felt like a princess. Maybe it was simply because it had been so long since she'd been on a date. Let alone one that was this perfect with such a handsome cowboy.

How else could she explain the way she was feeling?

She glanced over at Sawyer sitting next to her and felt her heart pound a little harder. There could be another explanation for the way she was feeling. Sawyer Nash could be her true hero, the cowboy she'd been waiting for to come galloping into her life all these years and sweep her up and ride away with her.

Crazy thinking. She was starting to sound like one of her sisters.

Embarrassed by the thought that a man could make her lose all sense, she started to look away when he reached for her. His large hand cupped the back of her neck as he drew her toward him. She looked into his gray eyes and lost another piece of her heart. He pulled her closer until they were a breath apart. Then slowly he dropped his mouth to hers.

Ainsley felt heat rush through her. His lips grazed hers. The anticipation was excruciating. His mouth took hers wantonly, sending desire rippling through her. The kiss was warm and sure and then altogether something else as he teased her lips open with the tip of his tongue. She let out a gasp as his tongue found the sensitive silken flesh of her mouth.

His reaction was to pull her closer, threading his fingers through her hair, as he deepened the kiss. The intimate taste of him sent a wave of pleasure through her. Fire ran along her veins as she arched against him, drinking him in with a need that shocked the old Ainsley Hamilton.

She wanted more. She wanted…him. "Please," she breathed against his mouth.

His hand went to her breast. She felt her already-hard nipple press against his warm palm through the thin fabric of her bra and the red dress. He thumbed over the aching tip, and she groaned with pleasure. He made small circles around it, and she thought she would die if he stopped.

She looped her arms around his neck, losing herself in the kiss until she felt his free hand on her bare knee. The palm felt scalding to the touch as he pushed the sheer fabric of the dress aside to move slowly up her thigh.

Don't stop. Please, don't stop. I want you to be my first.

He stopped.

She released a cry of frustration that came out a groan. When she met his gaze, she realized she'd actually said the words out loud.

Sawyer pulled his hands away and drew back. He was breathing hard, the look in his eyes as filled with desire as her own. From the expression on his face, he hadn't meant for things to go this far. He blinked as if bringing her into focus and let out a curse under his breath. "Ainsley, did you say—"

"Please."

He was shaking his head as if he couldn't believe it. "I'm sorry. I shouldn't have…"

She wanted to scream, "I just haven't met a man I wanted bad enough to…" But she didn't bother trying to explain all the reasons she hadn't. Opportunity. Desire. Or worse, some crazy, old-fashioned idea at the back of her mind that she wanted to wait for The One.

"We should go," he said, sounding almost as in pain as she felt as he reached for the key in the ignition.

Ainsley straightened her dress and sat back in the bench seat. She ached for the sweet release of his touch, and at the same time, she chastised herself. It might be old-fashioned, but she wasn't the kind of girl who went this far on a first date. Embarrassment added to the heat now flaring her cheeks. What was wrong with her? What he must think!

Sawyer put his window down to let the cold night air rush in. She did the same as he started the pickup. The windows were fogged over. No wonder she felt as if she was back in high school at the local make-out spot. Except, she hadn't been that girl. It was her sisters who got in trouble for going up on the hill with boys—not Goody Two-shoes Ainsley, who was at home waiting for them to get in before their father found out.

Because she'd done well in school, the only boys who'd asked her out were into computer programming, band and chess club. They never made a pass. She suspected boys were scared of her. At college, it was the same way. Miss Prim and Proper had stayed that way as if she had the word *untouchable* tattooed on her forehead. Until tonight.

With Sawyer, she felt alive. Sexy. Desirable. *Ready.* Right up until he stopped and drew back, as if he'd come to his senses at her words.

Ainsley suddenly felt like crying. Sawyer had opened up something inside her, a well of yearning, that she knew only he could satisfy. As he drove toward their cabins, she wished for the old Ainsley who'd lived for thirty-four years without really knowing what she was missing.

KITZIE COULD FEEL time running out. If Harry Lester Brown was on his way, then the sale was about to go down. She had to find out when and where. Unfortunately, the only way to tie Harry to the crime was to catch him in the act of receiving the stolen goods. Getting a conviction was tricky. The legal requirements were complex. That was why Harry had skated so many other times. It had to be proven that he knew the goods were stolen. Without serial numbers… She put on something sexy. Not quite as sexy as the red dress she'd sent Ainsley off in, but enough to tempt a man like LeRoy. She'd done this kind of work so many times that she didn't give LeRoy another thought.

Instead, her mind was on Harry Lester Brown as she sat down to wait for LeRoy to come back from the bar in town.

Harry had succeeded as a fence all these years because he had the entrepreneurial personality. He had resourcefulness, charisma, ingenuity and a good grasp of market practices and the competition. It was a matter of weighing the risks by both the thieves and the fence against a fair price for stolen goods. Usually the fence got fifty percent of the value unless dealing with amateurs, and then he could take as much as ninety.

So how much was he thinking he could fleece out of these thieves? They'd pulled off the mall burglaries so skillfully that she didn't think of them as amateurs. But often these kinds of thieves were anxious to get rid of the stolen merchandise before getting caught. They also often needed the money fast. From what she'd heard, at least a couple of them planned to skip the country.

It surprised Kitzie, though, that a well-known fence like Harry Lester Brown would be dealing with this bunch of thieves. He must have fallen on hard times, like Pete had said. Or...

She sat up abruptly and reached for her phone. "I need you to run some names for me."

"What are we looking for?" Pete asked.

"A relationship between my four suspects and Harry Lester Brown."

"I'M SORRY, I—"

"Please, don't apologize again," Ainsley said quickly. She was embarrassed enough. Why had she foolishly blurted that out? She didn't need Sawyer saying he was sorry. Her breast still ached in memory of his touch, and she didn't even want to think about where he had been heading with his other hand.

What hurt was that he'd stopped so abruptly.

He glanced over at her as he drove. "It's just that I hadn't meant for things to go that far."

She waved off whatever he was struggling to say. "We both got carried away. It happens." It had just never happened to her. She knew most women by the age of thirty-four had experience in this department. They'd either been married or had a live-in boyfriend.

Instead, she remembered sloppy French kisses

and uncomfortable gropes by young men with bad breath or too much aftershave. Or cowboys with a mouth full of chew who had to spit before trying to kiss her. Was it any wonder she hadn't felt attracted to any of them?

But sometimes she felt like a freak because she hadn't. She'd only mentioned that she was a virgin to one man she'd dated for a short while last year. He'd treated her as if she'd grown two heads and quit calling. So, what had she been thinking, telling Sawyer? Of course, his reaction would be the same.

She'd once mentioned that she "hadn't" a few years ago to her sister Bo. Bo had made it sound as if Ainsley's "condition" was a car with a faulty radiator. "You really should get that taken care of," she'd said.

Sawyer's guilty expression did not make it easier now. She kept thinking about the way he'd drawn back as if her words had snapped him out of a dream. And the way he'd looked at her…

She swallowed the lump in her throat and turned away to stare out the side window. Maybe if she had gotten it "taken care of," she wouldn't be feeling like this now.

Fortunately, Sawyer was quiet the rest of the way. The moment he stopped the pickup, she was out the truck door.

"Ainsley, please. Let me walk you back to your cabin," he called after her.

She shook her head, needing desperately to get to

the privacy of her place. "I'm fine, really. Thank you for dinner." And she was off, hobbling on the unfamiliar high heels to her cabin without looking back.

SAWYER WAS MENTALLY kicking himself all the way to his quarters when he spotted Kitzie. She had just slipped around a cabin he knew wasn't hers. He thought about confronting her about the red dress and how she'd tried to ruin his date with Ainsley. Instead, he'd been the one to ruin the date, because he'd forgotten for a while there that he wasn't here to date, let alone…

He was too upset with himself to get into it with Kitzie. Ainsley Hamilton was an assignment. Not officially, but in every other sense of the word. True, his plan to lure Lance Roderick out had worked. And dinner had been more enjoyable than any in recent history, but he should have left it at that. He shouldn't have stopped on that hill to watch the Northern Lights. He shouldn't have kissed her. Worse, he shouldn't have felt what he felt. He hadn't wanted to stop.

But once he had… Coming up for air, it hadn't helped though to see Ainsley wearing that damned red dress. Not that he hadn't desperately wanted to make love to her and still did. It wasn't lust. He'd lusted after enough women to know the difference. This was…something different, and it scared the hell out of him because he'd never felt it before.

Cursing himself, he stomped toward his cabin. Tomorrow he would deal with Kitzie and see if Ainsley was still talking to him. Tonight…well, tonight, he doubted he would sleep a wink. What he needed was a cold shower. Then a strong drink.

But before he could get either, he spotted a man stumbling drunk and heading for the cabin Kitzie had just sneaked around. He recognized Bobby LeRoy. He must have been passed out in his car when Sawyer had driven up. The door of LeRoy's car was standing open. There was no one else around, nor any lights on in the other cabins.

What the devil was Kitzie up to? He told himself that she knew what she was doing.

That's when he saw the other man come out of the darkness as if he'd been waiting for LeRoy. Sawyer swore under his breath as he watched the man fall in behind LeRoy and head for the cabin where Kitzie had gone.

The last thing he wanted to do was get involved, and yet all his instincts told him she was headed for trouble and didn't know it. She might have been expecting LeRoy, but she wasn't prepared for the second man who, he realized, was carrying a baseball bat.

"Hey, LeRoy," Sawyer called. Both men looked in his direction in surprise. Clearly neither had seen him in the darkness. Both had been intent on what they were doing.

LeRoy stumbled to a stop and squinted in his direction. The other one had stopped as well, hanging back in the shadows. As Sawyer walked toward LeRoy, he got the impression the man didn't realize he was being followed. The man with the baseball bat had frozen at the sound of Sawyer's voice.

Even feet from him, Sawyer could smell the alcohol. LeRoy reeked like a brewery. He moved to a spot where LeRoy would have his back to his cabin. Out of the corner of his eye, he saw the other man slink back into the shadows and disappear.

He and LeRoy had never actually met. It took a few moments for LeRoy to place him. "Oh, it's you."

"You didn't happen to see a woman, did you?"

LeRoy laughed. "I've seen a few. What did this one look like?"

He described Kitzie.

"Oh, that one," LeRoy said and winked. "Nice."

"I just wanted to see about getting something to eat. Isn't she in charge of the food out here? I'm starved."

"That's all you want with her?" LeRoy guffawed. "I'd want a lot more than that." Behind him, Kitzie slipped out from the back of LeRoy's cabin and into the night, but not before sending Sawyer a withering look.

"Maybe I'll just call it a night," Sawyer said, slapping LeRoy on the shoulder and turning toward his cabin. "Have a good one." As he walked away, he realized he didn't need the cold shower anymore, but he sure could use the drink. He had a feeling that he'd just saved LeRoy from a beating—if not saved his life from the man with the bat.

But it was Ainsley he was thinking about as he neared his cabin. He'd certainly blown things with her. He was giving himself hell when he saw that someone had left a note on his cabin door.

CHAPTER ELEVEN

SARAH COULDN'T SLEEP. She roamed the huge house, having sent the staff home for the night hours ago. Her mind raced, frightening her. She knew what she was thinking could get her killed. Or worse, get her daughters or husband killed.

Stopping in front of a mirror, she was shocked to see how much she'd aged. But then again, she still thought of herself as the age she'd been when the twins were born. There were still signs of that young woman in her face, enough to remind her of the woman she'd been. The woman who'd had six daughters with Buckmaster Hamilton.

She locked eyes with the woman in the mirror. Everything she'd learned about herself since Dr. Venable had been restoring her memory indicated that she'd been strong, determined, capable. So why didn't she feel that way now?

The answer was as clear as her face. Since her return almost two years ago, she'd been just letting things happen, waiting for the other shoe to drop. She'd depended too much on Russell. Now she had to take things into her own hands—no matter the consequences.

Turning from the mirror, she dug her phone out of her pocket, and hesitating only a moment, she called Martin Wagner's number, the secret number she'd gotten from him when his son and her daughter were in trouble.

She had met Martin Wagner her freshman year in college when the two of them were members of the anarchist group The Prophecy. He now went by Tom Durand, a successful businessman and, by all appearances, had put that part of his life behind him.

But she knew he was still involved up to his neck with The Prophecy. She suspected he provided the money that kept the anarchist group going.

Sarah was surprised when Martin took her call.

"Do you have any idea what time it is in Houston? Why are you calling me?" he snapped when he picked up.

"How can I find Joe?" she asked without preamble. It had been Joe who'd brought her into the group with his passion, his charm and his good looks. She'd been young, naive and ripe for the picking.

"I have to stop him."

Martin chuckled, and she heard the clink of ice against crystal. He hadn't been able to sleep either. "You try to stop him and he'll find *you*."

Fear paralyzed her at the thought of coming face-to-face with the man who was once her lover as well as her coconspirator. But that wasn't what terrified her the most. She wasn't just playing Russian roulette with her own life; there were her daughters and her husband to think about.

"Change your mind?" Martin asked with a chuckle. The ice cubes clinked, and she heard fatigue in his voice when he spoke again. "He won't hesitate to kill anyone who gets in his way. You should know that by now."

"That's why he can't know I'm coming until it's too late." She knew the risk she was taking, but she wanted to feel anything but helpless right now.

"You have no idea what you're suggesting."

"I do," she interrupted. "He'll kill us if he finds out, but isn't that better than continuing to go along with this?" When he didn't answer she said, "I need to know what he has planned."

"You're talking to the wrong person."

"Doc says he doesn't know either. I'm assuming that you've provided the money for whatever Joe has been doing all these years. Doc was with me in Brazil. So, what did you fund during the years I was...gone?"

She heard bitterness in his voice when he spoke. "A bombing somewhere in the world, an assassination, a group overthrown, another group armed."

"The Prophecy has been that active?" She wanted to believe that the group no longer had any power. That hope was now gone. If Joe really had managed all of those things, then The Prophecy was alive and well. If Joe was telling Martin the truth. "Then, why has it been years since anyone has even heard of The Prophecy?"

Martin sighed. She heard a chair creak as he relaxed into it. "I think he's waiting to make one big show, and then he will take credit for the rest of it. But that's just a theory."

Sarah thought about what she'd learned so far. "That big show has something to do with my husband and the election, doesn't it?" When Martin said nothing, she knew she was right. "How can we stop him?"

"No one can stop him. The election is only days away."

"What happens then?" Silence. "Martin, you have to help me stop Joe."

He sighed. "I already told you nothing can stop him. Don't you get it? None of this is like it was in 1979. We were kids playing at rebellion back then. Today's counterrevolutionaries are trained with the most modern weapons and explosives. They can do so much more damage than we ever dreamed possible."

"That's why he has to be stopped. We were idealists, no matter how misguided we were. Whoever Joe has working with him, they're terrorists."

Martin fell silent. Was she getting through to him?

"You don't want this any more than I do."

"Maybe, but I'm not going to help you. What you're asking is *suicide*. If Joe found out that we were even talking like this— I have to go. Sarah,

I don't know what he has planned, but it's too late. There is no stopping it."

"There has to be a way. This big event Joe has planned? Have you already sent funding for it?" No answer. "I can understand why you started funding our original cause, but not anymore." Still nothing. If she hadn't heard him breathing, she might have thought he'd hung up.

"Joe needs money to send to these…recruits," she continued, having given this some thought. "Without the money, they can't buy vehicles, weapons, explosives or fund the plan. Are you the only one who has been funding The Prophecy movement all these years?"

"No. That's why your plan won't work. A while back, Joe was bragging about how he had money coming in from places that no one would suspect."

Sarah felt deflated. Maybe he was right, and there was no stopping Joe and what he had planned. But she couldn't give up. "What kind of places?"

"He mentioned that he was getting money from lots of sources—drugs, money laundering, offshore enterprises, even a video production company."

That caught her attention. Ainsley was working for a company making a commercial. "Did he mention the name of the company?"

"Right. Joe and I are that close that he tells me everything. I got the impression it is just some small, fly-by-night company that made its real money on something other than commercials."

Sarah told herself there was little chance that the company was the same one that Ainsley was working on, and yet it would be just like Joe to see that Ainsley got hired on *his* video production company. Another way for him to control her family.

"He laughed and asked me the strangest thing. He said, 'When was the last time you went on a carnival ride, Martin?'"

"What does that mean?"

"I have no idea. Maybe it was just his way of telling me to keep my nose out of his financial business or I could find myself on some unfortunate Ferris wheel accident."

Which was why she had to stop Joe. None of them were safe, not to mention the rest of the world, as long as Joe was The Prophecy. "How did you send him the money?" she asked. "If we can track it..."

"Sarah, use your head. The moment he finds out what you're doing—"

"That's why I have to move fast and pray that he's busy with his big plan and won't notice until it is too late. Have you already sent the money?"

"I have another shipment scheduled. Sarah, if he doesn't get that money—"

"What if it is all a lie? What if he is putting that money away for himself and his escape? But if he's planning on the money you're supposed to send and it doesn't come, then it might make a difference."

"*Stop!* I'm sorry, but you really don't realize who you're dealing with, Sarah."

"Have you forgotten? Joe was my lover."

"What is it they say about a lover spurned? Trust me, he isn't the same man you used to know. I can't help you."

"You mean you *won't*."

"Good night, Sarah. Please. Don't call me again. Whatever Joe is planning, you can't stop it. None of us can."

BEFORE ANYONE ELSE got to the office the next morning, Sheriff Frank Curry finished typing up his resignation letter, double-checked it for any typos and then printed it. As he waited, he ran his thumb and forefinger down the length of his gunfighter mustache. This morning in the mirror, he'd noticed how gray it had become. Just like his thick head of hair, there was more gray than blond anymore.

It seemed to have happened overnight. He wondered sometimes how he'd gotten this old. The printer stopped. Getting up, he walked over to it, took the letter and reread it. The letter was short and to the point. He was done.

The thought gave him a start. He'd loved this job, worked hard at it for so many years... But it was time to move on. Swallowing the lump that had formed in his throat, he walked back to the table and carefully folded the letter and tucked it into the envelope.

Sealing it, he placed it in his drawer. The letter was postdated for the day after the election. Hell, if what he feared came true, he would be dead, and there would be no need for the letter.

But he'd promised himself that he'd see it through until then. In his heart, he feared the day after Buckmaster Hamilton was elected would be a dark one. But unless he could stop what he suspected from happening…

Either way, he wouldn't be sheriff after election night.

IN THE LIGHT of day, Sawyer was even more worried about Ainsley, given the note he'd found on his door last night.

> *Leave Ainsley alone. She deserves better than some two-bit cowboy. You ruin her, and I will take care of you—and her.*

This morning all he could think about was finding Lance and ending this. But so far, he hadn't been able to locate the man.

Lance's quick exit from the café parking lot the night before made Sawyer all the more convinced that he was Ainsley's stalker. He wasn't sure exactly what he planned to do when he met up with the security guard. He could always threaten him with arrest since it wouldn't take much to match Lance's handwriting to the notes—if not his fingerprints.

He also wanted to see Ainsley, but hadn't been able to find her either. What had happened last night—and hadn't happened—had been on his mind all day. He'd berated himself for handling it so badly. But he'd been so surprised—and yet, in retrospect, not surprised. Hadn't she said that she'd missed out on a lot, given that she'd always been the good girl?

But hearing her say it had stopped him, no doubt about it. Mostly, it had brought him to his senses. He'd come here to help her, not… On top of that, he was lying to the woman by omission. Worse, what had happened between them had rocked his world in a way he hadn't expected. He'd made it to thirty-eight without getting attached because he hadn't met anyone who even tempted him to ask her to move in—let alone propose. Then last night—

As he passed the kitchen, he decided to stop for breakfast in the hopes that Roderick would show up. Or Ainsley.

"We really have to quit meeting like this," Kitzie joked when she joined him at the table. "We need to talk," she said under her breath.

"Yes, we do," he said and gave her his sweetest smile. He still wanted to strangle her for the red-dress incident.

She ate in silence for a few minutes, as if realizing she wasn't the only one upset today. "How was dinner last night?" So like Kitzie to address the elephant in the room.

"Actually, it was wonderful."

"So, you liked the dress," she said, without looking at him.

"Actually, I hate the dress."

She seemed to flinch at his words. It had been a cruel trick, and she knew it. "Bad memories?"

He didn't bother to answer as he got up to take his plate to the back of the kitchen where her two teenagers were working. Kitzie followed him, and the two left the hotel.

"We should go to my cabin," she said.

He shook his head. "I want to walk." He turned toward the carnival rides. They looked even more dilapidated in the morning light.

"If you think I'm going to thank you for butting in last night," she said as they walked, "I happened to be waiting for LeRoy."

"I gathered that. But I don't think you would have been as happy to see who was following LeRoy with a baseball bat."

Her gaze shot to his. "Who?"

"I didn't get a good look at him, but the way he was following LeRoy—along with the bat—I think you owe me a thank-you."

She looked away. "Thanks."

He said nothing as they left the hotel behind and wandered through the rusting carnival equipment. She was only making this harder for him. The worst part was that she seemed to be enjoying messing with Ainsley. Kitzie was also something else he was keeping from Ainsley, another reason last night couldn't have happened until Ainsley knew everything.

He stopped next to the Tilt-A-Whirl.

Kitzie met his gaze. She looked regretful for a moment. "I'm sorry about the dress. But this is important. I think it's time you knew what was going on."

Sawyer didn't want to know, but at the same time Kitzie was here undercover. He couldn't leave another agent hung out to dry. If he could help with her assignment... Also the lawman in him was curious about LeRoy and the other man he'd seen last night.

"Not out here," she said, glancing toward the east. He followed her gaze to see a lone figure sitting on one of the rides as if waiting for the crew to appear. Neither of them had noticed him before then. It was that damned delivery guy with his hat on backward. He rose as he saw some of the crew members come out of the hotel and head in his direction. There was a hopeful expression on his face as if he thought he was about to break into the movies via this ragtag group.

"If you're afraid of what will happen if you come to my cabin—"

"Let's just make this quick," he said, turning back toward the cabins.

"Quick is good," she said, letting the sexual innuendo hang in the air as if she just couldn't help herself.

KITZIE OPENED HER cabin door, glancing back to see Sawyer following in long strides. The man moved like a mountain lion, all purpose, all predator. Her heart ached. She had the horrible feeling that she would never get over him, and she had only herself to blame for losing him.

Past him, she caught a glimpse of Ainsley Hamilton watching the two of them and smiled to herself. Sawyer stepped into the cabin behind her and closed the door.

She took a moment to catch her breath. Earlier she'd been so angry with Sawyer that she'd forgotten about the red dress. That had been dirty, she thought, and couldn't help but smile. She'd wanted to ruin his evening by reminding him of her. She hadn't wanted to remind him of their last fight, though.

Now she turned to face him. He was such a cowboy, such a man with his long legs clad in denim, his broad shoulders stretching the fabric of his Western shirt, his black Stetson cocked back to reveal a head of thick dark hair.

She just couldn't win for losing when it came to Sawyer Nash, she thought, feeling her eyes burn with tears.

"Have you seen Lance Roderick this morning?" he asked without looking at her. But as his gaze took her in, he asked, alarmed, "What's wrong?"

She turned away from him to wipe at the errant tears. "Allergies. Is Lance's car still here?"

"It is."

"He wasn't at breakfast." Kitzie could feel his gaze on her. She moved deeper into the cabin. "So, have you told her what's really going on?" When he didn't answer, she chuckled. "Should be interesting when she finds out."

He was still studying her, making her nervous because of the intensity of his look. "I'm surprised you've kept my secret."

"You have such high expectations where I'm concerned." Before he could respond to that, she said, "But with good reason, given how I've acted. Why don't we sit down? Don't worry, I'm harmless."

He laughed, buoying her spirits. "*Harmless* is the last word I would associate with you."

He took the chair, even as she patted a spot next to her on the couch for him. She smiled sadly to herself. When was she going to accept the way things were between them?

That was the problem. She'd never been good at that. When she wanted something, she went after it. That's how she'd gotten so far in her career. She just didn't quit.

"Did you try Lance's cabin?" she asked, not quite ready to tell him about her case.

"He didn't answer. The door was locked. Maybe it's his day off."

"I can check when I go back. I heard you're in another scene this afternoon. This could be a whole new career for you."

He smiled at that but quickly got back to what was on his mind, Ainsley and her stalker. "Roderick followed us to the café last night. I saw him drive up and went out to confront him, but he quickly drove away."

"So he's your man," she said, not really interested. Lance Roderick didn't seem like much of a threat to precious Ainsley. "I'm here chasing jewelry thieves, but I have them in my sights."

"Who?"

She shook her head. "I can't say just yet, but you might find this interesting. The fence they contacted? None other than the great Harry Lester Brown."

"*Harry Lester?* I thought he was dead," Sawyer said, his interest piquing.

She smiled to herself. This is what she and Sawyer had in common. They both loved their work. That was the bond they had that Ainsley Hamilton could never share. "I have it narrowed down to who I believe is involved, but unless we can catch them making the sale to Harry Lester…"

"When do you think it's going down?"

"Probably after the commercial wraps," she said.

Sawyer shook his head. "I'll be long gone by then. Once I take care of the Lance Roderick problem…" He seemed to sense her disappointment—and her surprise. "I'm on medical leave. I shouldn't even be here."

She couldn't argue that. But he was here saving Ainsley anyway.

"The sooner I'm finished and on my way home, the better." He got to his feet. "But I could use your help. I haven't been able to find Roderick all day.

I really could use a look inside his cabin. If what I think is in there, it would speed up the process. Any chance you could get the key?"

Kitzie rose as well, seeing that they were done. If she couldn't lure Sawyer back in with Harry Lester Brown, then there was no hope.

SAWYER COULD TELL that Kitzie was disappointed that he hadn't offered to help with her investigation. He was tempted. Harry Lester Brown? If Kitzie could bring him down, that would be huge. Harry Lester was suspected of fencing some of the largest jewelry heists on record.

But the ache in his leg reminded him that he was still on medical leave. Also, he knew that Kitzie would resent him getting in the middle of it. If she needed him, she'd let him know. As it was, he had no business even being here right now. Not that he wasn't glad when the sheriff had called. He was even gladder after meeting Ainsley.

His time here, though, was about over. He'd found her stalker. Once he put an end to it—putting Lance Roderick behind bars—he would tell Ainsley what he was really doing here. He suspected that wouldn't go well. Then he would head home. The chances of his and Ainsley's paths crossing again were...slim.

Unfortunately, that made him think of last night. He was still trying to understand why it was Ainsley Hamilton who'd brought out such passion and desire in him. A rebound from Kitzie? Or like Ainsley, something to do with him almost dying, when he was shot and fell off the moving train?

He couldn't have fallen in love with her. Not this quickly.

He pushed the thought away. "I don't know who that man was I saw following LeRoy last night, but if LeRoy is one of the jewel thieves, then he is the loose cannon. We can't be the only ones aware of that. His partners might have decided to cut him loose last night."

Kitzie seemed to think about that for a moment. "If he knows where the loot is, then I have to try to get close to him."

Sawyer shook his head. "The others would have to be fools to trust him. From what you've told me, these burglars are anything but fools. I think you're wasting your time with LeRoy. Worse, you're taking a hell of a chance. If I hadn't come along when I did last night—"

"I can take care of myself," she said, cutting him off.

He cursed under his breath, aware how much Kitzie and Ainsley were alike in that respect. "We all need help sometimes."

Her gaze met his. She looked chastened as if reminded that he'd had to save her not that long ago. "LeRoy is the weak link. The others will be harder to get close to, especially if we're right and Harry Lester is on his way here to buy the goods."

He couldn't argue that. "Just be careful."

She smiled. "So you do care."

"You know I do."

Her eyes glistened. "If you'd just given us a chance—"

"Let's not go there again."

"Because it's too late? Because you've fallen in love with someone else?" Her eyes widened. "Not Ainsley." She shook her head. "Men, they never know what's good for them."

Sawyer wasn't about to touch that. He rose from the chair and headed for the door. "Can you get me a key to Roderick's cabin?" He had to find Lance Roderick, and then his work here was done.

"If you'll help me distract Murph."

On the way to the main office, Sawyer tried Roderick's cabin again. Still no answer to his knock.

Kitzie's cell phone rang. She checked it and said, "I have to take this." Stepping away, she said, "What did you find out? So one of them is related. Which one?" She laughed. "That explains a lot. Yes, it will be most helpful." She disconnected and walked back to him smiling.

"A break in the case?"

"Guess who is related to Harry Lester Brown?" she said quietly.

He thought for only a moment. "LeRoy."

Her smile was sad. "That's why you and I were made to do this. It also explains why the other three put up with him."

"Until one of them decided to go after him with a bat?" Sawyer said. "That makes no sense."

She frowned. "I don't think the man you saw last night was one of the burglars. They would be fools to hurt him when they are so close to selling the goods."

He had to agree. "Then who the hell was that?"

"Someone with a grudge?" she suggested. "Or maybe the man with the bat wasn't after LeRoy, but someone else."

Sawyer had been so sure that the man with the bat had been following LeRoy, but he realized now that he could have been mistaken. If so, then he'd interfered with Kitzie's undercover operation. "I'm sorry about last night, then."

"Knowing what I do now, I will be going in with better intel. You probably did me a favor."

At the office, he cozied up to Murph, asking questions about the next shoot, if she knew of any other jobs, while Kitzie snatched a key to Roderick's cabin.

"Lance was scheduled to work today but didn't check in." She held up the key on their way to the guard's cabin. "I suppose he could be in his cabin drunk or passed out asleep. We won't have much time, but it sounds like you know what you're looking for."

"I do." Obsessed stalkers often kept photos they'd taken of their admired victim or other items they'd collected. The more evidence he had, the better to put Lance Roderick behind bars.

They walked in silence to the cabin. Sawyer stood

back and let her open the door. The smell hit him first. He reached for Kitzie's shoulder and drew her back before she could step in. "You'd better let me."

He knew before he entered the cabin what he was going to find. What he hadn't expected was the brutality with which Roderick had been killed. The man's facc was battered to the point that he was barely recognizable.

"Call the sheriff," Sawyer said over his shoulder to Kitzie. "Tell them a man is dead. Murdered."

CHAPTER TWELVE

As Kitzie made the call outside, Sawyer took a few minutes to search the cabin. He'd pulled off the bandana from around his neck that the assistant director had insisted on for the shoot earlier, and did a quick look around, leaving no prints behind.

If his knowledge of stalkers were correct, Roderick would have something of Ainsley in this cabin. At the very least, he would have photos, which were too easy to snap on a cell phone—even from a distance.

He found a photo of Ainsley hidden in the corner of a shelf in the bedroom. It had been taken near the barn. She was squinting at something. She'd taken off her hat and had a look on her face that he'd come to recognize. She wasn't happy. The photo had been cropped so he didn't know who she'd been talking to, but he was betting it was Devon Gunderson, the director. He'd seen her butting heads with him before.

The other photos had fallen to the floor, he realized. Picking them up, he saw that Roderick had taken some of everyone staying up here, including the teenagers from the kitchen and even the delivery guy. What the hell?

He found nothing else of interest, which surprised him even more than the man's death. If Lance Roderick had been tailing Ainsley for months and was obsessed with her, he would have printed up more than one photo. But maybe that was all he kept here in the cabin. And the other photos? How did Sawyer explain those?

There had to be more. Roderick, if he was the stalker, wouldn't have been able to help himself. He would have taken more photos of her. Sawyer was betting that there were more on Roderick's cell phone. Unfortunately, it seemed to be the only thing missing.

But why would someone take it? Unless Roderick had snapped photos of something that had gotten him killed. He thought again of the cell phone photos the man was taking from his car at the café. He had been shooting Ainsley sitting inside the café, hadn't he?

"His cell phone is gone," Sawyer said as he quickly stepped over the body and back out into fresh air. "But his wallet is still in his pocket with a couple hundred in cash."

Kitzie raised one finely shaped brow. "So it wasn't a robbery. Are you sure he had a cell phone?"

"I saw him taking photos with it last night outside the café." He frowned. "I just assumed he was shooting Ainsley sitting inside. But maybe he saw something else of interest and that got him killed."

"You're sure this wasn't Ainsley's doing?" Kitzie asked.

He shot her a look. "You seriously think she took a baseball bat to Roderick?"

She shrugged. "You know what they say about still water."

He shook his head, wondering if she was serious or if this was more about him and her. "I *saw* the killer. He was following LeRoy last night, but now I'm wondering if he realized he had the wrong man when I stopped LeRoy to talk to him and save your neck."

"You better hope your *stalker* doesn't blow my cover and my entire case." She glared at him. "This could end up with us both in hot water—if not fired."

At the sound of sirens, they both looked toward the road. It wouldn't be long, and everyone out here would know about the murder. Which meant hours of interviews by local law enforcement.

Kitzie must have been thinking the same thing. "I was so close to wrapping up this case," she said angrily as a sheriff's department vehicle pulled up followed by a coroner's van.

Sawyer thought that both of their covers would be blown shortly. "They'll know the moment they run you through the system. Me, as well." He was mentally kicking himself for not being honest with Ainsley. This was not the way he wanted her to find out.

"I only need another day," Kitzie was saying. "With all these suspects, it is going to take them a while. My burglars will have to move fast now. Sawyer?"

He nodded. "Go on, I won't involve you in finding the body. That will keep you out of it—at least for a while."

Just until Murph mentioned that it had been him and Kitzie who had been in her office, he thought, as Kitzie ducked out of sight and the first batch of cops made their way toward him.

THE FORK CLATTERED to the tabletop, making both women jump.

"What is going on, Nettie?" Kate French demanded. The mother of three had managed to get away to meet her friend at the café she owned in Beartooth. "I've never seen you this nervous."

Nettie picked up her fork but had lost interest in the cinnamon roll they'd been sharing. She put it down and sighed. "It's this upcoming election."

"Are you worried that Buck won't win? Or that he will?"

Nettie met Kate's gaze. She felt so fortunate to have her for a friend, especially given the difference in their ages. While Nettie was in her sixties, Kate was only in her thirties. Also, they'd gotten off to a rough start when Kate had first come to town.

"I don't care who wins," she said in a hushed whisper as she looked around the café. Most everyone in these parts was rooting for Buck to win. According to the polls, he would.

"It's about election night. You may have heard, Buck is planning to give his acceptance speech—if he wins—at the Beartooth Fairgrounds. Frank is beside himself trying to come up with a security plan."

"No wonder you're stressed, but the sheriff can't really believe anyone would…" Her words faltered as if she'd seen the answer in Nettie's face. "He thinks Buck might be in danger?" she whispered.

They were alone in the café except for a couple of ranchers at the front and a couple sitting in a booth along the other side of the room.

All Nettie could do was nod. "It's complicated."

"Apparently," Kate said thoughtfully. Her eyes brightened as an idea came to her. "It's Sarah, isn't it?"

Nettie picked up her fork again. She'd been sworn to secrecy about the investigating she and Frank had been doing in regard to the future president's wife. She couldn't even tell Kate, though she was dying to unburden herself with the young woman. Kate had a good head on her shoulders. Kate would give her good advice.

"Have you asked…" Kate motioned with her head toward Nettie's purse.

She quickly shook her head. "I threw it away." Nettie groaned at the memory. "Then I dug it back out of the garbage. I finally threw it back in the garbage, took the bag and—" she hated to admit what she'd done "—took it out to the burn barrel."

"Why would you get rid of the pendulum?"

Nettie looked at her as if she'd lost her mind. "Because it scares me. *You* wouldn't even touch it."

"Maybe it's good that you got rid of it. No one wants to know what the future holds unless it's something good."

"Exactly."

"And you don't think it's good," Kate said.

Nettie nodded. "I couldn't bring myself to ask it anything more, especially anything about Frank."

Kate looked at her watch and moaned. "I have to get back. Jack is great with the kids, but the twins are a handful right now."

Just the mention of her children and Kate seemed to glow. For not the first time, Nettie was envious of her having the children she'd dreamed of. Childless herself, she often wondered how different her life would have been if she and Frank had married when they were young and had the children they, too, had dreamed of.

But instead, Nettie had married Bob Benton on her mother's advice and regretted it for too many years to mention. Frank had married Pam Chandler on the rebound, and that had turned out even worse.

She and Frank were together now, she reminded herself, wishing she could forget the past. It bothered her some days, though, when she thought about how much time they would have together before something happened to one of them. They weren't spring chickens anymore.

"Don't look so down. You're worrying about something that probably won't happen," Kate said.

"I'd almost advise you to get another stupid pendulum just so you can quit worrying."

"But what if it told me that something happens to Frank election night?"

Kate reached across the table and squeezed Nettie's free hand. "You have to have faith that the two of you are going to come out of this just fine."

Nettie nodded, but she couldn't help having her doubts. Frank was worried. Worse, she sensed something in him that felt like…defeat.

SAWYER HAD BEEN anxious for more news about the murder, so he was glad when Frank finally called him. After being questioned, he'd gotten Frank on the line to let him know what had happened and asked for his help.

"It's complicated, but there is another FBI agent here working undercover, so we're both trying to stay under the radar. So any information you might be able to find out…"

"I'm sorry I got you into this. Also sorry you couldn't reach me right away. I've been working on security for election night. But with the future president's daughter from here and now out there working on the set, I'm sure the sheriff over there will cooperate."

That had been earlier today. Now Frank asked, "Are you sure this man's death doesn't have something to do with the other FBI agent's case?"

"I'm not sure of anything. I was sure he was our

stalker, but now I'm having my doubts. Have they established a time of death?"

"The coroner estimates somewhere around 10:00 p.m. last night. Apparently the heat was turned to high in the cabin, so the coroner couldn't be more accurate than that."

Sawyer shook his head. The smell inside the cabin had told him that Roderick had been dead for hours. He could have been killed right after he got back from town, and the killer tried to throw off the time by kicking up the heat.

"Do we know any more about him?" he asked.

"He'd been disbarred several years go. I talked to Buck, but he hadn't ever heard of him, so I doubt Roderick ever had a case involving Ainsley."

"What about Roderick's cell phone?" he asked.

"It hasn't turned up. But they know about at least one call he made. It was at eight." About the time he would have returned from town? If he had gone right back to his cabin. "He called his mother. According to her, there was a knock at his door during the conversation. His mother heard him let someone in before he said he had to go. She said the visitor had a male voice."

"Let me guess, Roderick lives with his mother. I'd love to see his room."

"He does live with his mother. Fits the pattern, huh. The local sheriff already checked out his room in the basement. He had apparently moved everything out before this latest job. She didn't know if he put it in storage or what."

"Did his mother say anything that could help?" Sawyer asked, thinking that the move might have signaled that he was ready to come out to Ainsley.

"According to her, he was in high spirits. He said he would be coming into some money soon, so for her not to worry. Apparently, he'd been supporting her until he lost his license to practice law."

"Money? Was there anything to that?"

The sheriff sighed. "Not that the local law has been able to find out. The sheriff down there thinks he was just trying to reassure his mother. The commercial was about to end and so was his job. He didn't seem to have any prospects."

Sawyer thought about the photos Roderick had been taking at the café. Maybe they had been of Ainsley inside the café just as he'd first suspected. Sawyer couldn't imagine anything else the security guard might have photographed that he could turn into cash.

Maybe he thought he and Ainsley had a future. Her father had money. Maybe that was what Roderick had been referring to. Or maybe he'd been lying. They might never know.

"So the knock at the door," Sawyer said. "It could have been someone he was meeting."

"Possibly. But no one on the production company told the sheriff over there that they'd been by Roderick's cabin last night."

Sawyer thought about that for a moment. Often people clammed up when the law got involved.

"The sheriff is looking into another suspect. It seems that after you saw Roderick in the café parking lot, he drove over to the bar where he proceeded to get into a brawl with one of the patrons over the music playing on the jukebox."

"Doesn't sound like a man excited about coming into money. Or getting the girl he's been following," Sawyer commented.

"No. Sounds like a man who is just looking for a fight. But if he'd seen you and Ainsley together, he could have been looking for trouble. Apparently, he found it."

"They think this local followed him back to his cabin?" he asked.

"They do since the man at the bar left right after Roderick—and he was still mad, saying he was going to kill him. Apparently, alcohol had been involved."

Sawyer thought of the dark shadow of a man he'd seen with the baseball bat. Maybe he hadn't been after LeRoy—but Roderick instead. "Have they picked the man up yet?"

"No, apparently, he came home that night with blood all over him from the brawl or the murder, got into a fight with his wife and left. She has no idea where he's gone. But they've put a BOLO out on him."

Was this it? Was it over? Roderick didn't fit the profile perfectly, but he was damned close. He'd followed them last night, he kept a photo of Ainsley by his bed, he didn't have a job and had been living with his mother, and he'd cleaned out his basement bedroom at his mother's… It all added up to a fairly good profile of an obsessed stalker.

"I take it you didn't mention what you were doing there?" the sheriff asked.

"I didn't lie to the local sheriff. I'm an extra on the film. I'm not here as any kind of law enforcement."

"So you haven't told Ainsley?"

He'd reached Ainsley's cabin and saw that her door was ajar. "I'm about to tell her now."

SHERIFF FRANK CURRY had just hung up and was reaching for his Stetson when his phone rang. "Sheriff Curry," he said, hoping it was some good news for Sawyer. He felt bad for getting him into this situation. But at the same time, he was glad that the agent was there with Ainsley.

He recognized the voice on the other end of the line at once. "What can I do for you, Warden?"

"I have bad news, I'm afraid. Two inmates have escaped. You should be getting the bulletin shortly. It happened an hour ago. Several guards were killed. I wanted to give you a heads-up because one of them has a connection to your area. Harrison Ames. You had talked to me about him some time back."

"Right," Frank said, his heart dropping at the news. "He's a former boyfriend of Emily Calder." Emily had started to get her life together again after going to jail because of Harrison Ames. Not only did Emily have a now five-year-old daughter, but she was involved in a serious relationship with Alex Ross, who owned Big Timber Java.

"As I recall, Ames had paid a friend to spy on her a while back," the warden was saying.

"Yes. I'd hoped that was the end of it." But now that Ames was on the loose... "I'll let Emily know. I'll put a deputy on her and her daughter until Ames is caught." He thought of Alex Ross, again. He would have to know, too.

"Might be a good idea to give her some protection," the warden agreed. "You know how these escaped criminals can be."

Unfortunately, after this many years, Frank did know. Harrison Ames was a bad one.

"They always have someone to blame for their problems. I'd hate to see the young woman pay the price of Harrison's self-inflicted misery."

"Let me know any further updates on his escape," Frank said. "The sooner we get that one locked up again, the better." He hung up, hating that he would have to tell Emily—and fearing what she might do. Harrison terrified her, and Frank didn't doubt that the criminal would use Emily's little daughter against her if he got the chance.

AFTER BEING QUESTIONED by the deputies in the conference room of the hotel about Lance Roderick's murder earlier, Kitzie was in the hotel kitchen when her cell phone rang. She stepped out the side door into the sunlight to take it. "Give me some good news."

"Okay," Pete said. "I've found out more about the connection between Harry Lester and his sister's youngest grandson, Robert Lester LeRoy."

Bobby LeRoy.

"He's got a long rap sheet, mostly kid stuff, but definitely headed for trouble. Makes sense that his great uncle might try to do something to help him if he asked."

She let the door close behind her and walked toward the pine trees at the edge of the meadow.

"Sounds plausible, but I have bigger problems here." She told him about Lance Roderick's murder.

"Do they have a suspect?"

"Not yet, but apparently Roderick got into a fight last night at the bar. LeRoy it turns out jumped in to help him. The fight was broken up and the crew left, but a man was spotted following LeRoy last night up here at the cabins. He was carrying a baseball bat, the apparent murder weapon."

"No ID on the man?"

"No, just that he was big."

"So, no connection to what is about to go down?"

"Who knows? Someone here also saw Roderick taking cell phone photos outside the local café last night. His phone is missing."

Pete let out a whistle. "So there could be more to the story."

Wasn't there always? She turned away to make

sure no one was within hearing distance. "You at the airport?"

"His flight is delayed."

Kitzie sighed. She needed a break. Finding out that LeRoy was related to Harry Lester tied up a few loose ends, but there was still too much she didn't know.

"Keep in touch," she said and disconnected. Turning, she saw Gun watching her and felt her heart drop to the pit of her stomach. The look on his face turned her blood to slush. He knew she'd been in his cabin. But how? She'd been so careful.

CHAPTER THIRTEEN

EMILY CALDER LOOKED up from her desk at the Sarah Johnson Hamilton Foundation as the sheriff came in.

She assumed he was looking for Bo Hamilton, her boss and the foundation director. She was about to tell him that Bo wouldn't be in today when she saw his expression. A bad feeling swept through her.

"It's Harrison, isn't it?" she asked in a whisper.

He nodded, his expression serious. "He and another inmate escaped from prison."

Her heart raced. All she could think about was getting to her daughter's day care. She needed to have Jodie in her arms. "When?"

"A few hours ago. He couldn't have reached here yet."

She looked around for her purse. "I have to—"

"Get to Jodie. I called her preschool. They know you are on your way and not to let her leave with anyone else."

She nodded, unable to speak around the lump in her throat. Her eyes blurred with tears. She'd known that one day her old boyfriend would get out of prison, but that was years away. Now to hear that he had escaped...

"He'll come here looking for me," she whispered, close to tears.

"And we will be waiting for him."

Her gaze locked with the sheriff's. "What are you saying?"

"You don't want to run. You'll be safer here."

She thought of the small house she rented. One of Harrison's friends had broken into it and taken a photo of her and Jodie last year. Even with security gates on the windows, she didn't feel safe—not with Harrison on the loose.

Her first instinct was to get her daughter and run. She had money saved in the bank. She could get in her car and—

Alex. The thought of the man she'd fallen in love with brought its own kind of pleasure and pain. She couldn't leave Alex. She couldn't break her daughter's heart. Jodie adored him. Emily had never loved anyone the way she did Alex. He was her one and only.

Nor did she want to uproot them. She loved her job, loved being back in this part of Montana. Her brother's wife and her boss, Bo, were going to have twin girls any day now.

Emily found her purse and clutched it to her. Get to Jodie and then... She looked up at the sheriff again. "Does Alex know?"

"Not yet. I thought you would want to tell him."

At the sound of the foundation's front door opening, they both turned abruptly. Alex Ross came in. Just the sight of him made Emily melt. She would never have guessed she could fall in love with such a straight-arrow guy. Harrison had been a biker, an outlaw, a worthless jerk. Like the many tattoos and piercings she'd gotten, he had been her outward sign of rebelling against the loss of her parents at such a young age.

But after Harrison had involved her in a robbery and she'd done time, she'd become pregnant with Jodie and knew she was no longer that girl.

She was still finding herself when Alex, the owner of Big Timber Java, had come into her life—and Jodie's.

"What's wrong?" Alex said now, instantly on alert.

"It's Harrison. He's escaped from prison," Emily said.

Alex's gaze went to the sheriff. "What are we going to do?"

"First, go pick up Jodie. Then I would like Emily to go to her house. We will have men surrounding it."

"Isn't Emily's house the first place Harrison will go? I don't like the idea of you taking a chance with the two of them inside," Alex said, shaking his head.

"I'd like you there, too. Harrison knows about all three of you. Separately, you make too good of a target. Together, we can protect you. Once he is caught—"

"Or dead," Emily said. "He always said he'd die before he went to prison."

"And yet he went to prison," Alex pointed out. "I suspect he won't choose going out in a blaze of glory this time either."

"The bright side is that he will get more prison time and less chance of getting out on parole because of this," the sheriff said.

"Let's go get Jodie," Alex said, reaching out his hand for Emily's.

Tears filled her eyes as his strong, warm hand enveloped hers. She instantly felt safer.

AINSLEY HAD HOPED that her family wouldn't hear about the murder. She'd just heard about it herself when she'd returned to the hotel and run into one of the kitchen workers. Fortunately, the teenager had filled her in on everything before Kat had called.

"They already think they know who did it," she tried to reassure her sister. All the talk around the hotel had been about the murder and what the local sheriff had discovered so far. "The victim had gotten in a bar fight earlier in the night. They think he was followed out of town last night after the man he'd fought with threatened to kill him. Both men had been drunk, apparently."

"So it had nothing to do with the commercial or... anything else?" Kat asked.

Kat knew that Ainsley had been followed for a while now. "Nope, has nothing to do with my...

secret admirer." She always tried to joke it off, telling herself the man was harmless. "And I'll be headed home in a few days. How is everyone there holding up with the election so close?"

"Sarah is doing a charity event in Big Timber. She's asked us to join her."

Kat refused to call Sarah Mother. Ainsley was used to it and didn't argue with her anymore about it. And like now, Ainsley didn't volunteer to help their mother. She needed some downtime and couldn't wait to get home and just relax. She wasn't going to get swept up in some political charity event. The old Ainsley would have felt guilty if she hadn't offered to help. But not this newer one.

"So you're all right?" Kat said.

"Fine."

"Really, you sound…funny."

Ainsley rolled her eyes. So like Kat to pick up on something in her voice. She knew she would have to tell her or Kat would keep digging.

"I met someone." The words were out before she could call them back. *Now*, she had Kat's attention.

"A man?"

Another eye roll before she said, "Don't sound so surprised. Yes, a man. It's nothing…serious, though. It's just a…fling." *Really?* She couldn't believe she'd said that. Did she wish that's what it was? Is that why she'd said that?

"A fling?" Kat sounded disbelieving. "You don't do flings."

"Maybe I do now. Maybe, now that my sisters are all settled, maybe I'd like to kick up my heels and… do whatever strikes my fancy."

Kat laughed. "*You?* I'd like to see this."

"I doubt you will because, like I said, it's not serious. I'm trying out a new me on this handsome cowboy I've met." She rolled her eyes again, wishing she would just shut up. What she was voicing was pure fantasy.

"*Really?* You and some handsome cowboy?"

That Kat thought she was incapable of such a thing made her more determined to convince her of it. "That's right. He's going to be my first." Ainsley slapped a hand over her mouth.

Silence on the other end of the line told her that her sister had suspected but hadn't known until that moment. She mentally kicked herself hard for opening her mouth.

"You're not serious? Ainsley, what do you know about this man? He might just be using you."

She laughed. "Maybe I'm using him and then moving on." She really had to get off the line before she dug herself in any deeper. "How's Max?" she asked, knowing that was the way to shift the conversation.

"Good." Kat's whole demeanor sounded as if it had changed. Just asking about her fiancé lit her up. Seeing her sister so in love made Ainsley happy. All of her sisters had found love. She couldn't have wished anything more for them.

The knock at her cabin door gave her the perfect excuse to escape. "Someone's here, Kat. I have to go. See you in a few days." And she was finally off the line. If only she had done that earlier, she was thinking when she turned and realized that she hadn't closed the cabin door all the way when she'd returned.

The breeze must have caught it because now the door was wide open, and standing in it was Sawyer.

Her heart dropped like a stone. She felt heat rush to her face. Her palms went clammy. *He'd heard. He'd heard every word!* She could see it on his face. He'd only knocked to make her aware of his presence. He'd heard everything she'd said to Kat.

She opened her mouth to explain but quickly closed it. One word and she feared she would only make matters worse.

But she realized that this newer Ainsley Hamilton wasn't one to keep her mouth shut. "I suppose you heard all that?"

Sawyer glanced down at his boots before lifting his gaze to hers again. "I didn't mean to eavesdrop." He looked embarrassed and yet almost…pleased. "I'm…flattered," he said and couldn't seem to help himself because he grinned. "I'd love to take you up on that, even though you plan to dump me and move on." He held up a hand to keep her from saying something stupid. "But there's something you need to know first."

GUN COULDN'T BELIEVE his bad luck. Things had been going so well, he should have known something would throw a monkey wrench into it.

He had only himself to blame. He'd had a strange feeling when he'd hired Lance Roderick. He hadn't been able to put his finger on it. Definitely not the law, he'd thought at the time, so he'd pushed his worry aside and hired the man.

Now Roderick was dead. Murdered. And the place was crawling with cops. He swore under his breath. The timing couldn't have been worse.

His special guest was flying in tonight. Now he would have to detain him until all these local yokels cleared out. Not that he thought any of them would recognize Harry Lester Brown. Few people had ever laid eyes on him, Gun included.

That was where LeRoy came in. If Gun could keep the bastard alive that long. Clark and Hale had reported that LeRoy had gotten into an altercation at the bar last night that involved Lance Roderick.

Apparently LeRoy had jumped in to save Roderick, but with so many witnesses, LeRoy would be a suspect in Roderick's death.

Gun had expected it would be Hale involved in a brawl. He reminded himself that it wasn't over. If he could get through this and the remainder of the commercial shoot, he would be home free. He just had to keep his cool. If only he could depend on the others to do the same.

Looking up, he spotted the local law headed in

his direction. One more day. Even now he could hear Hale over in the meadow working on getting all the rides ready for tonight. He'd gotten a hungover LeRoy and that delivery kid to help him.

SAWYER TOLD HIMSELF that he felt badly about eavesdropping on Ainsley's conversation with her sister. But at the same time, he had to admit that he'd enjoyed it. But why hadn't he just turned around and left instead of knocking? Partly because the darned cabin porch boards creaked with each step. The last thing he'd wanted was to get caught sneaking away.

Her cheeks were flushed, her blue eyes bright as stars. She couldn't have looked more beautiful. Had she really said he was going to be her *first*?

He still didn't see how that could be possible. A beautiful woman like her? But it would explain how she'd reacted the other night when he'd stopped himself from making love to her in his pickup. Was that really what she wanted? To use him and move on?

"We need to talk," he said, and she motioned him on into the cabin with an expression of dread. He was the one dreading this. He had to tell her the truth about why he was here. But after what he'd heard her say to her sister…

"You've heard the news about Lance Roderick, the security guard?" he asked.

She nodded. Ainsley seemed relieved to be talking about murder rather than what he'd overheard her saying to her sister. "I heard you found the body."

He'd been ready to tell her that he'd heard that the security guard hadn't reported for work and had gone to check on him—an explanation that had satisfied the chief of police—but she didn't ask how he had come to find Roderick.

"Do they know who did it?"

"Not that I've heard. They don't think it was anyone staying out here, so that's good. You just got back?"

"Scouting the last location shot." She finally sat down on the end of the couch. He took a chair at the small kitchen table opposite her. Last night during dinner she'd told him she had to get up early to look for another location for a shot the assistant director wanted. As far as he knew, she'd been gone all day.

"Did you find a location that is going to work?" Sawyer asked now.

"Several," she said. "Then I came back to find out that the security guard had been murdered." She shuddered. "I'll be so happy when this commercial is over." She looked uncomfortable and nervous around him now. He mentally kicked himself for letting her know he'd overheard her conversation.

"There's something I need to tell you."

"About the security guard's death?"

"No," he said with a shake of his head. "About me. I wasn't completely honest with you about why I'm here, and given what's happened, I need to be."

She sat back a little as if distancing herself from whatever was coming.

"I know someone's been following you."

Her voice came out a whisper. "You mean because of the day in the canyon."

"I knew before then. That's why I was there. Apparently you mentioned to your father that a man had been following you." She began to shake her head, her eyes wide with more than alarm. "Your father mentioned it to Sheriff Frank Curry and he—"

She made a broken sound and looked away. *My father paid you to look out for me?"* She seemed to be both surprised and angry. He could see that she was thinking of what had happened last night after dinner parked on that hill, as well as what she'd told her sister.

"No, not your father," he said holding up his hands in surrender. "Frank and I go way back, and he asked me to—"

"To *spy* on me." She shot to her feet as if her anger wouldn't let her sit any longer. Anger, hurt and embarrassment, he thought as he looked into her face. "To...*protect* me? That's why you asked me to dinner."

He was on his feet, as well. "No. Ainsley, this is why I didn't want to tell you."

"You need to leave now." She walked to the door and started to open it, but stopped to turn back and face him. "I should have known," she said, shaking her head again, this time in obvious disgust. "And last night when you...kissed me, when you..." She grabbed the door handle to throw open the door, but he stepped to her in one long stride and dropped a hand over hers.

"Please," he said. "Please, just listen to me."

She froze. Her eyes glistened with tears she was desperately trying to fight back.

"I kissed you last night because I wanted to. Trust me, it was the last thing I planned to do. That's why I stopped. I couldn't go any further...not with you not knowing the truth about why I came here."

She hadn't moved, hadn't looked at him. He prayed she was listening, really listening.

"Remember when I left you at the table before we ordered?" he asked, buoyed to continue. "I went out into the parking lot." She looked at him now, listening. "Lance Roderick's car had just pulled up in the parking lot. When I approached the car, I saw that he appeared to be taking photos with his phone. He seemed to be shooting you sitting in the café. Before I could confront him, he took off."

She stared at him. "So Lance Roderick *was* the man following me?"

"Like I said, it appears so." He hesitated for a moment before he said, "Did you sense that anyone followed you today?"

Ainsley gave it a moment's thought. "No." She sounded surprised by that. "I didn't even realize... It's been so long since I haven't felt someone watching me."

She glanced away for a moment, frowning, before

turning her gaze back on him. "So you suspected him right away?"

He had to improvise. Dragging Kitzie into this would only muddy the already dark waters. "I saw him watching you."

She nodded, then studied him, eyes narrowing. "Why would Sheriff Curry ask *you* to find this man?"

"He knew I was at loose ends." Sawyer motioned to his leg. She'd been polite not to question his limp. "I work in law enforcement, and he knew I was on medical leave and probably going crazy with nothing to do."

She nodded, her expression making it clear that this news wasn't pleasing her any more than the idea of him misrepresenting himself—especially after their date last night and what had almost happened between them.

"What I'm trying to say is that I didn't tell you because I didn't want to upset you. I thought for sure I would be able to neutralize the problem without you even knowing I had."

"Neutralize the problem," she repeated.

"I didn't kill Lance, if that's what you're asking."

"But now that the problem is…neutralized, you won't be staying on here," Ainsley said. "Is that what you're trying to tell me?" Anger made her blue eyes spark like hot flames.

"I'm not leaving until I'm sure that Roderick was the man following you. Once his cell phone is found, we'll know more. I'm not going anywhere until I'm sure you're safe." She couldn't know how dangerous that would be, given the way he felt about her.

CHAPTER FOURTEEN

EMILY CALDER HAD almost forgotten about her troubled past. She'd almost bought into second chances. Then the sheriff had shown up at her office with the news that her past had reared its huge head again.

Harrison Ames. She cringed, no longer able to remember what she had seen in the outlaw biker. She knew what counselors had said had caused her self-destructive behavior—the death of her parents and rebellion against her brother, Jace, who'd suddenly become her guardian.

Harrison had been dangerous. She'd climbed on the back of his motorcycle, not caring what happened to her. So it was no wonder he'd gotten her into trouble with the law.

But now she had Josie, she thought as she walked down the hallway to her room. She'd left the door open where she could hear her—even though her landlady had put metal bars on the windows after the last break-in.

Jodie was sleeping, one hand under her head, the other curled next to her face. She looked like an angel.

"She's beautiful," Alex whispered next to her ear from behind her as he pulled his arms around her.

She leaned back into him, thinking as she often did how inconceivable it was that they had gotten together. She with her tattoos and piercings. Alex in his chinos and button-down shirts as straitlaced as a man could be.

And yet, they had fallen in love. He'd taken to Jodie right away and the child to him. They'd become a family, something she'd never thought possible, given her past.

She'd never thought that she wanted normal, but she'd never wanted it more than she did right at this minute.

"She's all right," Alex whispered and pulled her toward the living room.

"I'm so sorry," she said, ashamed that this was all her fault. "If I hadn't—"

"Honey?" he turned her to look at him. "We all have pasts. It's what makes us the person we are today. I love this Emily." He touched her cheek, and she turned her face into his hand to kiss his palm.

"The sheriff will catch him. It will be over soon," he assured her.

Emily hoped and prayed that was true. Until Harrison was either dead or behind bars, she would live in fear.

THE CRIME SCENE tape came down before dark on Lance Roderick's cabin, and the last of the statements were taken. Everyone was told to go about his business again.

The pall that had seemed to fall over the place earlier disappeared by dusk. The kitchen was loud and noisy. Ainsley listened as the murder was discussed, suspect names were whispered at tables before bursts of laughter. She got the impression that everyone was trying too hard to forget about it, since as far as anyone had heard, the killer hadn't been caught yet.

She felt relieved that there was no one following her anymore. Not that she had wanted him murdered. She tried to relax. She hadn't seen Sawyer since their talk earlier. She was mortified that the only reason he was here was part of a job to look after her. Add to that what she'd said on the phone to Kat… She felt her face begin to heat and concentrated on her meal.

She'd left her cabin earlier because she couldn't sit still. While everyone else was on edge because of the murder, Ainsley felt safer than she had in months. Lance Roderick was no longer a problem. Also, she had her own guardian angel in Sawyer watching out for her. Everything should have been rosy.

On top of that, Gunderson had agreed much too easily to one of the locations she'd found. Maybe like her, he just wanted to get this commercial over with, now that someone had died here.

With the meal over, everyone wandered outside. Someone had built another bonfire. The crew seemed to gravitate toward the light of the roaring flames. She could tell that they felt safer where they could see each other. Darkness had dropped like a cloak over the valley. While they'd all laughed and pretended not to be bothered by the violence, it was clear that no one wanted to go back to their cabins.

Ainsley didn't feel up to joining them—not after the embarrassment of the other night. She left the hotel and headed for her cabin, wondering where Sawyer was.

She didn't have to wonder long. He appeared out of the night giving her the impression he had never been far away from her since their earlier discussion.

"Not in the mood to party tonight?" he asked.

She ignored him as he fell into step alongside her. In truth, she was like everyone else. Still a little spooked to have violence hit so close by. And while she resented being "looked after," she was smart enough to appreciate having Sawyer here.

As she unlocked her cabin door, he took the key from her and entered the cabin first. Since the cabins were small, she found that rather silly and said so as he motioned her in.

"What is the point? My stalker is dead."

"I'd feel better if you didn't stay until the end of the commercial."

She reared back like a horse given too much bit. "I signed a *contract*. I gave my word that I would see this through. I can be fined if I don't stay on. Not to mention the fact that I don't quit jobs in the middle of them. I know I've been acting…less like myself lately, but I don't take my responsibilities lightly."

He held up both hands. "Neither do I. I'm still worried about your safety."

She shook her head. "What is this? Lance is dead. Why are you still trying to protect me? I'm not *your* responsibility. You can tell Sheriff Curry and my father that I am perfectly capable of taking care of myself." All the fight went out of her as if, like him, she'd just recalled the rock slide, and her behavior after that that had ended with her naked in her bed and him sleeping on her couch.

"Under normal circumstances," she added under her breath, her cheeks flaming again.

"Exactly. These haven't been normal circumstances, as you just pointed out."

She saw something in his expression. "What is it you aren't telling me?"

FRANK FOUND HIMSELF wearing a hole in his office carpet. But he couldn't sit still. He paced, willing the phone to ring. He'd talked to the deputies around Emily's house. No sign of Harrison Ames.

Still he couldn't relax because no law officer had spotted the two escaped prisoners. The obvious explanation was that they weren't headed for Big Timber. Instead, they'd done the smart thing and had gotten out of Montana.

Otherwise, they should have been spotted. Every law enforcement officer in the state was looking for the two escaped prisoners and had a pretty good idea where Harrison would be headed—

When his phone rang, it made him jump. He quickly stepped to his desk and picked up. "Sheriff Curry."

"You wanted to know the moment I heard anything about Harrison Ames?" the warden said without preamble. "A gas-station clerk was just found shot to death outside of Basin, Montana."

"Basin?" He stepped to the Montana map on the wall. "That's as far as they've gotten?"

"The coroner estimated the clerk had been dead since late last night. So to answer your question, they hadn't gotten far probably because they cut across the mountains, and the snow is pretty deep up there."

"But that was late last night? They could be anywhere by now," Frank said. "Even right here in Big Timber."

"Doubtful. We know that they're taking back roads. We got a call from a woman who thinks she saw them. It's not confirmed—"

"Where?" he asked impatiently.

"Harrison."

Frank ran his finger down the map southwest of Butte.

"She saw two men stealing clothes off a neighbor's clothesline and called the Madison County sheriff. He gave chase but lost them near Norris. He thinks they're headed for Bozeman—"

"And once they get on Interstate 90, it won't take them long to get to Big Timber," he said with a sigh.

"I'm going to put a couple more deputies on Emily Calder's house."

"We're going to get them."

Frank wasn't counting on it as he disconnected and called two more deputies to come in and work tonight.

SAWYER BRACED HIMSELF for the anticipated explosion when he told Ainsley the rest. Motioning to the couch, he suggested she sit. Instead she crossed her arms defiantly and stood her ground in the small kitchen.

He had no choice but to stay standing, as well. "Earlier I told you that Lance Roderick *seemed* to be your stalker. I'm waiting on confirmation from the sheriff."

Her blue eyes widened in alarm. "But I thought—"

"Roderick fits the profile, but until his prints get run and compared to the note I sent to Frank…"

"Note?"

He sighed. "There's something more I haven't told you," he said, almost flinching from the look she shot him. "The man who followed you to the canyon left a note on your cabin. I found it taped to the door the night I carried you back here after your first attempt at skinny-dipping."

"A note to *me*? And you didn't see fit to tell me about it?" she demanded as she took a step toward him.

"I didn't want to scare you."

"*Scare* me? What was in the note?"

She listened as he told her and seemed relieved when he finished. "So the rock slide was an accident. He didn't want to harm me."

Sawyer hated to burst her bubble. "Here's the problem. From what I saw in his note, he appeared to be infatuated with you."

She laughed. "And this is a problem? Men have had crushes on me before." She sounded defensive, and she knew it.

"But they haven't followed you from town to town and never tried to speak to you," he pointed out. "I think Lance became obsessed with you. He put you on a pedestal."

"He also wouldn't be the first man to do that," she said as if more to herself.

"But after you had too much to drink the other night—"

"We don't have to recount my behavior," she said, looking away. "You're saying I disappointed him—"

"He left another note last night."

"*Another* note you kept from me?" Her words were clipped, her body appearing more rigid with either anger or fear. He couldn't tell which.

"I found it on my cabin door after we returned from dinner. It was addressed to me, but it was about you."

He saw her swallow before she asked, "What did it say?"

"That he blamed himself for your behavior the

night of the rock slide, but if you continued drinking and acting out, dressing the way you were at dinner, he would have to punish you and hurt me."

Ainsley stood for a moment perfectly still, then dropping her crossed arms, moved to the couch and sat down. "Are you trying to tell me that you think he is still out there?"

"I won't know until the sheriff compares Roderick's fingerprints to those he left on the notes."

"When will we know?" she asked, her voice sounding hollow.

He shook his head. "But until we have a definitive answer, I'm going to be here. Gunderson wants me for the final shoot at the carnival. I told him I would stay. So unless you want me sleeping outside your cabin for the remainder of our time here…"

She bristled, took in a breath and let it out slowly. "What am I going to have to do—shy of leaving my employment here—to keep that from happening?"

"You could let me sleep on your couch. I would be very discreet," he added quickly. "The worst that could happen is that everyone would think we were…romantically involved."

She looked away. "We wouldn't want them thinking that."

THE MEADOW HAD come alive in a kaleidoscope of lights and noise. Gun walked toward it, mesmerized. He felt like a kid again. Also, his optimism had returned. Hope soared through him. Not only would he finish this commercial on schedule, but also the rest of his life would fall into place, as well.

He prided himself on finishing what he started. That was the problem with Hale. He lacked whatever it was that made a man have pride in his work. A loyalty to what he did for a living—even if it was running a cruddy carnival.

The noise of machinery and carnie music filled the night air. Hale had all the rides going. Empty, they whirled and chugged and creaked and wheeled as if being ridden by ghosts that only Gun could see.

He saw them, ghosts grinning from grotesque faces in a kind of glee that he understood too well. Had he been planning to stay in the video production business, he would have bought this carnival for himself and hired someone to keep it running day and night until it rusted and fell to the earth.

His gaze fell on Hale, who stood next to the Ferris wheel as if he'd been waiting patiently for him. "Ready for that ride?"

Gun looked up as an empty chair rocked at the top before making its descent. "I've never been more ready."

Laughing, Hale brought the wheel to a stop with practiced ease and made a grand gesture at the empty chair before him. He noticed then that the man had a small handheld device and realized with a start that Hale planned to ride with him.

As he sat down, Hale slid in next to him, forcing him over. "Let's go for ride, Old Buddy." He didn't

bother laying the bar across them for security as
he hit the button on the device in his hand and the
chair began to rise. The music seemed to soar as they
climbed higher and higher.

Gun tried to relax as he looked out over the coun-
tryside. He could make out the lights of the town in
the distance, just as he'd known he would be able to
do. The night air was crisp and cold, with the smells
of fall. The lights, the music, the feeling of flying
would have all been magical had he been alone.

At the crest before the chair began to descend,
Hale brought them to an abrupt stop. The chair
rocked dangerously, groaning under the weight of
the two of them.

"Why did you stop it?" he demanded, annoyed as
he grabbed hold of the side to keep from falling off.

Hale almost dropped the remote device as he, too,
had to hang on without the bar down to keep them in
their seat. The chair rocked precariously, the wind
buffing it, and Hale hung on uneasily as if he didn't
like being up here. He seemed to wait for the chair
to quit rocking before he said, "We need to talk, and
I thought this would be a good place to do it. I guess
I forgot how damned high it is."

They were sitting so close that Gun would have
had to crane his neck to look at the man. Not that he
wanted to. If anything, he wanted to push Hale off
and watch him fall, hitting the next chair and then
the next until his broken body hit the ground.

But if anything, Gun was a pragmatist. He could

probably climb down from here if he set his mind to it, but he'd rather use the remote gripped tightly in Hale's hand. So he took a breath and let it out slowly.

"What is it you think we need to discuss?"

Hale cleared his throat. "Tell me I have nothing to worry about."

"I have no idea what you're talking about."

The older man chuckled. "How long have we known each other?"

He couldn't believe Hale wanted to talk about this now. A gust of wind caught them, making the chair swing back and forth, groaning as it did. The carnival music was starting to get on his nerves. He'd been looking forward to this, and now he felt anger building in him. Hale was spoiling it.

"Get to the point, then get the hell off my ride."

"*Your* ride?"

"Yeah, *my* ride," he said turning his head to lock gazes with him. "I'm paying for this. That makes it my damned ride." He watched Hale take a breath and let it out.

"I just wanted to make sure you weren't planning to screw me out of my share," Hale said, all his bravado gone.

In one swift movement, Gun grabbed the remote. The Ferris wheel shuddered and began to move again before he thumbed it to a stop. The chair rocked wildly. Hale was fighting to stay on.

"If I planned to cut you out of the deal, I would push you off this chair right now," Gun said. "I hope that alleviates your concerns, and we won't be having this discussion again."

With that, he hit the button again. The chair jerked as they began to descend. Once they reached the bottom, Gun said, "This is where you get off."

Hale was still clinging to the side of the chair as he shakily stepped off and, on wobbly legs, moved out of the way as Gun got his ride going again.

CHAPTER FIFTEEN

SHERIFF FRANK CURRY had been distracted all morning. He'd pulled off several men he had watching Emily Calder's house at first light. He didn't think Harrison was stupid enough to try anything until dark. He hoped he was right.

But what worried him was that he hadn't heard on those prints for Sawyer. He was thinking about calling the lab tech, when his wife interrupted the thought.

"You haven't touched your breakfast," Nettie pointed out unnecessarily. "I made your favorite."

He gave her a smile. "I know. Thank you. I'm just not—"

"Hungry. You're starting to worry me, Frank Curry."

Getting up from the table, he went to her, pressing her back against the sink as he cupped her face and kissed her. Desire stirred within him as strong as it had been as a teenager for this woman.

"What is it about you?" he asked. "Whatever it is, we should bottle it. We could make a fortune."

She laughed at that, as she always did. "Aren't you the charmer." But there was worry in her gaze.

"I'm fine. Just not hungry lately. Once this blamed election is over..."

Nettie locked her gaze on him. "You've been saying that for months. Are you sure that isn't all that's bothering you?"

"I might have a surprise for you," he said.

"I know that twinkle in your eye. You're trying to distract me from worrying about you."

He laughed. "Is it working?"

"A good surprise?" she asked, clearly playing along.

"I think it is. We'll see what you have to say once I decide to tell you." He moved away, anxious to drive by Emily's and make sure for himself that she and her daughter and Alex Ross were all fine. He knew what a man like her former boyfriend was capable of. As an escaped convict, Harrison would think he had nothing to lose. Men like him always wanted to blame someone else for the way their lives had turned out. Harrison would blame Emily.

"When can I expect this...surprise you have for me?"

He heard the fear in her voice, even as hard as she was trying to hide it. Both of them were worried about election night. "As a matter of fact, I thought you might want to go for a ride with me later. There's something I want to talk to you about."

"I would," she said sounding close to tears, which wasn't like her at all.

What did she think he was going to tell her? He thought about just blurting it out, but held his tongue. He shouldn't have said anything. Too late now.

He smiled and pulled her to him. "Everything is going to be all right. You'll see."

IT WAS OVER. The commercial wrapped earlier that afternoon. Everyone had gotten paid after dinner and now it was time to leave. The hotel was shutting down. A cleaning crew would be coming to clean cabins the next day.

Sawyer watched the carnival rides being taken down by the remaining crew. He noticed the two kitchen girls were also watching.

For the past two days, Ainsley had sworn that no one was following her. "I'd know, trust me. It had to have been Lance Roderick—just as you'd thought all along. Since his death, nothing. I haven't felt anyone watching me, and since no one has tried to kill you…"

He couldn't believe it was over just like that. For Ainsley's sake, he was glad. But still it didn't feel right. Maybe it was because he hadn't been able to confront Lance Roderick that it felt…unfinished.

He tried to relax. The local sheriff's department hadn't been able to find the man who Roderick had fought with that night at the bar. Burt Jenkins seemed to have just dropped off the face of the earth. Or, more than likely, had taken to the mountains and was hiding out, which made him look all the more guilty.

Sheriff Curry hadn't gotten back to him on the prints yet from the notes. That's all he needed to finally quit worrying.

So why couldn't Sawyer accept that it was over?

He knew the answer to that. Ainsley. If his work here really were done, then this would probably be the last he ever saw of her. She was planning to leave tonight—unless he could change her mind.

As he walked toward her cabin, he glanced over at Kitzie's. It was dark inside. He hadn't even seen her for the past forty-eight hours. With the commercial done, what happened now with her case? he wondered.

He tapped at Ainsley's cabin door to find her packing. The sight reminded him how he'd failed. He'd done what he came here for. He'd discovered her stalker. Unless, of course, it hadn't been Lance Roderick, a little voice in the back of his brain reminded him.

Frank still hadn't called on the fingerprints. He wondered what was taking so long. Once he had verification that the prints from the notes matched Lance Roderick's, then maybe he could relax.

"I wish you weren't leaving tonight," he said, surprised at how much he hated the thought of this woman walking out of his life. Since he'd overheard her on the phone with her sister Kat, she'd been...

distant. He'd told himself that was probably best. Best to keep his distance and let this play out.

But he feared that once they left here, he wouldn't see her again. Even if he followed her back to the family ranch outside of Beartooth, he wasn't sure she would want to see *him* again. Unless he could turn things around between them.

You still have time.

"I think we need to go out again," Sawyer blurted out, hating this pathetic attempt to postpone the inevitable.

She stopped packing to look at him. "That's not necessary. You're off the hook. My stalker is gone. No more babysitting."

"You know it was more than that."

Her gaze said she didn't before she turned back to her packing.

"I enjoyed having dinner with you the other night," he said, taking a step toward her. "In fact, it was the most fun I'd had in a long time. I'd like to do it again. You don't have to leave tonight, do you?"

"Dinner. That's…all you had in mind?" She kept her back to him as she finished folding a shirt and putting it into the suitcase.

"I wouldn't mind having you in my arms again."

Her back stiffened. "Is this about what you overheard me say to my sister, because if it is—"

"Then we should do something about it."

Ainsley turned around to look at him. "I beg your pardon?"

"Why not do what you said you were going to do?" He held out his arms in a welcoming gesture.

Her face reddened. "You misunderstood what I—"

"Then let *me* be clear. I want you." He shrugged as he took another step toward her. "Any way you want me—even if you plan to use me and move on—is okay. Though if I had a choice, that wouldn't be it." His gaze held hers. He didn't realize he was holding his breath until Ainsley released hers. He saw her struggling as if the old Ainsley, the one who'd always been the good girl, was fighting toward the surface.

"Cut loose, let your hair down, kick up your heels, unless you're afraid to take a chance with me. That is what your sister was worried about, right?"

"So you heard *everything*."

Sawyer closed the distance, taking her shoulders in his big hands. "I wanted you long before that. I can't bear the thought of you walking out of my life right now. Ready to live a little dangerously?" he asked. "Unless the new you isn't up for it."

Her chin went up. "Are you actually daring me again?"

He grinned and lifted a brow. "Maybe we can kill two birds with one stone."

She gave him a horrified look.

Sawyer laughed. "I meant, maybe we can flush out your stalker if Roderick wasn't the man and he's still out there *and* have a wonderful dinner, as well." He did his best to look innocent.

Ainsley was eyeing him skeptically. "Why do I get the feeling that you're enjoying my embarrassment?"

He shook his head, sobering. "Not at all. I would be honored to be your first. That isn't why I stopped the other night. Like I told you, I couldn't, not until you knew why I was here. Stopping was the last thing I wanted to do and if I had another chance…"

She shook her head. "It is so kind of you to want to…help me out," she said, her words heavy with sarcasm.

"My pleasure." His grin broadened. "I'll let you get ready for our date while I go change. If you need me—"

"I HAVE YOUR NUMBER." Boy, did she, Ainsley thought as she watched him head for his cabin. What was she thinking? Was she really going through with this?

She was. She knew it sounded crazy what she was about to do. But Bo was right. Her virginity was something she needed to get taken care of, and who better than a handsome cowboy with no strings attached?

For a moment, a sadness filled her. After tonight she wouldn't be seeing Sawyer Nash again. She'd heard him take a call just yesterday from someone asking when he would be ready to get back to work. Apparently they needed him as early as next week for another special assignment.

Ainsley closed the cabin door and turned to her

closet. She'd been packing up everything she'd brought. The red dress Kitzie had lent her and the high heels were all that was left in the closet. She needed to return them, but not now.

Tonight she wouldn't be wearing a sexy dress. Tonight she would wear one of her Western shirts and a pair of jeans and her best boots. Tonight she would be herself, the new, hopefully improved Ainsley Hamilton, a Montana cowgirl at heart. The other night hadn't been the real her, and she wasn't going to change for any man. Not that Sawyer would be around long enough to get to really know her. But that was okay, she told herself.

In truth, she had enjoyed wearing the red dress. It had made her feel like someone else. Someone sexy and desirable. But tonight she would see if it had been the dress—or the woman in it.

Are you sure you can do this and not want more than Sawyer was offering? She wasn't, but she had no choice. She tried to think of it as just taking care of business. Once they'd completed this… arrangement, they could go their separate ways, even though he said he didn't want it that way. It wasn't like any of this had been serious. Also, she suspected he would feel differently in the morning.

She dressed and glanced at her watch. Shouldn't Sawyer be back by now?

KITZIE COULD TELL that she was the last person Sawyer wanted to see when she'd cut him off before he could reach his cabin. She'd made it sound urgent, insisting she needed his help.

She knew him well enough that he wouldn't be able to turn her down. She'd seen him whistling as he walked to his cabin after leaving Ainsley's. She knew his good mood could only mean one thing. One last hot date.

"What's up?" he said now as she motioned him into her cabin and quickly closed the door after him, locking it.

"I was wrong. I need your help on this case."

He looked as surprised as she knew he would.

"It's more…dangerous than I thought." She met his gaze. "I need to tell you what's going on."

Sawyer glanced at his watch.

"It won't take long. Sit down. I don't know about you, but I could use a drink. You have time for one drink and what I have to tell you, don't you? Or would you rather have coffee?" She knew him so well. He'd think she was trying to seduce him with a drink. But not with coffee.

"Coffee would be great." He sat on the edge of the couch as if anxious to get going. This wouldn't be easy, she thought. Not even what she had to tell him might not keep him from Ainsley tonight. Apparently this was more serious than she'd thought.

Her stomach roiled at the idea that Sawyer could fall for someone so quickly. Especially when he hadn't fallen for her as close as they'd been. Anger heated her skin as she stepped into the tiny kitchen to get them coffee.

She wondered when she'd see him again. She wouldn't if he had his way, she thought bitterly. Look how hard it had been to just get him to step into her cabin. He couldn't wait to get away from her.

He was all cleaned up. He smelled so good it made her hurt inside. She turned to see him sending a text. Not doubt to Ainsley saying he had gotten held up but wouldn't be long. She'd been right about the hot date.

As she filled Sawyer's mug with instant coffee, she saw her bottle of prescription sleeping pills sitting on the counter next to the sink. She'd lured him in with her jewel thieves case. She knew where the man's true heart lay. But she could tell he was anxious to get to his precious Ainsley. Kitzie still couldn't imagine what he saw in the woman. She was pretty, if you liked that bland girl-next-door type, but the two had nothing in common. What was Sawyer thinking?

"So what was it you had to tell me?" he asked, shifting impatiently on the couch.

Her anger and jealousy got the best of her. She opened the sleeping pill bottle, took out two, then changed her mind and dropped a third one into the mug of hot coffee. A half of one of the pills laid her out for twelve hours. Three should do the trick and then some for a man his size. Fortunately, they were very fast-acting, she thought as she added a little sugar and cream, just the way he used to like his coffee, and turned to smile at him.

"I told you that Harry Lester Brown is related to Bobby LeRoy, but it turns out that he also has a Montana connection we hadn't known about." She gave the pills another moment or two to dissolve, stirred his coffee and put the spoon in the sink. "He recently purchased a house on Flathead Lake. Apparently he's planning to spend at least part of the year here. That's probably why they're doing the deal here in Montana. I'm waiting to hear from Pete. He's following Harry Lester, who flew in late last night and is staying in a Butte hotel."

"So Harry Lester Brown is already in the state?" Sawyer asked. She heard the interest in his voice and smiled. "This grand nephew and Montana are what brought Harry Lester out of retirement, you think?"

"It's still pretty hot," she said of the coffee she'd handed him. "You might want to let it cool a little," she said as she took her own over to the end of the couch and, sitting, tucked one leg under her to turn to face him. She knew he could never wait until the coffee cooled.

"That's the theory." Kitzie watched him take a drink. He didn't look quite as impatient now that they were talking criminals. It was something they shared. She was glad she could remind him of that. "I expect the deal to go down tomorrow—if not to-night." She smiled at Sawyer.

He suddenly looked nervous. "Kitzie, I can't—"

"I don't need you to do anything tonight," she quickly assured him. He took another drink of his coffee. "I just need to cross all my t's and dot my i's on this bust. I need an ID on my fence. You're one of the few people who has actually laid eyes on Harry Lester."

"But that was years ago. It's hard to say how much he might have changed."

"Pete should be sending me a photo any minute." She glanced at her cell phone. "He called right before I caught you to say Harry Lester had left his room to go down to the dining room." She could see that Sawyer was anxious to see the photo. But he was also anxious to leave.

"Should be just a minute," she said, putting her phone back in her pocket and stalling for time.

Sawyer seemed to relax as if relieved she really did have something she needed his help on. What did he think? That she got him into her cabin to seduce him? Or worse, drug him, she thought with a stab of guilt. Too late now. The damage was done.

"You must be excited about this bust. Nice work," he said as if he meant it.

"You can't believe what it took to talk my boss into letting me go undercover on this. That's why I have to succeed, whatever it takes." She couldn't help but smile. "I'm close. By tomorrow…"

Sawyer let out a chuckle. "I know how you love being right."

She smiled and took a sip of her coffee. He took

a healthy gulp. "I'm sorry. It should be just a few more minutes." Outside, she heard a vehicle pull up to one of the cabins. Everyone would be gone soon, except for Gunderson and his cohorts. "You leaving in the morning?" she asked, even though she suspected the answer.

He nodded, his eyelids drooping for a moment. He glanced at his watch, but she could tell he wanted a quick look at the photo before he left. "I have a few minutes." He yawned and took another drink of his coffee.

She saw him fighting to keep his eyes open. She got up to take her cup to the kitchen. "How's your coffee?" she asked, looking back at him.

"Fine," he said. "If you don't hear from Pete soon, I might have to…leave." His words slurred, and she saw something flash in his eyes. He knew.

Sawyer put down the cup, sloshing what little was left of his coffee, as he tried to get to his feet. "What the hell, Kitzie?"

She turned her back, pretending not to hear him or notice that anything was wrong. She heard him trying to get up, trying to talk, but failing at both. Those pills could put down an elephant, she thought. She hoped she hadn't killed him.

When she finally looked in his direction, she saw that he was out cold. Still, she waited to make sure the pills had done their job, before she walked back over to him.

"You might as well be comfortable." Picking up

his boots, she swung his legs around so that he was lying on the couch. She lifted his head, tempted to kiss him, as she put a pillow under it. But she was still too angry with him. He thought he could dump her and then fall instantly in love with someone like Ainsley Hamilton? Not without consequences.

She pulled off one boot, then the other. He stirred, but only to groan before quickly falling back to sleep. Getting up, she took out the bottle of whiskey and two glasses. She put them on the floor next to Sawyer. She waited until he began snoring softly before she unsnapped his shirt, baring his big strong, suntanned chest.

Maybe two pills would have done it, she thought as she checked his pulse, then pulled out his phone. Knowing him, she doubted he had changed his security code since the two of them were together. She was right, she saw, not only about his password. Sure enough, the last text he'd sent was to Ainsley saying something had come up but that he would be there soon.

She began to type: Tying up some loose ends with Kitzie. Maybe we could

Smiling, she left it unfinished, put his phone back and hurriedly changed. Sawyer was out for the night, and if she knew Ainsley, she'd be here soon.

Not ten minutes later, there was a knock at the door. Kitzie shot a look at Sawyer, but he didn't even stir. He was sprawled on the couch, his shirt open, his boots off, sound asleep.

"Just a minute," she called. Then, wearing nothing but her robe, her hair in a towel as if just coming from the shower, she opened the door a crack—just enough so that Ainsley would be able to see Sawyer, his boots, his bare chest, the whiskey and the glasses, and come up with her own conclusions as to what had been going on here.

"Hi, is Sawyer…" Ainsley's eyes widened as they took in Kitzie in her skimpy robe and then Sawyer passed out half dressed on the couch.

Kitzie hurriedly blocked Ainsley's view of Sawyer with her body. "He might have had too much to drink. Was he supposed to stop by your cabin before you left?"

"No, it's fine," Ainsley said. "We already said everything we had to." She took a step back, disappointment marring her pretty face.

Kitzie felt a moment of guilt. But Ainsley was all wrong for Sawyer. It was better this way. She was actually saving Ainsley a lot of heartache since Sawyer wasn't the marrying kind. Kitzie knew that only too well.

"Have a nice trip home," she said to her, then closed the door and looked to the couch with Sawyer sprawled on it. He really was too damned handsome for his own good, and Ainsley was the kind of woman every man wanted to rescue, especially a man like Sawyer. She feared he had it in his head that he was in love with Ainsley. Well, she doubted he'd be hearing from her again.

"*Now* you and I are even," she said to the sleeping cowboy before going to get dressed and packed. She didn't plan to be here when he woke up.

CHAPTER SIXTEEN

FRANK HAD JUST come in the door from a long day and hung his Stetson on the hook by the door, when his cell phone rang. He shot a look at Lynette, shrugged and, with a sigh, took the call. He was tired, more tired than he thought he'd ever been. He was more than ready to retire. Only a few more days, he told himself.

"Sheriff Curry," he said into the phone.

At the sound of the warden's voice, his fatigue instantly dissipated. He straightened, the cop in him desperately needing some good news for Emily and her daughter's sake, and Alex Ross's, as well. "Is there word?"

"They were spotted in Wilsall trying to steal a pickup. No doubt they realized they needed another vehicle, since we had the plates and description of the last one, even though they got away."

Frank knew the small western town of Wilsall well; it wasn't far from Beartooth.

"A sheriff's deputy spotted them and gave chase."

He couldn't bear to hear that the two convicts had evaded capture again.

"They lost control of the stolen vehicle just outside of Clyde Park. Rolled a half dozen times to come to rest against a tree next to the Shields River."

"Are they—"

"Dead. Would have called sooner, but I wanted to be sure we had positive identifications on them both before I did. You can tell that young woman that Harrison Ames won't be bothering her anymore."

Frank disconnected and turned to find Lynette standing in the doorway waiting anxiously.

One look at his expression, and she rushed to him to throw herself into his arms. "He's dead?"

"I need to call Emily and tell her the news."

"I know how relieved you are." She stepped back. "Make your call. I'll have a beer waiting for you in the kitchen. By the way, I made your favorite, pot roast. I just had a feeling you might need it tonight."

He smiled at her, feeling blessed to have her, before he made the call, then asked to speak to one of the deputies guarding the house. After he told the men they could step down, he started to put his phone away when it rang again.

More good news, I hope, he thought as he answered. It was finally the lab tech calling.

"You said you wanted to know as soon as those fingerprints were compared to the ones taken from the notes?"

"Yes?"

"They don't match."

"Not those from the second note either?" There

had been only two sets of prints on the second note Sawyer had sent him. One set had matched those from the first note. Those were the prints he'd been praying would match Lance Roderick's.

He hung up and called Sawyer's cell. It went straight to voice mail. He left the message, hoping that Sawyer got it soon. "The prints don't match. Lance Roderick isn't Ainsley's stalker."

IT WAS TIME. He quivered at the thought of how he would punish Ainsley for her behavior. He'd been away for several days getting things ready for when he finally introduced himself to her. After he'd been questioned by the local sheriff, he'd thought about giving up, moving on. But he'd always prided himself on finishing whatever he started. True, things weren't turning out like he'd planned with Ainsley. Her own fault.

Had she not made such bad choices, she could have been his. He would have treated her like a princess. He would have bought her pretty dresses, proper dresses, and he would have showered her with little gifts and special moments. He would have knelt at her feet, idolizing her.

But apparently it wasn't meant to be. It wasn't the first time he'd been wrong about a woman and had to change his plans. But this one hurt more because she'd seemed so perfect. He sighed, thinking of Sawyer Nash. The man had ruined everything.

Anger made him flush. He balled his hands into

fists, then quickly opened them at the thought of his mother. She had tried to beat the anger out of him throughout his childhood.

"It's for your own good," she would say as she pulled out the belt with the silver buckle. The time he'd been so angry that he'd kicked a hole in the wall, she'd made him pull down his pants, and she'd used the buckle end on him. He hadn't been able to sit down for days. She'd called the school and told them he had the flu.

It was nothing compared to the time, though, that she'd caught him alone in his bed thinking about one of the girls at school and —he couldn't bring himself to recall what she'd done to him.

Instead, he thought about his precious Ainsley and what he would do to her as he drove back toward the cabins through the darkness. Everyone would be leaving. But he knew she hadn't left yet because he'd put a tracking device on her car. Her car hadn't moved.

Maybe she was waiting for him to save her. The thought cheered him. Maybe he would go easier on her. He thought of his mother and realized that would be wrong. Ainsley needed to be punished, and he was the man to do it, just as his mother had taught him.

AINSLEY COULDN'T BELIEVE what a fool she'd been. She stomped back to her cabin, fighting tears of anger and humiliation. She'd trusted Sawyer. He was going to be her first. Then after tomorrow, she would never have to see him again.

But that was what hurt so badly, she realized as she reached her cabin. This wasn't casual for her. She wanted him. And not just for a night. She thought that after they made love...

What? That he would be so enamored with her that he couldn't let her go? He hadn't even shown up for their date tonight!

She remembered the way he'd asked her to dinner, the way his gaze had locked with hers, the promise she saw in those beautiful gray eyes. Her heart had pounded at the thought of being with him tonight. She'd wanted this...desperately. She'd wanted *him*.

But then, apparently, he'd wanted Kitzie and Kitzie had wanted him. Ainsley had seen the two of them together before. She remembered seeing him come out of Kitzie's cabin. What a fool she'd been for not realizing that Sawyer was double-timing them both. Now that she thought about it, she'd seen the way Kitzie had looked at him. But what woman wouldn't want him? Sawyer Nash was...gorgeous. Not to mention he was sweet. He made her laugh. Even the memory made her smile now.

She quickly replaced that memory with one of him passed out on Kitzie's couch and Kitzie fresh from the shower. Her heart broke. She'd never wanted anything this badly in her life. No man made her feel like Sawyer did. Maybe no man ever would.

That thought brought fresh tears. "Fool, fool,

fool," she muttered as she opened her cabin door and stepped in.

The dark figure came out from behind the door so quickly, Ainsley didn't have time to move, let alone scream. He grabbed her, forcing a wet, smelly cloth over her mouth and nose. She struggled, but it was useless.

THE SUN WAS up by the time Sawyer stirred from the dark depths of sleep. He sat up, making his head swim, and looked around, momentarily confused. All the cabins were identical, but he knew at once that this wasn't his. This one had the distinct smell of Kitzie's perfume.

He swore as he remembered what he'd realized just before he'd passed out. He struggled to his feet. The bitch had drugged him? Looking down, he saw that his shirt was unsnapped. He quickly snapped it, telling himself nothing had happened between him and Kitzie. She just wanted him to think something had.

Drawing on his boots, he promised himself that when he got his hands on her... But he suspected she was long gone. Had she even been here chasing jewel thieves? Had any of it been true?

Throwing open the cabin door, he squinted into the bright sunlight. He'd known it was morning, but he hadn't realized how late it was. Given the angle of the sun... He glanced at his watch and swore.

His heart wanted him to run to Ainsley's cabin,

but his body refused. Anyway, he knew it would be too late. She'd think he stood her up last night, and, given their plans, she would never be able to forgive him.

But he had to find her. She had to know how much last night had meant to him and what a fool he'd been. He'd deal with Kitzie later. He saw a cleaning crew going into one of the cabins. The driver of a large truck was pulling away with one of the last of the carnival rides. The commercial was wrapped. Only a few vehicles remained. Kitzie's car wasn't one of them.

He assumed that she'd probably split last night after she'd done her worst. Never underestimate a woman scorned, he reminded himself as he stumbled like a drunk over to Ainsley's cabin. He knocked, then, feeling foolish for doing so, tried the door.

It swung open. "Ainsley?" His voice echoed in the cold, hollow space from inside. Stepping in, he already knew what he would find. There was no sign of her, no sign that she'd ever even been there.

He stood in the empty cabin, mentally kicking himself for trusting Kitzie last night. He still felt woozy. What had she drugged him with, anyway?

Pulling out his cell phone, he cringed when he saw the last text message on the screen. Kitzie. Of course she would text Ainsley. If he could get his hands on Kitzie right now, he would ring her neck. She had no idea what she'd done last night, he thought with a curse.

He had to assume that the text had gotten Ainsley to come over to Kitzie's cabin where she would have seen him passed out on the couch, boots off, shirt open... Of course she had thought exactly what Kitzie had wanted her to think. He could even imagine what Kitzie would have been wearing when she opened the door.

He cursed and keyed in Ainsley's number, only to have it go straight to voice mail. He didn't leave a message. He had to do this in person. It was the only hope he had—and not much of that. He'd stood Ainsley up on the most important date of possibly either of their lives. It was unforgivable. Maybe if he had warned her about Kitzie... Not that it mattered now.

He started to put his phone away when he saw that he had a voice mail from Sheriff Curry. Hurriedly, he played it, praying for the good news he desperately needed right now.

His heart dropped, all the breath in him going with it. The fingerprints didn't match. Lance Roderick wasn't Ainsley's stalker! Which meant her stalker was still out there.

He stood in the middle of her cabin trying to tell himself that Ainsley was all right. She'd gone home to the ranch. All he had to do was call the ranch and—

He saw something lying on the floor between the bed and the wall in the tiny bedroom. Like a sleepwalker, he moved to it, a knot in his chest as he prayed it wasn't blood.

Even before his fingertips touched it, he knew it wasn't blood—but it was no less terrifying to find. He picked up a ragged scrap of thin red fabric. The edges appeared to have been slashed with a knife. Kitzie's red dress. He saw there were more small jagged pieces caught at the edge of the bare mattress.

His pulse lurched. Ainsley, no matter how angry she'd been last night, wouldn't have cut up the red dress with this kind of fury. There was only one man capable of this. The man who now had Ainsley.

EMILY HEARD HER daughter's sweet giggle and looked up as Jodie came into the room, Alex right behind her. "What are you two up to?" she asked, seeing the twinkle in her daughter's eyes.

"Nothin'," Jodie said, then looked at Alex and started to giggle again. Emily could tell that the girl could hardly contain herself.

Being locked up in the house with deputies outside, Emily had worried that it would frighten her precocious five-year-old. But Alex had been amazing, keeping Jodie occupied making cookies, playing games, pretending everything was as normal as possible.

"We have a secret," Jodie burst out.

Alex put a finger to his lips. "Remember," he said.

Her daughter nodded and looked so serious that Emily had to laugh.

"Okay, what's going on with you two?" She still couldn't believe how blessed she and Jodie were to have a man like Alex Ross come into their lives. Sometimes she had to pinch herself. She'd never dreamed she could be this happy—not after what she'd gone through with the loss of her parents and then the downhill slide that had landed her in jail.

Alex looked to Jodie, before dropping to one knee in front of Emily. Her pulse took off like a shot. "Alex?" she whispered, as goose bumps rippled over her body.

"I've been wanting to ask you to marry me, but I was waiting for the perfect time," Alex said. He shook his head at his own foolishness. "There is no perfect time. I should have done this months ago."

Emily's eyes widened as he turned to hold out his hand to Jodie. Her small hand dipped into the pocket of her overalls and came out with a small velvet box. She handed it to Alex and began jumping around in circles.

"Emily Calder, will you marry me and make the three of us a family?" Alex asked as he opened the box. The ring was a Montana agate. It was so beautiful that Emily began to cry. Then she raised her gaze to Alex's and felt her bubble of happiness pop.

"If you're only doing this because Harrison has escaped—"

"I'm doing it because I don't want to spend another minute away from you and Jodie. Harrison only reminded me how precious our time together is. Marry me."

Tears filled her eyes again as Jodie stopped jumping to say, "Marry us, Mama."

Alex laughed. "Well, Emily?"

Her throat was so tight, she couldn't speak. She nodded and Alex slipped the ring onto her finger. It fit perfectly. Then she was in Alex's arms, and the three of them were hugging and laughing.

She looked into their faces and prayed nothing could spoil this. That Harrison couldn't spoil this.

Her cell phone rang. She looked at the screen, then up at Alex. "It's the sheriff."

SAWYER TRIED AINSLEY'S cell again, even though he knew it was useless. Again it went straight to voice mail. He called the Hamilton Ranch on the chance that he was wrong. He was told by one of the staff that Ainsley wasn't there.

"Has anyone seen or heard from her since last night?" he asked.

"Maybe you should speak with her mother."

When Sarah Hamilton came on the line, Sawyer quickly told her that he was a friend of Ainsley's and concerned about her. "Have you seen or heard from her today?"

"No. Actually I thought she'd be here by now. Do you want me to have her call when she arrives?"

"Please."

"Is there a reason you're concerned?" Sarah asked.

"Just let me know if you hear from her."

He hung up and called Sheriff Curry and quickly

told him what he'd found in her cabin. "I think her stalker has her."

"You were having doubts before this?"

Sawyer hated to admit that he was. "But Ainsley was so sure that she was no longer being followed."

"We need to give it at least a few more hours before I put out a missing person's BOLO on her," Frank said. "With the election so close…"

Sawyer knew what he was saying. He could be wrong about all of it. On the off chance that Ainsley was fine and just didn't want to talk to him, he didn't want to blow this up so close to the election. And yet, he feared to the depth of his soul that the stalker had her. That her life depended on him finding her.

Noticing a car parked beside the hotel, he walked over there on the chance that someone had seen Ainsley leave.

Murph was still behind her desk putting paperwork into boxes and sealing them. She looked up when he came in.

"I thought everyone had gone," Murph said, clearly surprised to see him.

"I was wondering if you've seen Ainsley Hamilton this morning?"

Murph shook her head. "I saw her leave last night."

"You did? Was she…alone?"

The woman raised a brow with an expression of both humor and curiosity. "As a matter of fact, she was not. Afraid you lost out. I thought for sure you had swept her off her feet. But apparently you lost out to the grocery boy." She grimaced. "That has got to hurt."

He stared at her. "She left with the *delivery guy*?"

CHAPTER SEVENTEEN

FRANK SWORE AS he took in the area around the Beartooth Fairgrounds. It would be impossible, even with all the manpower they had, to keep it secure.

Damn you, Buck.

He wanted to blame it on the man's arrogance, and yet he didn't believe that was the problem. Buckmaster Hamilton refused to admit that anyone would want to kill him. Or at least that's what he wanted everyone to think. But Frank knew late at night, lying next to Sarah, Buck had to question just how safe he was.

Love. It sure as hell was blind.

"This is what you wanted me to see?" his wife asked as she joined him.

"I needed to come out here, but this isn't why I brought you here," Frank said.

"Why are you so worried about the perimeter?" she asked. "If you're right, the real threat will be standing next to him when the election results come in, and the next president is announced."

He glanced over at her. Everyone called her Nettie, but she would always be Lynette to him. Of course, she was right. But she didn't know that the threat could be much bigger than even Sarah.

"What does your…pendulum say is going to happen?" he asked only half joking. He didn't believe in any of that hocus-pocus stuff, as he called it, but right now he would love to see into the future. "Or have you moved up to a crystal ball?"

She slapped playfully at him. "I threw it away."

He stared at her in surprise. He hadn't been happy when she'd confessed that she'd bought the stupid thing. Worse, that she believed it was always right.

"Why did you do that?" he asked as he turned to look toward the Crazy Mountains. The snow-capped peaks gleamed in the afternoon sun. No storms loomed over them. They'd been fortunate that winter hadn't come early. But maybe if it had, Buck wouldn't be making his acceptance speech from here.

"It was silly," she said, drawing his gaze back to her. "And…scary."

He felt his heart drop. "What did it tell you, Lynette?"

Her jaw set, but tears glistened in her eyes. He'd seen her cry only a few times in all the years he'd known her. Most recently when she'd fallen into his arms in tears after they'd both almost died.

She shook her head. Lynette was strong. Seeing the tears about broke him.

"Tell me," he said, scared to touch her for fear the dam would break. She would be even angrier with him if he made her cry when she was trying so hard not to.

"I was too afraid to ask what I desperately need to know," she said and finally turned to look at him. The wind coming down out of the Crazies, as everyone called the mountain range, lifted her auburn hair, whipping it around her face.

"I'm going to be fine. *We're* going to be fine," he said with all the certainty he could muster. He lived with a fear that The Prophecy was going to try to bring the country down, and there wasn't a damned thing he could do about it.

What little he knew about the group had come with no proof of what they might have planned. The FBI didn't see them as a threat. Most of the original members would be in their fifties by now, so what few members weren't in prison couldn't do much, right?

"I just can't bear the thought that something might happen to you," she said, her voice breaking.

"Nothing is going to happen to me," he said, putting his arm around her. "But there is something I should tell you." He felt her tense. "I'm going to retire after the election." She didn't react. She knew how much he loved his job. She'd been afraid that he wouldn't be happy if he retired.

"So, it's decided?" she asked in a weak voice.

"But we're not really retiring. I have a plan for the two of us." She finally looked at him. He could see that she was waiting as if for an ax to fall. "I want us to be partners in the new venture."

One eyebrow shot up as if she thought he was about to tell her that he was going to buy the Beartooth General Store where she now worked part-time after being the owner for years.

"Curry Investigations. We'll both need to get our PI licenses but—"

"Wait, you're serious?"

He laughed and turned her, so they were facing each other. The tears were gone, leaving her eyes bright. Her cheeks were flushed, but it could have been the cold wind.

"You're the best investigator I've ever known," he said with a chuckle. "I want you by my side. And you know neither of us would be happy retired with nothing to do. This way, we can take only the cases that interest us."

She looked as if she might cry again. "Do you have any idea how happy you have made me?"

"I was afraid you wouldn't like my idea."

"*Like it?* I *love* it! Getting paid to snoop into other people's business?"

He laughed and pulled her closer. "I should have known you'd be up for it."

"Everything is going to be all right as long as we're together." She hugged him back tighter than usual.

As he breathed in her perfume, he told himself they would get through whatever was coming. They had to. He'd been dreaming of the two of them working together for months now. He couldn't wait to start looking for a building to rent and put a Curry Investigations sign out front.

But first, they had to get through election night. He couldn't shake the feeling that something bad was going to happen—and he would be right in the midst of it.

Frank feared he would never see that Curry Investigations sign, but he wasn't about to voice it, especially to Lynette. In his heart of hearts, they would survive all of this and get to solve cases together long into their old age.

GUN TOOK HIS time packing. He had never owned much clothing, but what he did, he valued. Now he carefully folded each piece and tucked it neatly into the suitcase.

"You are one freaking weird kid," his stepfather used to say. "Margie, have you seen the way this kid butters his toast? There is definitely something wrong with him."

Gun had dealt with him by keeping his head down, letting Ray run off at the mouth all he wanted and telling himself that his stepfather's day was coming.

"I think he's a sissy," Ray would goad. "No real boy keeps his room all nice and neat like that. We got ourselves a pantywaist, Margie."

"Leave the boy be," his mother would say but not

with enough conviction to make any difference. She had loved Ray—even at the cost of her son.

Not that Gun felt any animosity toward his mother. She'd done what she had to survive. If anything, she'd taught him well. Also, he'd known that one day he would show Ray just how much of a sissy he wasn't.

And he had. He still remembered the look on his stepfather's face when he realized what was about to happen. By then Gun's mom had been gone to an early grave. Ray was living off social security and hanging out at some seedy bar down the street.

Gun had waited for him to come out of the bar. Ray had only been a little drunk, having run out of money before he could finish the job. But he was cocky and arrogant and thought he could take up where they'd left off before Gun had left home.

He smiled now, relishing the memory of Ray's surprised expression the moment before Gun had hit him. It was that memory of Ray blubbering on the sidewalk, begging for his life, that always brought him peace. He finished packing, closed his suitcase and set it by the door.

His smile faded quickly, though, at the thought of Kitzie. When he'd asked Murph if he could see what information she had on the crew as far as backgrounds, she'd given him one of her "Trouble?" looks.

He'd waved it off. "Nothing I can't handle." Once he'd realized that Kitzie had been in his cabin, he'd wondered not just who she was—but if she was working alone.

Most undercover cops had partners. He'd seen her with that cowboy Murph had hired for the commercial. Gun hadn't thought anything about it at the time. Murph had been right about Sawyer being perfect for the production.

First he checked what Murph had come up with on Kitzie. One glance at her so-called background and he knew it was all staged. If he were to call one of her references, he'd get just what was on the page, though. That would be a mistake, since it would only alert whoever she was working for that he was on to her.

He took a look at the cowboy's information. Murph hadn't gotten much on him. Gun could usually spot a cop a mile away. He thought about Sawyer Nash's limp. Was that why he hadn't considered that he might be the fuzz? He had the air about him of law enforcement, but the limp had been real—just as the occasional wince of pain had been. No agency would send an injured lawman.

But it had him questioning his instincts. He'd hired Kitzie, even when he'd sensed he shouldn't. Something had been bothering him about her, but he hadn't listened to his gut that day. A big mistake, as it turned out. Swearing, he looked at the rest of the crew, stopping on the only one who he hadn't considered. A man named Jason Bowman, the late-thirties odd-job man, who had been delivering their supplies during their stay here.

"Murph, where did you find this guy?" he asked.

"Jason? I thought *you* hired him. He showed up one day with a couple of cases of water, introduced himself and then asked what else we needed. I sent him into the kitchen to talk to Kitzie." She must have seen his expression, because she instantly started apologizing.

He held up a hand to stop her. He didn't have to tell her what was at stake here. He trusted Murph with his life. Jason had conned his way in. The fact that he seemed harmless should have been a clue.

Gun now thought of all the times he'd seen the young man hanging around watching them shoot the commercial. He'd shown an interest, pretending he wanted to get into the business. He hadn't been the first looky-loo who thought they could make commercials. Gun hadn't thought anything of it.

"Have you seen Jason today?" he asked Murph.

She shook her head, looking even more upset with herself. "The cowboy was here earlier asking if I'd seen Ainsley. I told him that she left last night and that she wasn't alone. She left with Jason."

He stared at her. "Ainsley and Jason?" What would the future president's daughter be doing with Jason unless he was an undercover cop and he was just getting her out of here before the shit hit the fan?

Gun stepped to the window and looked out on the bucolic scene. His gaze scanned the mountainside.

Something caught the light on the side of the mountain across from them.

He turned quickly. "Pack up," he ordered. "We're moving now."

"But I thought—"

"Go to Plan B. Let everyone else know. Now!"

KITZIE HAD HATED to leave last night, but she'd had no choice. Her job in the kitchen was over. Staying around would only make Gun more suspicious, and he was suspicious enough as it was.

She raised the binoculars again, focusing in on the hotel and the cabins behind it from her spot on the mountainside across the way. Gun still hadn't left. Neither had Murph. But the rest had scattered to the wind—including Sawyer.

Kitzie figured that he would be headed for the Hamilton Ranch over by Beartooth. But she doubted chasing down Ainsley was going to do him any good. *Maybe someday he'll thank you for saving him.* Or not.

She called her partner. "Anything going on there?" she asked Pete.

He sighed. "Nothing."

"You're sure he's still in his room?"

"From where I am, he can't leave it without me seeing him. He's still there. What about Gunderson?"

"He just loaded his suitcase in his car and went into the hotel. Murph is still in there. If the loot is here, they should be loading it soon," she said.

"You'll be able to follow them?"

"I'm staying with Gun, no matter what," she said. "He isn't going to let anyone else make this deal for him. I saw his cohorts with LeRoy. I would imagine they are staying with the nephew until the deal goes down, then cutting him loose."

"Or killing him. Gunderson has never left any loose ends."

Across the way, she watched first Murph come out with a box of what looked like file folders. She got in her car and drove off. Finally Gun came out of the hotel and walked toward his car. "We're movin'."

AINSLEY CAME TO in darkness. She blinked, confused as to where she was and what was going on. A strange smell made her wrinkle her nose. She tried to sit up, but with a stab of horror, she realized her wrists and ankles were bound to a bed. She tried to open her mouth to scream and couldn't. What little sound she'd been able to make came out muffled from the duct tape over her lips.

Her terror rose as her eyes began to adjust to the blackness. She was in a stark, small room. The windows were covered with dark cloths that kept out the light. She knew immediately that she'd never been here before.

Last night came to her in a miserable, terrifying wave. Her throat ached, and her voice broke as she tired to cry out for help. She heard a sound beyond the room. A moment later, the door opened.

At first all she saw was a dark figure silhouetted against the daylight. For a moment, she thought it was Sawyer come to rescue her—until she was reminded of how he had betrayed her. Sawyer wouldn't be coming for her. He was with Kitzie.

The man turned on an overhead light, blinding her momentarily.

She blinked in surprise when her gaze lit on the man. She'd seen him numerous times over the past few days, but she hadn't paid any attention to him. He always had his earbuds in, his baseball hat on backward. When they'd passed each other, he would nod and she would do the same. He'd appeared… harmless before. He didn't now.

"So you're finally awake," he said as he stepped into the room. "I can't tell you how long I have been waiting for this moment. I'm sorry. We haven't officially met. Let me introduce myself. Jason Bowman. I'd shake hands but…" He shrugged, indicating her bound wrists. He no longer was wearing his baseball cap on backward, just as he no longer was dressed in jeans and a T-shirt with some band's name on it. The earbuds were also gone.

He looked much older in slacks and a button-down shirt. All the other times when she'd glimpsed him following her, he'd been wearing a cowboy hat. He'd stayed in the shadows all these months. But even before he'd become the delivery guy, if she had passed him on the street, she wouldn't have recognized him. The man was so…average. Just as she hadn't recognized him as her stalker when he'd shown up at the commercial shoot as the man who delivered the groceries.

He stepped forward. "I'm going to remove the tape from your mouth. I just want you to know it won't do any good for you to scream. No one will be able to hear you down here."

An icy sliver of fear raced up her back to curl around her neck. Had she been the first to wake up in this bed? She had a bad feeling she hadn't. She cringed as he leaned forward, grabbed the end of the tape covering her mouth and ripped it off.

Ainsley had told herself she wouldn't make a sound, but a cry of pain escaped her lips anyway. She swallowed. Her mouth felt dry as dust. She licked her lips and found her voice. "Why are you doing this?"

"Because you failed. I spent all that time hoping you wouldn't disappointment me, but ultimately you turned out to be like the others. Now you have to be punished."

"You've been following me."

He smiled down at her. "I couldn't help myself. You probably don't remember the day we met. It was in Livingston. I had dropped a bunch of papers, and you stopped to help me pick them up." He stared down at her as if hoping she would remember. She didn't, and he must have seen it in her expression, because he instantly looked upset. "I didn't expect you to remember, but it would have been nice."

"I'm sorry." She hated the weakness she heard in her voice, in her words.

"So am I," he said with a sigh as he ran a finger down her cheek.

Ainsley flinched in spite of herself, and he drew back his finger. His eyes were dark with a sick hatred. She didn't kid herself. The man could profess how much he wanted her to like him, but he was a predator, and she was his defenseless prey.

She tried to fight her panic, but it was useless. The pounding of her heart was deafening. She felt cold, her weak limbs trembling. She couldn't have been more terrified.

That's when she saw the baseball bat leaning against the wall. Her eyes widened in alarm at the dark spots on it. Blood. Her pulse jumped with the realization. Jason had killed the security guard, Lance Roderick.

He followed her gaze to the baseball bat and smiled. "Another casualty, I'm afraid. I could tell right away he was suspicious of me. I'd seen him taking photos with his phone but hadn't thought much of it until that night at the restaurant. He knew. I can't imagine how, but he knew I wasn't who I appeared to be."

Jason Bowman was a killer. Worse, he had some crazy idea that she needed to be punished. Punished before he killed her? Her blood ran cold at the thought.

"I couldn't let him spoil everything," he was saying as he stepped over to the windowsill and picked up a cell phone. "Not just that. He'd taken photos of you." He shook his head. "I couldn't have that either. You have to understand. I still had hope that you would come to your senses." He laughed, an odd, high-pitched sound.

She realized she'd heard it before and not on her job at the cabins. "I *do* remember you from that day in Livingston."

He looked skeptical. "You don't have to pretend—"

"No, you were wearing a uniform."

He nodded, looking delighted. "I was working as the city dog catcher. I quit my job that afternoon. I had to go wherever you went. I had to know if you were the one."

"The one?" she managed to ask around the lump in her throat. Again she tested the tape binding her.

"You mustn't keep doing that," he said, looking down at her wrists bound to the bed frame. "You'll chafe your soft, tender skin." He ran a finger along her bare arm, stopping at the tape.

Bile rose in her throat at his touch, but this time she didn't flinch. "You have to let me go."

"I can't do that. Like I said, I had to know if you were the one. The one woman I would be proud to take home to my blessed mother if she were still alive." He met her gaze. Something dark and damaged lived in those eyes again. "Unfortunately, you failed me. You aren't the one. And now you're going to have to be punished. Mother wouldn't want it any other way."

CHAPTER EIGHTEEN

KITZIE KEPT GUN'S large black sedan in sight as he drove out of the mountains along the narrow dirt road that wound along the creek. Clouds scudded across a pale blue fall sky. Gusts of wind made the older model SUV she was driving shudder. A tumbleweed cartwheeled across the road. She dodged it, telling herself it would have been bad luck to hit it today.

She'd never been superstitious, but today she wasn't taking any chances. Excitement rippled through her. This would be the biggest bust of her career. Instantly, she thought of Sawyer.

He should have been the one she celebrated with later tonight. Instead it would be Pete. Or maybe she would be alone in her apartment in Billings.

That thought was like a bucket of ice water on her excitement—until she reminded herself how envious Sawyer would be when he heard. She knew he hated being sidelined with his injury.

He must be pretty down right now. He'd lost Ainsley, and he hadn't been the one to bring down Ainsley's stalker. Someone else had ended it for him when they killed Lance Roderick. She almost felt sorry for him. That reminded her that she should keep a safe distance from Sawyer until he got over her little… trick she'd pulled on him.

She was smiling again when her cell rang. "Tell me something is happening at your end," she said to Pete.

There was a smile in his voice. "He just came out. Yep, there's a car pulling up now. Three men. I can ID at least two of them from the photos you took of them. Looks like Nathan Grant is driving and the one with the ponytail, Clark? He's riding shotgun. Or at least he was. He's getting out."

"Should be Clark, Grant, the nephew LeRoy and Hale. Are you sure there isn't a fourth man in the car?"

"Yep, Clark got out to let Harry Lester in the front seat. There's a heavyset guy in the back with the nephew."

"Don't lose them," Kitzie warned. "I'm still on Gun. He's headed that way. Won't be long now once we get out of this mountain pass."

She disconnected as the road narrowed even more as it cut through the narrow winding canyon. There was no other traffic on the road and in the canyon she was out of the wind. She didn't realize how much she'd been fighting it until she got to release her death grip on the steering wheel.

Only now she had to slow down because of the curves in the snaking road—and she was only getting glimpses of Gun's sedan when he came out of a bend ahead of her.

That made her a little nervous, but there was nowhere for him to turn off until they got out of the canyon. Also, she knew where he was going, and Pete had Harry Lester. The two of them had this. She just needed to relax. She moved her shoulders, sitting back and taking a breath. Soon, she said to herself. Soon.

Kitzie thought she was seeing things when the first boulder came bouncing across the narrow dirt road to crash down into the creek. She hit her brakes as another boulder followed and then another. One landed hard in the middle of the road just inches from her bumper.

What in the...? With a jolt of panic, she suddenly remembered what Sawyer had said about Ainsley's stalker almost killing her in a rock slide.

She threw the SUV into Reverse and had turned to look behind her when a huge boulder crashed into the side of the SUV, caving in the roof and sending glass flying as the side windows exploded. She was slammed against her door as the rock drove the SUV several yards toward the creek.

Stunned by the blow, it took her a moment to realize what she had to do. She quickly unbuckled her seat belt and grabbed her door handle, telling herself she had to get out now! If she didn't, she could end up in the creek and drown or be buried alive in rocks.

She jerked on the door handle. Nothing happened.

It was jammed! More boulders were slamming into the side of the car, throwing her around like a rag doll. She could hear more rocks coming down.

The windshield smashed when one of the boulders bounced off the hood. A shattered web, the windshield was still intact. She tried to push it out with her hands. Failing that, she managed to get a foot up as more boulders crashed into the SUV, driving her closer and closer to the creek.

All it took was one kick before the entire windshield dropped out onto the dented hood. Another boulder crashed into the car, pushing the SUV off the road.

Now leaning precariously over the creek, she climbed up on her seat to look up the mountainside where the boulders had been coming from. She spotted a figure and hesitated a moment too long because of her surprise. *Murph?*

An avalanche of boulders and dirt came careening off the side of the mountain. Kitzie started to scramble out, but it was too late.

The landslide hit the car, and the next thing Kitzie knew she was lying on the headliner of the SUV in the creek bottom and ice-cold creek water was rushing in.

Dazed and bleeding, she managed to get her cell out of her pocket and key in Pete's number. "I'm in trouble. You're on your own," she cried into the phone an instant before a huge boulder crashed into the car, jostling the phone out of her hand and knocking her unconscious.

"YOU NEED TO let me go," Ainsley said, trying to keep her voice from cracking. She'd never been so afraid, and yet a part of her mind warned herself to keep calm. She couldn't afford to panic. If it was possible to reason with this man... "My family will be looking for me."

Jason shook his head. "No, they won't. That is another thing that I loved about you. Your independence. I would imagine they aren't expecting you until election night. Maybe if you didn't show up then, they would start looking for you. So we have lots of time."

She feared he was right. No one would be looking for her. Especially not Sawyer, who was probably still with Kitzie. Ainsley shoved that thought away, recoiling from the pain it brought.

"Just tell me what you want from me," she said.

"If only it was that easy. You were the kind of woman I wanted to take home to my mother, God rest her soul. I watched you for months. You were so nice. You didn't dress trashy like so many other women. You were a hard worker. You were kind to others. I could see us having children together. We would raise them like my mother did me. She only punished me when I deserved it. She would cry, saying punishment had to hurt and leave scars, or what was the point?"

She shuddered to think how Jason had been raised, let alone what his mother had been like.

"But then that cowboy came along." He shook his head, his expression bitter. "Sawyer Nash."

"Nothing happened between us," she said, feeling the weight of those words.

"But look how you behaved. You were…were… wanton."

Ainsley almost laughed. No one had ever called her wanton. Or ever would again—if she managed to get away from this obviously psychotic man.

"That red dress! It showed…*everything*." He shuddered, but she saw naked lust in his gaze. That scared her more than waking up bound to this bed. Her heart began to pound harder, her mouth going even drier. If she hadn't realized how much trouble she was in before, she did now.

"It wasn't mine. That dress. Kitzie—"

"Oh, yes, Kitzie. You should have seen what she had in her closet. Tramp."

She felt her eyes widen. "You were in her cabin?" Of course he was. He had been waiting in her own cabin for her. "How did you—"

"Get the master key?" He laughed. "You really underestimate me. I brought Murph her favorite treat—chocolate and caramel ice cream. I would bring her a gallon, so she would sneak down to the kitchen to get more. She didn't want anyone to see her eating it so she'd hurry, leaving the office door open. It was our little secret."

And while she was gone, he would take the keys.

Ainsley told herself not to underestimate him again. He was smarter than she'd thought. He'd spent months trailing her and had been within inches of her without her being any the wiser.

"I cut that red dress to pieces, slashing and slashing and…" He stopped as if realizing how crazy he was starting to sound. "I left it for your cowboy to find. Imagine what he thought when he saw it."

"I hate to disappoint you, but I doubt Sawyer saw it. Like I told you, nothing happened between us. He wouldn't have come looking for me, so he wouldn't have seen the dress."

If he had, would Sawyer think that she had cut up the dress after seeing him with Kitzie? If so, then he didn't know her at all. Just thinking about him brought tears to her eyes. If only she'd gotten that one night with him.

"I don't want to talk about him," Jason snapped. She flinched at his sudden touch as his finger traced along the inside of her arm. "Mother used to find those sensitive places on my body when she punished me," he said in a singsong voice. "She always said that punishment should hurt in a way that a person never forgot." His gaze came up to meet hers. "Don't you agree, Ainsley?"

SAWYER FELT LIKE an insane man. He'd driven too fast out of the mountains earlier, taking some curves on the narrow canyon road so erratically that he thought he'd end up in the creek if he didn't settle down.

He had to find Ainsley.

It was his only thought. He'd had no clue where to look. Murph had said that she left with Jason, the delivery guy. He'd called Frank as he'd left. I need everything you have on a Jason Bowman. He's Ainsley's stalker."

Frank had come back with more than he'd expected. "A little over two years ago he was working as an animal control officer in Livingston, Montana. He quit one day without any notice."

"About the time Ainsley said she felt someone following her."

"About the time Sarah returned and the Hamilton family was in all the news," the sheriff said. "Only known relative was his mother, Clare, deceased a year before that."

"By any chance, was he still living in his mother's house when he worked as a dog catcher in Livingston?" Sawyer asked, betting money he still did.

Frank read him the address of a property under the name of Clare Bowman. He knew the area. Livingston had been a railroad town. Many of the buildings had small houses behind them that had been constructed for railroad workers. Clare Bowman's house was on one of the alphabet streets.

"I'm on my way there," he said.

"Are you sure you don't want me to send backup?" the sheriff asked.

"I'll call you if I need it, but I don't want to take that chance with Ainsley's life. This man is obsessed and angry with her. He won't kill her unless he is forced to. I don't intend to give him that option."

"KITZIE? *KITZIE!*" called a young female voice.

"I wouldn't go any closer," warned another young woman. "She's got to be dead. It's going to be so gross. Can't we just call someone? Or maybe—"

Kitzie thought she must be dreaming. It sounded like the two teenagers she'd hired to work in the kitchen.

"Help!" Her voice came out like a hoarse croak. "Help me!"

"See, she's alive. We have to help her. I think the two of us can move this rock if we both push."

There was a lot of grunting. Metal creaked and groaned. Something large fell into the creek with a splash that sent small waves across the headliner of the SUV and Kitzie lying on it. But Kitzie could see light from where the boulder had been moved out of the way.

"I'm here," she cried through the hole they had made. She could feel cold air rushing in and breathed deeply, amazed she was alive. She was soaked to the skin, wedged against the headliner by part of the steering wheel.

She'd tried to move when she'd first come to, but when she had the car had shifted, and she'd frozen in place. There hadn't been anywhere to go anyway. Any exit was blocked by boulders.

Now, though, she was able to shimmy out from under the steering wheel toward the hole the girls had made.

"You look awful," the tall one named Penny said.

"Can you crawl out?" Jennifer asked. She was short and blonde and perky.

Kitzie realized that she'd underestimated Jennifer and now felt badly about it as the girl helped her squeeze through the hole.

She cried out and realized that several of her ribs were either cracked or broken. Her slacks were torn, her right leg cut and bleeding, and she hurt all over. On the whole, she just felt lucky to be alive.

"Are you all right?" Penny asked.

"I've been better. Can you reach my phone?"

"I'll get it," Jennifer said and slipped into the smashed car to retrieve it.

Kitzie wished she had paid the girl more. "I thought you two had already left."

"We had, but Penny forgot her makeup bag in the kitchen. She was hoping someone would still be around to get it for her," Jennifer said.

"I'll probably never get it now," the teen lamented.

Kitzie looked toward Penny's car. "I'm going to need your car."

"We can take you to the hospital," Jennifer offered.

"I'm not going to the hospital. I'm FBI. I have to go after the people who tried to kill me."

Penny's eyes widened in shock. "Someone tried to kill you?"

"I'm going to need your car. I'd take you as far as town, but I'm afraid it might be too dangerous. Walk on up the road to the hotel. There are still people up there cleaning. If not, you can break into the hotel and stay there until I send help for you."

Penny looked like she wanted to cry.

"We'll be fine," Jennifer said. "Go get the bad guys."

Kitzie smiled. "I will." Her phone had somehow escaped the creek water. She called Pete as she hobbled to the car.

CHAPTER NINETEEN

SARAH HAD FELT defeated and helpless after her call
to Martin. At times like this, she missed Russell the
most. She'd been able to talk to him. He'd known
there was darkness in her past. He'd said they would
face it together.

She ached at the thought of him not remembering
anything they'd shared. So many days she wished
she'd married Russell. How much easier her life
would have been. The Prophecy would still have
tried to use her through her children to get to Buck,
but Russell would have helped her deal with it.

What now? *Wait and see what happens election
night?* When she'd voiced concerns about security
for election night, Buck had insisted that it was all
taken care of, and there was nothing to worry about.
She knew that there would be dozens of Secret Service brought in, and Sheriff Curry had told her he
would have all his men available plus the agents and
the National Guard.

Still, she feared it wouldn't be enough.

She'd promised Buck when they'd gotten married
that she wouldn't have any further contact with Dr.

Ralph Venable, the man who had stolen her memories and kept her away from her family for twenty-two years.

Her fingers were shaking as she keyed in his number. If Buck found out, it would destroy the fragile start of their remarriage. As it was, he didn't trust her. Who could blame him, given her past? But if she didn't try to stop The Prophecy, she feared none of them would live past election night anyway.

The phone rang four times before going to an automated voice mail.

"We need to talk," she said into the phone. "You're going to help me stop Joe. Call me."

Her hands were shaking so hard that she almost dropped the phone. Every instinct in her told her that she'd just made a huge mistake. Doc would tell her former lover Joe. Joe would retaliate. Why hadn't she simply left her name?

Not that it probably mattered. Martin had more than likely called Joe and told him about their conversation. In for a penny, in for a pound, she thought, fearing she had set something in motion that she would regret.

She waited for Doc to call her back, wondering if instead he was now on the phone with Joe. Only months ago, Joe had kidnapped her daughter Cassidy. What would he do now, if he thought she was again trying to stop him?

Her cell rang. She jumped and attempted to pull herself together. She didn't recognize the number.

She let it ring a second time before she answered. "Hello?" Someone was breathing on the other end of the line. "Hello? Doc?"

The party on the end disconnected.

Sarah stood holding the phone, suddenly terrified. Had that been Joe? Or Buck? Why had she asked if it was Doc? If it had been Buck and had merely been a bad connection...

She could no longer live with all the lies, all the—

Her phone rang again. She snatched it up but said nothing.

Again she heard breathing. She disconnected. It rang again almost at once. Her nerves were frayed, but from somewhere deep inside came a surge of not just determination, but anger. She'd been Joe's puppet for too long.

"Hello?" she said into the phone. Her voice broke. She didn't sound as strong as she told herself she was. She didn't sound like a woman capable of anything, especially a woman able to take down a terrorist group. She sounded as terrified as she felt.

"I warned you about going against Joe. He knows you tried to get Martin to help you." Dr. Venable sounded old and tired and scared. "Do you have any idea what you've done?"

"I have to stop him. If that means getting back the rest of my memory, of being this anarchist Red again, then—" Joe was so sure that once she got her memory back, she would again join him and be the anarchist she'd been all those years ago.

"Oh, you'll be Red again soon. Sooner than you think. God, help us all." With that, Dr. Venable hung up.

Her heart was pounding so hard, she couldn't catch her breath as she disconnected. Like a pebble thrown into a still pond, she'd started ripples that were growing wider and wider. Joe knew. The question was, what would he do now?

"I NEED TO use the bathroom," Ainsley said when Jason returned to the room. He'd left earlier, promising to come back.

She'd been working at the tape binding her to the bed frame until her skin was chafed and aching. There was no getting loose without him cutting the restraints.

Now, he eyed her suspiciously. "If you're thinking that I will cut you loose and you'll overtake me and escape…" He shook his head. "I don't want to have to cut you, slice that beautiful skin to shreds, but I will. I will leave you in a pool of your own blood so helpless and in pain…"

She couldn't imagine being any more helpless than she was now. "I won't try to get away," she said, sounding as helpless as she was. It was a lie. She would do whatever she had to.

He studied her for a moment. "Okay, but if you're naughty, you know what happens."

She'd already been naughty, according to him, and needed to be punished. He just hadn't told her yet what that meant. But from what he'd said about his mother and the way he'd smiled when he'd said the word, it made her quake inside.

Jason pulled a knife from the scabbard on his belt. The shine of the deadly looking blade seemed to catch his attention and hold it for too long. He ran his thumb along the sharp edge of the blade. A trickle of blood appeared. He sucked the blood into his mouth, his attention finally coming back to her.

Ainsley had been watching, sickly mesmerized and equally terrified. Now he moved toward her. She closed her eyes, telling herself that she didn't want to see this. She felt the blade slice through the tape binding one wrist. She wriggled her fingers to get some life back into her hand.

Opening her eyes, she watched him cut her ankles free, then her wrist.

She had to get away from him, but she had no idea how she was going to do that. He was much larger and stronger than she was, and he knew it. Also, he was armed. *Bide your time. Just don't do anything stupid.*

Ainsley watched him, aware of the knife in his hand and the look in his eyes. He wanted her to try to escape. But she refused to give him that pleasure. She rubbed her hands together for a moment, then slowly sat up. "Where is your bathroom?" she asked.

"I'll show you." He sheathed the knife and reached for her hand.

Wanting him to believe she was docile, she put her

hand into his. Just touching him made her sick to her stomach. But she didn't recoil. She let him lead her out of the room to a bathroom right outside the door.

"There's no way to get out," he noted, but she'd already seen that there was no window, no other door in the small utilitarian bathroom to escape from. "Also, there is nothing in there you can use as a weapon." That she had suspected, as well. If Jason was anything, he was thorough. He'd probably learned the hard way with the others.

She shuddered as she stepped into the bathroom and closed the door, telling herself not to think about the others. Not to think about what had happened to them.

"There isn't a lock either," he called through the door, sounding way too proud of himself.

Ainsley didn't bother to look for a weapon. He'd even taken the top off the toilet tank as if he thought she might try to hit him with it. She suspected someone had done just that.

She took the opportunity to do what she needed to do. Then washed up as best she could. He'd left her a towel. As she dried, she tried not to panic.

So far, he hadn't done anything to her. But she knew that once she stepped out that door...

He knocked on the door. "Don't make me wait too long. It will only force me to punish you much worse."

She cringed at his words and wondered again how many times he'd heard those same words from his dear mother. She hoped the woman was rotting in her grave right now.

Bracing herself, she opened the door to find him lighting a cigarette. He removed it from his mouth to stare at the red-hot end. "Did I mention that my mother smoked?"

GUN COULD ALMOST smell the tropical breezes. In a matter of hours, he would turn the commercial over to the editor. After that, he'd only have to hang around for a few days to okay the final cut.

Then he would announce that he was taking a long vacation. He had his passport ready. His bags were packed. The money from the burglaries would be tucked away until he needed it. He was too smart to blow it all.

He feared that the others weren't that smart, though. LeRoy would shoot his mouth off, sure as hell. But let his uncle Harry Lester deal with that. By then Gun planned to be out of the country and unreachable. He couldn't wait to toss his cell phone into the ocean, he thought as it rang.

"Gunderson," he said into the phone.

"Plan B?" It was Clark. "Why? What's going on?"

"Just a precaution. This will be over soon. Just follow procedure." If he had a dime for every time he'd said that, he'd be filthy rich.

"Okay," Clark said, though he didn't sound happy about it. Gun could hear Hale in the background. That was something else he wasn't going to miss.

With luck, he would never have to see the man again in this lifetime.

"I'll see you soon," Gun said and hung up.

Ahead, the old mining city of Butte, Montana, loomed up from the horizon. He could see where the mountain had been gouged out to make the mile-deep famous Berkeley Pit. A few old mining rigs stood higher on the mountain, dark silhouettes against the daylight.

What an appropriate place for this to end, he thought, smiling. He'd always been fond of Butte. It was rough around the edges, and he liked that, just as he liked the old buildings, the sense of history, the kick-your-ass people who lived here.

He drove up Montana, turned, to go by the Copper King Mansion, and thought of the city fathers who had pillaged the state's treasures for over a hundred years. They were thieves just like him, he told himself as he turned into one of the old brick houses along a side street.

He parked, sitting in the car for a moment. Murph had called earlier to say that she'd taken care of their little Kitzie problem. Everything was going as planned.

A curtain moved on the first floor of the house. He caught a glimpse of red.

"As weird as you are, you're never going to have a girlfriend," his stepfather used to tell him. "No woman with any sense would want you."

The curtain moved again. Molly waved at him

from the window as she pulled her long dark unruly hair up into a high ponytail. "Wrong again, Ray."

KITZIE GAVE PETE the abbreviated version of what had happened to her. "The bottom line is that I lost Gunderson. Tell me you still have Harry Lester."

"I'm on his tail right now."

"Where are you?" she asked. It hurt to talk. Her ribs were killing her. She ached all over, and there was a knot she'd found on the side of her head along with several abrasions that had bled. But she was alive, she had her weapon, and she was almost to Butte.

"Leaving Butte," Pete said.

Kitzie thought she'd heard wrong. "*Leaving* Butte?"

"Headed out of town on the road toward Helena. We just topped the hill. Wait a minute. They're turning."

Turning? She quickly thought about what was up there. "He's headed for Our Lady of the Rockies?"

"What?"

"That Madonna-like white statue high on the mountain. That's Our Lady of the Rockies." A bunch of miners got together and had it built after one of the men lost his wife. She'd wanted something like it put up there, only she'd envisioned something small. How surprised she would have been to see what her small wish has become. "It's a tourist site now, but

I don't think they have tours up there this time of the year."

"You think that's where he's heading? They turned off on a road. I'm stopped, but I can see they are headed up the mountain."

"There are a few cabins on that road, but I'm betting he'll go clear to the top of the mountain. The problem is that there is a locked gate. How—"

"There's a gate all right, but it's standing open. Someone must have opened it for him—and Gunderson..." Pete said. "That must mean that Gunderson isn't here yet?"

Kitzie's head ached. "Stay with him. I'm driving a blue VW bug. I'm on my way."

She disconnected, wondering where Gunderson was right now. Or Murph, for that matter. Kitzie had known that Murph had worked for Gunderson for years, but she'd never thought she was involved in the burglary part of the business. But now she knew.

In the rearview mirror, she caught a glimpse of her face. Her left eye was almost swollen shut. A scratch on her chin was bleeding. But all that was minor. Each breath was a labor. She could still fire a gun, she told herself. Turning her attention back to the highway, she concentrated on getting all of them. Now they'd made it personal.

SAWYER DID HIS best not to speed as he drove to Livingston. Clare Bowman's house was in an older part of town near the Yellowstone River. Fog moved up from the river to crawl through the neighborhood like searching spirits.

He drove by the house, not surprised to see that there was no car parked out front. The garage door was down. He couldn't see through the dirty windows to tell if there was a car parked inside or not.

A block down, he parked and popped the trunk. It was still early in the sleepy, slightly run-down neighborhood. Nothing moved in the fog. He suspected most of the residents were older and that their Christmas tree lights stayed up all year.

Getting out, he moved to the trunk and took off his jacket. From the hidden compartment, he pulled out his Kevlar vest, put it on, then his jacket again. Loading one of the handguns, he stuck it under his jacket, then he closed the trunk.

Would Jason be expecting him? Probably not. In the first place, Jason didn't know he was a lawman. He didn't know about the resources Sawyer had at his disposal. Also, he probably didn't think that Sawyer cared enough about Ainsley to come looking for her. Given what he knew about stalkers, Sawyer was pretty sure that Jason thought he was the hero of this story. Sawyer couldn't wait to see his face when he realized he was the villain—and the victim.

He just prayed that the man hadn't hurt Ainsley yet as he moved down the street and then turned up the alley behind the house. Fog moved in wisps past him. The air was colder this close to the river, but he hardly noticed. He knew he wouldn't have but a few moments to make the decision once Jason saw him. The problem with this kind of psychopath was that you never knew what they were going to do. Sawyer would have preferred a straight-up hardened criminal any day over one of these nutcases.

At the back of the house, he carefully opened the gate. It creaked only a little, the fog muffling the sound as he slipped through and moved toward the back door. He'd just reached it when he heard Ainsley scream.

CHAPTER TWENTY

GUN GOT OUT of his car as Molly came running from the house. She threw herself into his arms. He caught the sweet citrusy scent of her perfume as he wrapped his arms around her and buried his face in her wild curly head of coal-black hair.

His heart swelled to bursting. He'd never known such love, and for a moment, he almost chucked this deal and walked away. But at the thought of Hale and the others, he knew he still wouldn't be safe. If only he had met Molly before all this.

"I didn't think you would ever get here," she said, smiling up at him. Her beautiful face was freckled, her green eyes wide and luminous, her lips were bowed and the faintest pink.

He kissed her, whirling her around, before setting her down again. He had to finish what he started. "I just stopped by because I missed you so much. I have to run an errand, but when I get back—"

"No," she cried. "Whatever it is, I'm going with you."

"Molly—"

"You have to stop protecting me. Do you hear

me?" She touched his cheek, turning his face down until their eyes locked. "I know you, Gun. I love the man you are. Stop trying to hide from me."

What was she saying? "Molly—"

"Take me with you. You promised that we would be together after today," she said, shaking her head. "Let's be in this together from this moment on. No matter what."

She knew. He wasn't sure how, but she knew. His heart plummeted for a moment. She was too smart.

He heard his stepfather. "No *smart* woman would ever fall for you."

"Wrong again, Ray," he said under his breath.

Molly looked at him quizzically. "Talking to your stepfather again?" She laughed. "You do it in your sleep. I hope you killed that bastard."

Gun let out a laugh. "You really do know me, don't you?"

She nodded, holding his gaze again. "You don't need to keep secrets from me. I'm on board whatever you want to do."

"I am the luckiest man in Butte, Montana. Hell, the world." He picked her up and kissed her hard. When he set her down, he said, "Get your coat. I assume you're packed?"

"Of course," she said with a grin.

"Then let's go finish my business and start really living. I need to pick up a few things I hid in the house."

KITZIE TOPPED HOMESTAKE PASS to see Butte in the distance. Around the next curve, she got a glimpse of Our Lady of the Rockies. The ninety-foot statue gleamed in the morning sun from atop the Continental Divide.

She kept going straight on the interstate past the Berkeley Pit off to her left until she saw the turnoff and swung onto the dirt road.

Her cell phone rang. She didn't check caller ID, just answered, thinking it was Pete with an update. It was Pete, but it wasn't the update she had been expecting.

"I just heard that Ainsley Hamilton was taken captive by some guy who was stalking her," Pete said.

"No, Lance Roderick was stalking her, and he's dead."

"Apparently, it wasn't him. I just heard on the scanner that Sawyer called for backup. The man has Ainsley in a house in Livingston. You must know him. He delivered the groceries to the hotel for you."

Kitzie had been having trouble breathing because of her broken ribs. But now, she couldn't draw a breath for the life of her. "Are you sure?" she managed to gasp.

"Sawyer is probably breaking down the door right now. Where are you?"

She was trying to process what he'd told her when she came around a corner and swore. "The gate's back up and locked." That meant that the last person of the group, probably Gunderson, had locked it.

"What are you going to do?" Pete asked.

Kitzie slammed the gas pedal to the floor. "See if this VW can take it out."

But as she sped toward it, she was thinking of Ainsley. Kitzie had been so sure that she was safe. Now she feared that she'd played a part in getting the young woman abducted—if not killed, and Sawyer, too. What had she done?

SAWYER CALLED FOR BACKUP, but he wasn't about to wait for help to arrive. He rushed the back door. Crashing into the old flimsy door, he heard it splinter, but only found himself on a back porch. He tried the next door, knowing it would be locked. It was. This door was solid wood.

He started to put a shoulder to it, but saw a large window that looked out on the porch. Picking up a chair from the porch, he put it through the window. The glass shattered, sending shards flying. He quickly beat out most of the broken glass and dove through the window to land in the kitchen.

Immediately, he knew he'd hurt his leg again. He lay listening, waiting for the pain to subside. Jason had to have heard him enter the house, and yet he heard nothing. He had to get to Ainsley.

No sound came from within the house. It was the silence that scared him. Jason knew he was coming. He would be ready. What terrified Sawyer was that he might kill Ainsley simply out of meanness. If he couldn't have her, no one would.

He was on his feet, limping badly, but moving. The scream he'd heard had been muffled. She wasn't being kept on this floor or upstairs. He spotted the door to the basement, limped to it and, standing off to the side, opened it.

A gust of stale musty air rushed up at him. He listened, heard nothing and started to step through the door when he heard Jason's voice.

"Come join us, cowboy. But first, throw your gun down or I will cut out Ainsley's black heart before you can reach us."

Sawyer felt the weight of the gun in his hand. It was his only defense, given that his leg might fail him. But he had no choice. He tossed the gun down the stairs. It hit a lower step, bounced, hit another stair and then clinked down on what sounded like concrete floor.

He heard a shuffling sound. This time, Jason's voice was closer. "Ainsley can't wait to see you. Sounds like that leg of yours is bothering you, though. Be careful on the stairs. I wouldn't want you to fall and break your neck."

Gingerly, he took a step with his good leg. His wounded one roared in pain. He braced himself, determined that Jason wouldn't see just how badly he was hurt as he took the next step and the next.

AINSLEY SMELLED HER burning flesh, felt the searing pain, her eyes brimming with fresh tears as she looked at Jason Bowman.

When she'd come out of the bathroom to find him smoking a cigarette she'd thought about making a run for it, screaming her head off as she headed for the stairs. She'd realized that she was in a basement. She just had no idea where.

What had stopped her was Jason. He'd grabbed her and pressed the end of the burning cigarette into the underside of her wrist. She'd screamed in pain before he'd dragged her back toward the makeshift bedroom.

This time, he'd shoved her down on the bed and quickly bound her ankles together with the tape. But this time she'd fought him, kicking and hitting at him, catching him off guard.

He'd slapped her senseless, then stopped for a moment before taping her wrists together to admire his handiwork. His gaze rose to hers. The cigarette had dangled from one lip, before he slowly took it again in his fingers.

She'd seen what he planned to do. She knew from the way Jason had looked pressing the tip of the searing hot end into her flesh that he enjoyed this too much. He would do it again. And again. Just as it had been done to him as a child.

Ainsley had screamed and tried to hit him, clawing at him, this time in anger and anticipation of the pain. He'd put the cigarette down to grab one wrist, then the other as she flailed at him with her fists. He'd only wrapped the tape around her wrists above the burn twice when he heard the noise from above them. He froze.

Ainsley had heard it, too. It sounded as if something had crashed into the house.

The only thing that had stopped him was the sound of someone breaking into the house. She'd felt her heart soar for a moment.

"Looks like we have company. Want to guess who it is?" He sounded too happy.

No, it couldn't be Sawyer. How could he have possibly found her? But suddenly she was weak with worry. Jason had expected someone to try to save her. He'd expected Sawyer. Hoped he would come.

She heard a sound that broke her heart. The intruder upstairs had a distinct limp. "No," she cried as Jason pulled his knife.

A door opened above them.

"Don't come down!" she yelled when she'd heard the groan of the top stair under a heavy tread.

Jason backhanded her, making her cry out in surprise and pain, and called to Sawyer to throw down his gun and join them.

The sound of the weapon tripping down the steps made her jump.

Jason smiled and hurried to pick it up before returning to her. "Come on down, cowboy!"

At the noise from above them, Jason had stopped taping her wrists. He wasn't paying any attention to her now. He had a new victim. Her heart broke at the thought. She struggled to free her wrists and felt the tape give a little.

She'd heard how badly Sawyer had been limping on the creaky old wooden floor above them. Jason, she knew, had heard it, as well. From his expression she could tell that he thought Sawyer would be easy prey.

Jason had easily overpowered her. She feared what he would do to Sawyer in his injured condition.

The tape gave a little more. She worked her hands. Just a little more and she thought she could slip it off.

Sawyer limped farther down the stairs, but she could tell it was taking everything in him. She wondered at what cost to him. Her fear had shifted from herself to him the minute she'd realized he was the one who'd come to save her. At the thought that Jason would kill him...

She freed her hands, keeping an eye on Jason. He had his back to her. He was listening to Sawyer's awkward descent. She couldn't bear it as she hurried to free her ankles.

Sawyer might have broken her heart, but he'd also stolen it. And there was nothing she could do to help him unless she could get free of the tape.

KITZIE DROVE AS fast as she could up the switchbacks. The road was narrow and rough, with large rocks sticking up. Fortunately, the VW was small and went around most of them. Also, it sat high enough that the undercarriage didn't scrape on anything.

"I just came out in an open spot up on top. I'm going to hide my rig in the trees and go on foot from here," Pete said when he called with an update.

"I'm not far behind you."

She concentrated on her driving as the road climbed in twisting turns up and up. She caught a glimpse of the valley far below a couple of times. No wonder this was where Gunderson was meeting Harry Lester. The top of the world and with no one around this time of year since the guided trips up here were only seasonal.

With every turn, though, she felt the pain in her chest. Her right arm was growing numb. Good thing she was left-handed and was a crack shot on the firing line. She tried not to think about Sawyer or Ainsley and the part she had played in their current circumstances, because it made her feel sick and weak, and right now she had to be strong.

As she came out of the pines in an open spot near the top of the mountain, she got the call from Pete.

"It's going down! I've got it on video. I'm going in!"

Kitzie sped up. She wouldn't have time to hike to the base of the statue even if she wasn't so beat up that she wasn't sure she could make it. There was only one thing to do. She raced up the dirt road and came around a curve.

There was the back of Our Lady of the Rockies perched on the edge of the mountaintop. The gleaming white statue towered high into Montana's big blue fall sky.

In front of the statue, the small group of people gathered turned in surprise at the sound of the VW's roaring engine.

Kitzie sped at them at full spccd. Off to her right, she caught movement as her partner, Pete Corran, came out of the nearby pines, gun drawn.

SAWYER REACHED THE bottom of the stairs and turned toward Jason. Ainsley appeared to be bound on the bed. Jason was blocking his view of her. But he could tell that she was alive. At least for the moment.

He could see that she'd been crying and still looked as if she was in pain. Jason stood a few yards from her, holding a knife. Sawyer didn't see the gun he'd tossed down the stairs, but he knew that the man had it.

"I've called for backup."

"No, you haven't," Jason said with a laugh. "You knew what I would do if I heard even one siren headed this way."

"So, what now?" Sawyer asked, taking a couple of painful limps forward. He wanted to be within striking distance, but Jason halted him by pulling the gun with his free hand.

"Stay right there. I can kill her before you can reach me. I want you to watch what happens to this woman you...soiled," Jason said.

"You're mistaken. I did nothing to her."

The man's face reddened with anger. "You cheapened her by putting your hands on her, by kissing her, by…" His words came out in sputters that sent saliva flying. "Now she has to be punished."

Sawyer shook his head. "You're the one who needs to be punished, you sick son-of-a—"

"I adored her. I would have treated her like a princess."

Out of the corner of his eye, he saw that Ainsley had managed to free her hands. But she pretended they were still bound by hiding them in her lap, waiting. Waiting for him to make his move.

He'd been in situations like this before with his job, but never had he felt so helpless. Jason had already hurt her. He'd made up his mind that she was ruined. Even now, he could see the man struggling with his need to punish her against his obsession with her.

Sawyer took a step. His leg gave out under his weight, and he dropped to his knees. Just as he'd planned, the move forced Jason to turn his attention away from Ainsley.

"What did you see in him?" Jason demanded of Ainsley over his shoulder as he moved away from her and closer to Sawyer. "Look at him. He's *weak*. What you need is a man who can—"

Sawyer pulled the gun from the top of his boot and fired point-blank into Jason's chest. Just as he'd known would happen, the bullet didn't stop him. Jason kicked him in his bad leg, managing to knock the gun from his hand as he came at him. The gun skittered a few feet away, but Jason didn't seem interested in it.

The pain of the kick to his bad leg set stars dancing before his eyes. Everything threatened to go dark as he did his best to hold Jason off. The man was strong, the gunshot seemingly doing nothing to weaken him. Jason was frantically stabbing at him with the knife as if he knew that eventually through blood loss, he wouldn't be able to fight.

Sawyer managed to grab the man's wrist holding the knife. He felt the tip of the blade pierce his shoulder an instant before he heard the earsplitting second gun blast and looked up to see Ainsley standing over them, his gun in her hand. But the bullet found its mark just as the first had. Only this time, it took some of the life out of Jason Bowman.

He fell to one knee. The knife clattered to the concrete floor. With a shove, Sawyer sent Jason falling backward. He hit the floor hard, his head snapping back and smacking the concrete.

It took more than effort to get to his feet with his bad leg. Sawyer grimaced but managed to rise and work his way to the man on the floor. He could hear sirens in the distance.

Jason's eyes were open. He looked from Sawyer to Ainsley, who was still holding the gun on the man and crying softly.

"Too bad we didn't have more time," Jason said, his words strained. "I would have left you with a lot more scars to remember me by."

She glared down at him. "I've already forgotten you," she lied.

Jason laughed and closed his eyes. Sawyer watched the rise and fall of the man's breathing stop before moving to check for a pulse. Then he limped over to Ainsley. She met his gaze and began to cry harder as he took the gun from her and pulled her into his arms.

CHAPTER TWENTY-ONE

GUN'S FIRST THOUGHT, when he heard the approaching vehicle, was to curse himself for bringing Molly with him. No matter what took place, he couldn't let anything bad happen to her.

He'd been so sure that he hadn't been followed. With a silent curse, he realized that it was Harry Lester who must have brought the tail. He'd thought the old man was smarter than that. Or maybe his worthless nephew.

"What's going on?" LeRoy asked, looking from his uncle to Gun and back.

"What the hell do you think?" Harry Lester demanded.

"One of you was followed," Gun snapped as he reached down to pick up the briefcase full of money. He grabbed Molly's hand and started for his own vehicle. "Let's get out of here." Harry Lester was already starting toward his car after loading four boxes of the loot from the trunk of Gun's car.

"Hold on," Hale said. "You aren't taking all the money with you."

The sound of the approaching vehicle was growing louder—and closer. "Don't be a fool, Hale. We have to get out of here. Now!"

The carnie came after Gun, latching on to his arm and swinging him around to face him. "This is a trick so you can take off with all the money, and we'll never see you again."

Before Gun could respond, a man came out of the trees with a gun yelling, "FBI. Hands up!"

Gun tried to free himself from Hale, but the fool wouldn't let go. He swung the briefcase, catching the carnie in the side of the head and breaking his grip. He pushed Molly toward the car, saying, "Run!"

Behind him, Hale stumbled under the blow but quickly recovered and plowed into Gun from behind, sending him sprawling. Gun came up with his weapon, and as Hale launched himself at him, fired three quick shots.

Hale's momentum had him still coming. Gun rolled to the side as the older man hit the dust.

"Get to the car and go!" he yelled at Molly as he heard shots over the roar of the approaching vehicle. Looking up, he spotted a blue VW barreling down on them. The federal agent had taken cover behind a low wall at the edge of the parking lot. He was firing at LeRoy, who was making a run for it.

Harry Lester had made it as far as the car. He was trying to get in as if he thought he could still get away. LeRoy went down, grabbing his leg. Any minute that FBI agent would be firing on him.

Gun turned to find Molly standing behind him.

Hadn't she heard him tell her to get to the car? "I told you to—" The rest of the words died on his lips as he saw the gun in her hand.

"FBI," she said.

He stared at her, so stunned that she easily took his weapon from him. He'd told himself that she was too good to be true, but he'd hoped that maybe his luck had changed.

"Apparently my stepfather was right," he said as he met her green-eyed gaze.

"You have the right to remain silent," Molly said over the roar of the VW as it came to a dust-boiling stop just yards from them, and Kitzie stumbled out, weapon in hand. *"Molly Griffin?"* She swore under her breath before she collapsed.

AINSLEY TRIED NOT to look at the cigarette burn on her wrist. Jason was right. The scar would always remind her of him—and Sawyer.

"Did you hear about the bust?" Kat asked excitedly as she joined her sister on the couch at the main house on the ranch. Ainsley knew she was trying to keep her mind off what had happened to her.

"Spotlight Images, Inc. Isn't that the company you were working for? They were *jewel thieves.* The FBI busted them and the leader—" Kat took a breath "—had a tattoo of a pendulum on his ass." Kat seemed to be waiting for Ainsley to react. *"The Prophecy?* Is any of this ringing any bells?"

"I honestly don't know what you're talking about."

Kat stared at her in disbelief. "No one's told you that Sarah has a tattoo of a pendulum on her backside? I know you've heard about The Prophecy."

"Dad told me that some of the members tried to frame her, but that she wasn't involved."

Her sister rolled her eyes. "And you believe that?"

Ainsley didn't know what to believe. Her own ordeal had left her shaken. She had to admit, she wasn't that concerned about some anarchist group from the 1970s.

"Max and I have been digging into Sarah's past for months," Kat said excitedly. "We even talked to two of the men in prison, Mason Green and Wallace McGill. You should have seen their faces when I walked in. I look enough like Mother—Sarah—" she corrected herself "—that their eyes about popped out of their heads. They confirmed what we suspected. The Prophecy has something big planned, and it's connected to Dad. That's why there is going to be so much security election night. We think that's when they will make their move."

Ainsley chose her words carefully. "If any of this is true, why hasn't Mother been arrested?" Ainsley asked. She saw her sister's expression and didn't wait for an answer. "Because you can't prove any of it."

"The members of The Prophecy covered for her. If I told you everything we've found out about Sarah—"

Ainsley raised a hand to stop her. "Kat, this obsession with Mother's past has to stop."

"She was the *leader* of The Prophecy and probably still is. I saw a photo of her and the men. One of them was apparently her lover. They were responsible for killing two people in a bombing right before Sarah headed for Montana and married our father. She used to go by the name Red."

Ainsley got to her feet. She couldn't bear to hear any more of this. "Kat, I was just abducted by a man who was obsessed with me after one chance meeting. He followed me for months. He…" Tears burned her eyes. "You have to stop this. If there was any proof, Mother would be behind bars. By the way, where is she?"

"Off to some fund-raiser in town for Dad's campaign. She wanted me to go. I suppose she didn't ask you in your condition. But Harper and Cassidy were both going to be there." Kat shook her head. "It's all going to come out, and when it does, I worry what it will do to Dad. Max will break the whole story and has promised to do his best to protect all of us."

She'd been through enough lately that she didn't want to even contemplate her mother being a terrorist.

"Max has bought a half dozen weeklies, including the local one," Kat said, sounding full of pride. Her happiness bubbled over, and Ainsley found herself wanting to hug her sister. "I'm going to be his head photographer."

This Kat was…beautiful, full of hope, not obsessing over some conspiracy theories. She stepped to her and hugged her tightly.

"What was that about?" Kat asked in surprise.

"I just felt like hugging you. I'm happy for you and Max. He's good for you."

SARAH KNEW SHE should be concentrating on the charity event as she drove toward town. But she was too livid as she made the call. She didn't give her former coconspirator a chance to say more than hello before she launched in. *"You called Joe!"*

"Sarah?" Martin asked tentatively.

She had been trying to reach Martin since her talk with Doc. But he'd been avoiding her, letting his phone go straight to voice mail every time she called.

"I talked to Doc," she said as she drove.

He let out a curse. "I told you all hell would break loose if you did this. But I didn't call Joe. I haven't said a word to him or to anyone else. Do you think I'm crazy? So if he found out—"

She let out a curse under her breath. "He's got our houses bugged."

Silence on the other end of the line.

"Get out of the house," she said. Her mind was racing. When would a bug have been planted? She thought of all Dr. Venable's visits. Of course it had to have been him following Joe's orders.

"Just a minute." On the other end of the line, she heard the sound of footfalls, a door opening and closing. "I'm in the stairwell at my office building." She could hear the echo. "Sarah, what have you done?"

"That's basically what Doc said to me. He told me that I'll be getting my memory back. Soon. He and Joe are convinced that I'll become Red again, that I'll be that young girl I was in college who believed I could change the world by any means."

"What if they're right, Sarah?"

It had been something that had kept her up at night. "I don't believe it. Buck and my children changed me. That's why you have to help me bring down The Prophecy."

"I told you, I don't know anything about what Joe has planned. Did you really think he would share that with me?" He sighed heavily. "I've been thinking… I can hold up the money. Joe will know right away. I'll make myself scarce, so he can't find me until after the election."

"Thank you." It wasn't a lot, but it was something. If she could just loosen one wheel in Joe's runaway train before the election… "What changed your mind?"

"The FBI arrested some jewel thieves trying to fence stolen property. The men were part of a video production company shooting commercials in Montana called Spotlight Images, Inc. I think it might be the one that has been supporting The Prophecy."

"That's the company my daughter Ainsley was working for," Sarah said, trying to still her racing heart. "They were jewel thieves. I saw it on the news this morning."

"The owner, a man named Devon Gunderson, had a tattoo on his butt cheek."

"A pendulum," she said, thinking of her own tattoo, another surprise to her when she'd been told of its existence after her return almost two years ago. "Was there any other connection to Joe?"

"Not that I know of, possibly someone Joe recruited…"

"Wait, wasn't there a Gunderson we knew at college?"

"You're thinking it might have been a relative?" Martin asked.

Sarah wondered how far Joe's tentacles reached across the country. The only way to stop this was to cut off the head—her former lover Joe.

"Because of that bust up there in Montana, Joe needs my money even more than he did before," Martin was saying. "If you're right and Joe's been listening to all our conversations…"

"He'll know I'm the one who asked you to get involved. I'm sorry, Martin. But with the election so close and another member of The Prophecy arrested, they will be tracking where the money from the video production company was going. Joe's house of cards will come tumbling down."

"Not before election night," Martin said, bringing her back to earth. "From every indication, he has something big planned."

"How am I going to stop him?" She held the phone so tight her fingers ached. Maybe delaying funding wouldn't have any effect at all. It might get Martin killed instead. It might get them both killed or put another of her daughters in danger. Was she kidding herself that anything could be done?

"I doubt he can be stopped. He's a fanatic. Given the current climate in this country..."

"Martin, Joe isn't trying to change the world. We really did want to make this a better world. But Joe, he's just playing God because this is about him and his need to be somebody. What?" she asked when he let out a bitter chuckle.

"Just that you don't know how close you just came to the truth. He's not exactly playing God himself, but Joe is definitely on that team."

"What?"

Martin sighed. "When we almost lost our kids last summer? I was leaving the hospital in Houston when I saw this priest—"

"Are you telling me Joe is a Catholic priest?"

"Who knows if it was real or not, but he was dressed like one. He called himself Father John David Williams."

"What was he doing at the hospital?"

"What do you think?" Martin said with a groan. "I talked him out of killing Jack and Cassidy. But he said if they ever remembered what they'd uncovered about The Prophecy and their...parents—"

Sarah felt sick. "That's why he has to be stopped.

He would kill us and our families without batting an eye. You don't believe that it is for some great change for our country, do you?"

"No," he said after a minute. "Not anymore."

"Father John David Williams," she repeated. "If he really is a priest, he shouldn't be that hard to find."

"Which is why I'm sure he was only in disguise to get into the hospital that day."

"Martin, if you know anything else that will help me…"

"Help you get yourself and your family killed? No."

"Don't forget, your son and my daughter are in love and planning to get married. Whatever Joe has planned, I think you're right, and it will happen election night. *Jack and Cassidy will be there*."

"I'm so sorry I ever got involved."

"There is no changing the past," Sarah said, having that same regret.

"I'll make sure none of my money gets to Joe," he said. "But it means that I'll have to get out of the country. I won't be able to come back."

"Unless I can stop Joe. I'll do everything I can to make sure you see Jack again and our future grandchildren."

"You just take care of yourself. Whatever happens to me… Good luck, Sarah. You're going to need it."

She thought of Dr. Venable and wondered why he hadn't contacted her again. He'd said she would be seeing him soon. But how could he when since Buck had become the Republican candidate, the ranch had been crawling with Secret Service. Two of them were following her right now.

Doc had to find a way. "Once I get my memory back—"

"You could be more dangerous than Joe."

KITZIE HURT ALL over, but her physical ailments were nothing compared to her anger. "Molly Griffin? Our boss sent her undercover without telling us? I told you he didn't trust me to make this happen."

Her FBI partner, Pete, shook his head from the chair beside her hospital bed. "A lot more people could have been hurt or killed if she hadn't been there. She certainly took Gunderson down without a fight. Did you see the look on his face? She could have shot him, and I don't think he would have been as surprised."

"I find no humor in any of this. We could have handled that takedown. We had it under control."

Pete lifted a brow but was wise enough not to say anything more about Molly. She and Molly had been adversaries since their early FBI training. "Did you hear about Sawyer?"

She groaned as she remembered the part she'd played. "Is Ainsley all right?"

"He saved her from her crazed stalker."

Of course he had. She felt a huge sense of relief. If the stalker had killed Ainsley... She didn't even want to think about that. If she hadn't sandbagged Sawyer, then he would have been with Ainsley. Instead…she closed her eyes, groaning with a new pain. He was going to kill her for what she did, and she wouldn't blame him.

"What did you do?" Pete asked with a sigh.

"They are all wrong for each other."

"Kitzie."

"So she's all right?"

"Sawyer got there in time," Pete said.

"Doesn't he always," she said under her breath. "What about Murph? Did they catch her?"

"Got her before she could get on a plane. Recovered the stolen goods, arrested the jewel thieves and Harry Lester Brown." Pete sounded way too chipper, all things considered. "You sure you're all right?"

She nodded, feeling close to tears. She'd lost the man she loved, and now she'd have to share credit on this bust with Molly Griffin. Not to mention living with the guilt of what she'd done to Ainsley—and having to face Sawyer.

"Have you seen Sawyer?" she asked.

"He's in the hospital in Livingston. He reinjured his leg."

SARAH COULDN'T BELIEVE it as she stared at the Road Closed sign ahead. She was already running late for the charity event. Just as she was leaving the house, the phone had rung. She'd rushed back inside to answer it, thinking it might be something about the benefit. Or Dr. Venable. She couldn't understand why she hadn't heard from him by now.

But when she'd answered, there hadn't been anyone on the other end of the line. At least no one who said anything. She'd repeated "Hello?" several more times, a strange eerie feeling coming over her before she'd hung up.

She told herself it wasn't Joe calling. If it had been, he would have said something. Otherwise, what was the point? Just to scare her? Just to put her on edge?

Her conversation with Martin at least had gone well. Now, as she backed up, she motioned to the Secret Service men to do the same. They had wanted to drive her, but she'd put her foot down. It was bad enough having them shadowing her all the time.

She knew she would have to take a longer route into Big Timber. She questioned whether she should even go to the benefit. Superstition aside, the way this morning was going, she'd been hesitant to leave the house again.

It was crazy thinking. She *had* to go. They were expecting her, and, knowing Jerrod, there would be media there. She practiced her smile. It came out a grimace that made her laugh. This was her future if she wanted to be at Buck's side. Benefits, fundraisers, hosting dinners with dignitaries from around the world, every kind of charitable work imaginable. Some days, it seemed too much to bear. But she loved Buck, and she would do whatever it took to make him happy.

Being on the campaign trail had forced her into the role. She could do this. She *would* do this, even if it killed her.

But as she looked in her rearview mirror, she told herself she would do it without the two government goons following her. She knew these roads. At least that part of her memory was just fine. There was no way she couldn't lose these guys, she told herself.

That thought picked up her mood as she tromped down on the gas, dust boiling up in a dark cloud behind her.

Once she reached the armory where the benefit was being held, she was forced to park in the far back. She'd lost the men following her, but she knew once they found their way to town, they'd show up. They'd tell Buck and he wouldn't be happy, but too bad. She'd enjoyed herself. In fact, she felt like her old self again.

She'd just gotten out of her car when she saw the hunched-over old man.

He wore a large slouch hat and overalls. He appeared to be struggling with a box full of something… dolls, she realized as one of them fell out.

"Excuse me," he called to her in a crackly voice. "I'm sorry, but could you help me for a moment?"

As late as she was, she had no choice. He had stopped next to an old blue van and now leaned against it as if the effort of carrying the box was too much for him.

"Here, let me get that," she said as she rushed to him and reached for the box, but he pulled it away.

"If you could just get the one I dropped," he said without looking up at her. He sounded winded, but she did as he asked, bending to retrieve the doll from the dirt.

The blow took her completely off guard as the box connected with her back. She sprawled into the dirt, the doll's arm clutched in her fist. Stunned and confused, at first she'd thought the man had lost his balance and accidentally hit her.

That was until she heard him say in his normal voice, "It's been a long time, Sarah."

Joe Landon. Because of that, she wasn't even that surprised to feel the knife at her throat.

CHAPTER TWENTY-TWO

"I'm sorry I got you into so much trouble," Sheriff Curry said as he pulled up a chair next to Sawyer's bed. "I heard you were suspended."

"None of that matters. Ainsley is safe. I hate to think what would have happened if I hadn't gone up there."

"I'll have a word with your boss," Frank said and raised his hand to stop Sawyer when he started to protest. "You deserve a medal."

He chuckled at that. "I knew I wasn't near a hundred percent. I guess I'm learning the hard way to listen to my body."

"How is the leg?"

"The doctor says if I stay off of it and let it heal, it will be fine."

"Why do I get the feeling that you aren't going to do that?" the sheriff asked.

Sawyer shook his head. "I need to see Ainsley. Things got left...unfinished."

Frank was smiling at him. "I thought you two might hit it off."

"Yeah, that didn't quite happen. I'd hoped to talk to her before election night."

"Have you called her?"

He shook his head. "She came to see me here in the hospital. She thanked me and said she was sorry about my leg and that she wished me well and left."

"So it's like that?"

"Worse. While she was here, my boss came in, giving me hell for playing hero. Ainsley seems to think that I'm some Casanova who saves women, gets them to fall for him and then moves on to his next conquest."

Frank said nothing.

"Okay, maybe that is the way it seemed in the past. But I've changed. Once I met Ainsley..."

The sheriff picked up his hat resting on his knee and rose. "Get well. Time often helps. Time and space. She's been through a lot. Once the dust settles..."

Maybe, Sawyer thought as he watched Frank leave. But he'd never been good at sitting around waiting.

KITZIE TRIED TO call Sawyer, but his phone went straight to voice mail. She knew he was mad and probably not ready to deal with her. She couldn't blame him.

As soon as she was released from the hospital, her ribs taped up and all her other minor injuries taken care of, she called Ainsley and asked her to coffee. Ainsley agreed to meet her at the Branding Iron Café in Beartooth.

The other woman was already seated in a booth by the window when Kitzie arrived. After everything Ainsley had been through, Kitzie was surprised she'd be up to meeting her.

"I was going to call you about your red dress," she said the moment Kitzie joined her. "I'm afraid my stalker destroyed it."

Kitzie would have never worn it again anyway. "Don't worry about it. That isn't why I asked you to coffee."

"Oh?"

"No, I need to apologize for the last time we saw each other," she said.

Ainsley looked away. "There's really no need."

"I'm afraid there is. I gave Sawyer enough sleeping pills to kill a horse that night, so he wouldn't make his date with you."

"What?" Her blue eyes flashed. "Why would you do that?"

"Because you two are all wrong for each other," Kitzie said, then drew in a sharp breath and let it out. "I still believe that. Sawyer and I have a history. I screwed up on a case and he saved me. We started seeing each other. I was in love with him. Unfortunately, he wasn't with me. The truth is, I wanted to get back at him when I saw that he was interested in you."

"Sawyer didn't mention that you were both FBI or that you had a history."

Kitzie took a sip of her coffee before she spoke again. "When I heard that your stalker was waiting for you back in your cabin that night—"

"He would have taken me one way or another. If Sawyer had been with me, things could have gone much worse, especially for Sawyer," Ainsley said.

"You're letting me off the hook. Why?"

"Sawyer wasn't honest with me. If he had been..." They locked gazes for a moment.

"Then you would have known I was up to something," Kitzie said, smiling. "You wouldn't have bought my act."

Ainsley smiled, too, and nodded. "And I think you're right about me and Sawyer."

"Really?" Kitzie had expected the woman to be angry with her. "I was all ready to warn you about him, but it sounds like I can save my breath. You've already figured out that he falls for the women he saves. There will always be someone else he needs to save." She shrugged.

Ainsley finished her coffee. "Well, we both survived."

Kitzie's gaze went to the young woman's wrist. Ainsley quickly covered the scar and rose. "You must be excited about election night. From what I've heard on the news, your father is going to win by a landslide."

Ainsley looked at her watch. "I should get going.

It was nice meeting you, Kitzie. Maybe things will work out with you and Sawyer after all."

She laughed. "You don't know Sawyer. If anything, he'll never forgive me for what I did." Kitzie watched the other woman leave, wondering if she hadn't made a mistake about the two of them. What if there really was something lasting between Sawyer and Ainsley? What if that was the reason she'd done what she had? She sensed it. And now she'd managed to destroy it because of her jealousy?

STILL STUNNED BY the blow, Sarah didn't speak, couldn't, as Joe pulled her to her feet. She felt the blade prick her skin as he pulled her close. Something warm ran down her neck. She told herself that he wasn't going to cut her throat. But then again, she could feel anger vibrating through his body like a live wire.

Her surprise and fear at finally coming face-to-face with this monster had left her weak and trembling. But she gathered her strength and told herself that she would do whatever it took not to show him just how much he terrified her.

"You don't know how long I've dreamed of this," he said next to her ear.

"Holding a knife to my throat?"

He chuckled, and she felt some of the tension in his body relax a little. "A necessity, since I didn't think you would go with me willingly."

"What makes you think I'm going to now?" But

when she looked around the parking lot, she saw no one. Crying out for help would only get her killed. He was holding her so tight, the knife against her throat a painful reminder that fighting him was also a crazy idea.

"I have two men inside the charity event who are watching your daughters Harper and Cassidy. One word from me, and they will see that both of them disappear and are never seen again."

She'd forgotten both daughters had said they would be there. "I think you're bluffing," she lied.

He laughed. "No, you don't. You *know* me. I don't bluff. I have the upper hand. I've had it for a long time. So stop thinking you're going to outsmart me. Not only do you know me, but I know *you*." He chuckled. "That's why we're going to get into your car like we are old friends. Then we're going for a ride."

"I don't think so. Why don't you just kill me right here and save us both some time?"

"*Kill you?* Sarah, why would I do that after waiting all these years to see you again? Anyway, that would let you off way too easily. You've hurt me, Sarah. All these years we could have been together. We could have done amazing things."

"Those years are gone. So, what is the point now, Joe?"

He turned her so that he was facing her, but he still held the knife, the tip of it wet with her blood. "I *want* you, Sarah. That's all I've ever wanted. We can conquer the world, literally."

She started to speak, but he put a finger to her lips. "Don't. We'll have plenty of time to talk. Don't make me hurt you. Get into your car, Sarah."

Every victim knew that you did everything possible not to let a criminal get you into a vehicle. Once you did that, you were as good as dead. So instead, the good advice was to fight and scream and run!

The second blow did more than stun her. She staggered back, slamming into the side of the van. Her head snapped back, thudding against the metal. Stars danced before her eyes, then dimmed.

"You've been so anxious to get your memory back. Did I mention that Doc will be joining us?"

She felt Joe grab her and duckwalk her to her car before shoving her into the backseat. He leaped on her, quickly binding her hands and then her feet, before plunging a hypodermic needle into her arm. She watched it all happening as if in a paralyzed dream.

"It's going to be all right now, Red." He stepped out, picked up the box of dolls and tossed them in after her.

As the car door slammed closed, her head lolled to the side. On the floorboard, two dozen dolls looked at her from glassy dull eyes. She could feel the drug coursing through her body, but she was too weak to struggle, even if she hadn't been bound. Panic ricocheted through her before her eyelids crashed down, dropping her in a sickening, terrifying darkness.

CHAPTER TWENTY-THREE

Sawyer tried to take the sheriff's advice and give Ainsley time. But this couldn't wait. He'd considered going out to the ranch, but the only reason his doctor had let him out of the hospital was his promise to go straight home and put his leg up. He had to talk to her.

He called the ranch number, got a staff member and requested Ainsley. When asked who was calling, he said, "A friend. I just happened to be in town..."

"Just a moment," the woman said, and Ainsley came on the line.

"Ainsley, I need to see you."

"Sawyer?"

"Meet me somewhere so we can talk. Please."

Silence, then, "Kitzie told me what she did to keep you from making our date."

"She did?" That surprised him more than he could say. Instantly, he wondered what her angle had been. It wasn't like her.

"It really was no big deal," Ainsley said.

"Like hell it wasn't. Did she tell you that the only reason I went to her cabin was because she said she needed my help on the case she was working? She told you she's an FBI agent?"

"Yes, I saw it on the news."

He was still trying to figure out Kitzie's angle when she said, "She told me how you'd saved her once, you both being agents."

Sawyer swore under his breath. "She told you that's my MO. I save women, seem to fall in love with them, then when another woman in peril comes along, I'm off again, right?" The silence on the other end of the line was deafening. "She told you that because she knows this time is different. She can't stand the idea that I have fallen in love with you."

"We barely know each other," Ainsley said.

"I've seen you naked."

"You had to remind me, didn't you?"

"Ainsley, we have...*something*. Come on, you wouldn't have agreed to our last date unless you believed it, too."

"You forget, I was only going to use you and move on."

"You aren't the type to give away a piece of your heart or your trust to just any man." More silence. He thought that he might be reaching her. "Can't we meet and—"

"I'm really busy right now. The election is tomorrow. Let's see how we both feel after that." He started to argue that he couldn't wait. He needed to see her, when she said, "Sawyer? I can't thank you enough for finding me and getting me away from...

that man. You really are good at your job. I'll always be grateful to you."

He swore under his breath. Gratitude was the last thing he wanted from her. "You know it was more than a job," he said, but realized she'd already hung up.

"Was that him?" her sister Cassidy asked. Her other sisters had met at the house and were now sitting around the living room.

Ainsley nodded into the silence. They'd just had lunch together. Their father had hired an in-house nanny so they would be free to attend election events. Just moments ago they'd been talking about how their mother hadn't made the charity program.

Something had come up, was all they'd been told by one of the organizers. Since then, she hadn't returned to the house. But one of the staff said that she'd gotten a call from their father's campaign manager saying he needed her in Helena, and she would be back before election night.

With Sawyer's call, it was clear her sisters had lost interest in talking about their mother.

"Why didn't you meet him? That is why he called, right?" Harper asked. "Clearly you care about him."

Ainsley groaned as she took her chair again. "It's complicated."

Her sisters all laughed and began to talk at once about what they'd gone through when it came to love. "We've all been there," Olivia said once the roar of conversation had died down. She laughed. "Look what I went through! You want to talk *complicated*."

"This is different," she protested. "Sawyer is an FBI agent. He loves his job. He loves…saving people."

"He sounds horrible," Kat joked.

"He fell in love with the last woman he saved, then moved on, she said, when he found someone else to save."

"*She* said?" Bo asked. "You would take the word of his former ex? Really, Ainsley, you need to go with your heart. I made that mistake years ago with Jace. If I had followed my heart, I could have saved us both a lot of grief."

"Bo's right," Harper and Cassidy said in unison, then both laughed. Harper motioned for Cassidy to go first.

"With Jack, it was love at first sight. I swear. It was like we had always known each other. We still pinch ourselves because it was like that for him, too," Cassidy said.

"Well, that's a little different from what some of us went through," Harper said. "Brody and I had all kinds of obstacles to conquer and still do. But ultimately, it is about love. Do you love Sawyer?"

"I barely know him."

They all laughed again. "We all said that at some point," Kat said. "But it comes down to this. Do you think about him all the time? Do you feel like something is missing when you aren't with him?"

Ainsley felt tears burn her eyes. "I wish it was that simple. I'm not sure I can trust him."

"Or is it yourself you're afraid you can't trust?" Kat asked.

The room fell silent. She looked at each of them and saw compassion and understanding. It was true most of them had been there before they'd finally let themselves fall in love.

SAWYER WAS SURPRISED when the sheriff called him.

"There's something I've been debating if I should tell you," Frank said. "It's about election night."

Sawyer heard the concern in his friend's tone and voiced his immediate thought. "Ainsley will be there."

"It would be better if she wasn't," the sheriff said.

What was Frank saying? "With all the security…" He realized that he'd heard more than concern in Frank's voice. He'd heard fear. "What are you expecting?"

"Possible trouble."

"*Trouble?* You mean from non-supporters or—"

"A terrorist group."

Sawyer let out a curse. "Well, if you think I can stop Ainsley from being at her father's acceptance speech…" He realized he'd been so out of touch that he'd completely forgotten about the election. "Where is it being held?"

"At the Beartooth Fairgrounds in the rodeo arena."

"You can't be serious. Whose dumb idea was that?"

"Our future president's."

"Well, once he's aware of the danger—"

"That's the problem," Frank said. "He doesn't believe it."

"What kind of security do you have?"

The sheriff told him. "I even called in a bomb defusing expert. I've done everything possible, but I don't have to tell you that that doesn't always work, especially when dealing with extremists."

"Short of kidnapping Ainsley..."

"I thought you should know," Frank said.

Sawyer thought of Ainsley. "I'll be there."

"Your doctor—"

"I'll be there on crutches, but I'll be there."

"I'll see that you have access to the family."

SARAH WOKE AND sat up abruptly in a narrow bed. She'd expected to find herself in some kind of dungeon or, at the very least, locked up in a dark basement somewhere. Nor was she bound. Another surprise.

Instead she was lying on a daybed in what looked like a nice guest room. The walls were painted a pale yellow, and pretty paintings hung on the walls.

"Glad to see you're back again. I was afraid I might have hit you too hard or overdosed you," Joe said, getting up from a corner chair.

She recoiled, backing away from him until her spine pressed into the wall.

He stopped a few feet from her, shaking his head and tsking as if disappointed. "Really, Sarah. You have no reason to be frightened of me."

"I beg to differ. Where am I?"

"It doesn't matter, because you'll be returning to your family very soon." He turned to pull up a chair next to the bed. "Please, relax. I'm sure you're thirsty and probably hungry. I will take care of both after we talk."

She didn't want to talk. Nor did she believe he would be returning her to her family. "Everyone will be looking for me. I was supposed to be at that charity event. Once they contact Buck—"

"It's been taken care of," he assured her. "Everyone believes you had to go to the capital for another event."

Sarah leaned back against the wall. "They will check on me to make sure I'm all right." She wasn't confident of that. It wasn't like she was close to her children.

"You'll be back home before that. I promise you this won't take long."

She stared at the man she'd once had a torrid love affair with—her first. Joe had swept her off her feet. The fact that he wanted to change the world with her had made it all the more exciting and passionate. He was still a handsome man. But the electricity she'd once seen in his blue eyes seemed to be an eerie high voltage now.

"You will come back to me," Joe said confidently. "I had hoped it wouldn't take…extreme measures— that you would have realized by now that Buckmaster Hamilton was the wrong man for you." He shrugged. "How is your head?"

"Fine," she lied. The headache was like a hammer inside her skull. She wanted to lie back down and close her eyes. Wait, *extreme measures*? Her heart was suddenly a thunder in her chest. Sweat broke out under her arms. She looked into his eyes, and any doubts she had about his intentions were gone. She'd thought he wouldn't kill her, but now she knew that if he didn't get Red back, he would.

"Joe—"

He leaned toward her to put a finger to her lips. His blue gaze was like a laser boring into hers. "You will come back to me. We are supposed to do this together. Once you see what I have planned, the work I've done all these years behind the scenes will be worth it. You and I will emerge victorious against a country that needs us more than ever."

AINSLEY COULDN'T RELAX after her sisters left. It felt strange to be home on the ranch again—let alone staying by herself in the condos her father had built for his six daughters. Her sisters were either married or living with their boyfriends. Only Ainsley was still single. Not just single, she reminded herself with a groan.

"Just get through election night," she said to herself as she looked out at the ranch the Hamiltons had spent lifetimes building.

With the election tomorrow, it would soon be over. But then what? She had no job, no plans. Bo had told her that their father was planning a short surprise honeymoon after the election and before he was sworn in as president.

So if she stayed on the ranch, she would be here alone. Her sisters were all busy with their families or fiancés. And there was really nothing for her here.

Moving away from the window, she knew she was just trying to keep her mind off Sawyer. She wished she'd never met him, until she remembered that she'd probably be dead—or worse—if it wasn't for him. He'd left an ache in her chest at the thought of him, one she didn't know how to extract.

"You need to get a job," she said to the empty room. Doing what? She'd put her life on hold for the past two years, she realized now. Scouting for movie and commercial locations had been fun for a while. It had been fine after she quit law school. She'd wanted something that required little effort on her part. Also, she'd enjoyed the hours she'd spent on horseback exploring the state.

But now she yearned for something she could sink her teeth into. With a groan, she realized Sawyer had come back into her thoughts.

Earlier she'd noticed that Bo had been uncomfortable, and they'd joked about her going into labor. She picked up the phone and called Bo, only to get her husband, Jace.

"Bo's napping," he said. "I hate to wake her since she is having such a hard time sleeping with the babies due so soon."

"No, don't wake her. Just tell her I was thinking about her when she wakes up," Ainsley said.

"She's insistent on going out to the fairgrounds to be with all the family for your father's acceptance speech. Unless she has the babies first."

"Knowing her, she will have the babies right there on the stage," Ainsley said. "It will make a great story when the kids are older."

Pocketing her phone, she saw that it was dinnertime. She started to walk the short distance over to the main house, knowing there would be something in the refrigerator to eat over there.

Her cell phone rang, startling her. She looked to see who was calling. Her heart rose like a helium balloon in her chest. Sawyer. She debated taking the call as it rang a second time.

"Hello?"

"Ainsley." He sounded relieved that she'd picked up. "It is so good to hear your voice."

She held the phone, telling herself she shouldn't have picked up.

"I know you said we couldn't see each other until after the election..."

B.J. DANIELS

Just the thought of seeing him almost made her weaken. "I can't imagine what we have to say to each other—"

"Is there any chance I could talk you into running away with me?"

She laughed. "Seriously?"

He sighed. "It was a thought. Actually, if we could get together…"

"How is your leg?" she asked, changing the subject before she agreed. The problem was that she feared she couldn't trust her heart with him. She'd thought she could make love with him and then walk away. She knew better now.

"It's okay."

She didn't believe him.

"I'm worried about you. I talked to Sheriff Curry and—"

"If this is about election night, the sheriff has already talked to us about this. He would prefer the family not come."

"I know, so—"

"Precautions have been taken. There is nothing that can keep us away, short of nuclear war."

"I was afraid you would say that. I'd still like to see you. Let me prove how wrong you are about me."

Her heart begged her to say yes. Foolish heart. "I'm sure we'll see each other sometime, but right now…"

"All right." He seemed to agree too readily. "But

I miss you." With that, he disconnected, and she realized she'd lost her appetite.

"You can't keep me here," Sarah said as she looked past Joe Landon to the door, realizing he could probably do anything he wanted to her—and he knew it. She had no idea even where she was.

"I told you that I don't plan to keep you here," he said as if amused by her fear. "I know you don't believe this, Sarah, but I'm doing you a favor. Once Doc gives you back the memory of who you were, who *we* were…" He smiled. "Well, you and I are going to rule the world."

"You've lost your mind. Rule the world by killing a bunch of people?"

"You have a better idea?" Joe asked, his smile fading.

"Anything would be a better idea."

"Well, you always *were* the smart one. But together we were a force to be reckoned with. You might have been the true leader of The Prophecy after everyone thought I screwed things up, but you needed me. You will always need me."

"Joe—"

"I know. You don't remember us. Not really. Once you do…" He moved to a laptop computer sitting on the table.

For a moment, she thought about rushing him, but a wave of nausea forced her to stay where she was.

He opened the laptop and turned back to her. "Let

me show you. I've run The Prophecy now for years without you, even though I don't think you have a lot of faith in me. But take a look at this."

He brought the laptop over to the daybed. "On election night as your husband is about to make his acceptance speech, the world is going to blow sky high. See all these places? That's where bombs will be going off. Countries will fall. In the US alone, more than a dozen key spots will be hit. It will be like the Fourth of July. At a touch of a button, we will start the apocalypse. My people are all waiting for my go-ahead. At a touch of a button…BOOM!"

She tried not to show her horror. "And then what?" she said, her voice sounding relatively calm even to her ears.

"And then chaos, and out of that will come a revolution." He closed the laptop. "I want you with me, by my side. This is what we used to dream of, Sarah. This is our chance. Together there's nothing we can't accomplish."

She closed her eyes, the headache worsening, and opened them only when she heard the door open. Her heart dropped at the sight of Dr. Venable. He'd been the founder of The Prophecy, the oldest of the group back in the 1970s. He was still tall and lean with kind blue eyes, but with a determined look in his face.

Joe rose. "Get me Red back. Whatever it takes. Don't fail me, or you know what will happen," he said to Doc as he put the laptop back on the table by the door and left.

Sarah tried to get up, but Doc stopped her with a hand on her shoulder. He was still strong for his age. While she might be able to overpower him, there would be no getting past Joe outside the door.

"Do you know what he has planned?" she demanded, still in shock at the connected deadly attacks that Joe had orchestrated. It would take nothing more than Joe hitting a button to make it all happen. "He just showed me on that computer over there. We can stop him. We can—"

Dr. Venable pushed harder on her shoulder. "Stop it, Sarah," he snapped, then winced as if in pain.

"Doc—" She saw that his left arm hung limply at his side. "What happened to your arm?"

His gaze me hers. "You have to ask? *Joe* happened. If you doubt what he will do to you and your family, let me show you." He pulled up his sleeve.

She shuddered in horror at the mass of black-and-yellow bruises. It looked as if someone had crushed his arm in a vise. "Don't fight this, Sarah. This is how it has to end."

"No, we can stop him. We can stop all of this. Martin has promised not to send any funding and together—"

He shook his head sadly. "Martin is dead. And in a few minutes you will be Red again."

CHAPTER TWENTY-FOUR

BUCK LOOKED AROUND the rented apartment to see if he'd left anything behind. He wouldn't be coming back here. Catching his image in a mirror by the door, he stopped. He'd aged since this whole political career had begun. But he'd done it. He'd done what his father hadn't been able to accomplish. He'd stayed in the race, and now if the polls were right, he'd be the next president of the United States.

It was a dream come true, and yet there'd been too many times when he'd almost backed out, given it all up, told himself he'd been a fool to run.

But he'd hung in, and now he had his family back and the presidency almost at his fingertips. Just the thought of his wife, though, came with concern. He still didn't believe that she really wanted to live in the White House. He would have given it all up for her. Maybe he wasn't so different from his father, who'd chucked his chances over a woman.

He tried Sarah's cell phone. He hadn't been able to reach her earlier, but by now the charity event should be over. Maybe she would pick up. It went straight to voice mail, and he felt a pang of worry as he pocketed the phone.

He needed to hear her voice. He was flying home tonight. The security detail would be driving him back to the ranch, but he had still wanted to remind her what time he should be arriving. He wanted her there waiting for him. He needed her now more than ever.

Even though the polls had him so far ahead that his election seemed to be a slam dunk, he wouldn't relax until the results were in. He feared that because of what the polls were all saying, a lot of people wouldn't bother to vote, and it could go either way.

"Don't worry about it," Jerrod had said. "We have this one in the bag. You did it—in spite of everything."

Speaking of his campaign manager, he thought, as he heard the knock at his door. Jerrod had been in high spirits for a few days now, so at least he wasn't worried.

"How are you doing, Mr. President?" Jerrod said in greeting and quickly added, "I know, I know. Don't jinx it." He reached for Buck's bag. "A car's waiting to take you to the airport."

He pulled out his phone. Maybe he would try Sarah one more time.

"If you're calling your lovely wife, she probably isn't going to answer," Jerrod said. "I had a last-minute request from a group of Republican women in Helena." He shrugged. "I should have told you. She might not be back until tomorrow."

Buck tried to hide his disappointment.

"But then the two of you will be together and headed for the White House."

"Actually, I'm planning a surprise honeymoon before then," he told his campaign manager. "I'm going to whisk her off for a few days."

"Terrific idea," Jerrod said as picked up Buck's suitcase and ushered him toward the door.

"I wasn't that difficult, was I?" Buck asked on the way to the car.

Jerrod laughed. "Six daughters, one wife, one former wife, one scandal after another. Let's just say that it took some tap dancing to keep abreast of it."

"Well, you are one excellent dancer," he told Jerrod. "I'm sorry I put you through it. You know there will be a place for you on my staff."

Jerrod shook his head. "Thanks, but I might try something else. I've actually thought about going abroad for a while." He shrugged. "Not sure yet."

Buck was surprised by that. He'd assumed Jerrod had been waiting for a position. Clearly he was wrong.

"Will you be coming to the festivities election night?"

"A cold night in Montana? Not a chance. I'll be watching it from a warm bar somewhere. My job is done. Now it's up to you."

Yes, Buck thought as they reached the car and

Jerrod handed off the suitcase to the driver. Now it was up to him. "Well, good luck with whatever you decide to do."

"Thank you, Buck," Jerrod said and shook his hand, giving him the impression that they wouldn't be seeing each other again.

THE NEWS OF Martin's death hit Sarah hard. She lay back against the wall, all hope rushing from her like air from a punctured balloon. Martin hadn't managed to get away. She thought of his son. Poor Jack. At least he had her daughter Cassidy, and he would have the Hamiltons—if any of them survived this.

"There isn't anyone left to stop Joe," Doc said, not unkindly. "Mason Green and Wallace McGill are in prison, Warren Dodge will be, once his trial is over, and John Carter is dead. Joe's recruited more followers, but trust me, you would be wasting your time with them—if you even knew who they were."

Sarah had hoped that by cutting off Joe's funding… But now Martin was dead, and clearly from what Joe had shown her on the laptop, he was moving ahead no matter what. She'd never felt so helpless. "Joe will destroy the world."

"It's the revolution we used to dream of," Doc said wistfully. "Maybe once you're Red again, you'll want to help change things. Or at least finally realize how fighting Joe will only bring you pain and sorrow. Joe is determined you will be by his side—one way or the other."

"Why didn't you and I just stay in Brazil?" she asked, close to tears. She'd brought all of this on her family.

"You know why. Joe found us. He forced me to give you back your memories of your daughters and Buck, because he needed you and Buck back together again. That's why his wife, Angelina, was eliminated."

She shuddered at what Joe had already done as she saw how the events had all come together. "That's why after Brazil I was parachuted back in Montana. Dropped off with no memory of where I'd been or who I'd been those twenty-two years."

Doc nodded. "It wasn't my idea. Joe was obsessed with you. He wouldn't let it go. A committed anarchist. Now, he wants his pound of flesh, and he will get it—if I can't give him back the woman he knew as Red."

"What if you can't?" she asked, grasping on to that thin thread of hope.

"Then we are both as good as dead. People we care about will also die."

She could see that there was no way out. "So all those years ago, Joe must have thought I was coming back to him after I made sure that Buck's father, J.D., became president." She couldn't believe that she'd actually "targeted" Buck, planning to use him in the name of The Prophecy.

Instead, she'd fallen in love with him, had six children with him.

Doc sighed. "No one would have foreseen your father-in-law falling for the teenaged girl next door, dropping out of the race and ending up dead. Clearly, Joe hadn't known what to do then. But he never gave up. When he came to you twenty-three years ago, he wanted you to encourage Buck to run for office. When he realized you were in love with your husband and no longer interested in him or The Prophecy, that's when he...snapped."

"You saved me the night I tried to kill myself," she said, realizing how true that was now. She'd called Doc after a hermit living on the edge of the river had fished her out of the freezing water. Dr. Venable was the only one she thought she could trust. Doc had been working at a clinic in White Sulphur Springs, Montana, experimenting with brain wiping. He believed he could take away bad memories and replace them with good ones.

She'd hated him for what he'd done, but Doc swore that she had pleaded with him to take away her memories because she couldn't live, knowing that she had a husband and six children she loved. For twenty-two years, she'd lived and worked with Doc in South America, not knowing about Buck and her children, but aching for something. She just hadn't known what.

Then one day she'd found herself in the woods. She hadn't known where she'd been. She certainly hadn't known that she'd lost twenty-two years of her life when she'd stumbled out and into the middle of a narrow dirt road outside of Beartooth and into Russell Murdock's life.

Russell had almost hit her with his pickup. He'd thought he was seeing a ghost because he'd been at her funeral twenty-two years before, after her body hadn't been recovered from the Yellowstone River.

She'd been in bad shape. Russell had taken her to the nearest house, where a doctor and his wife had lived. All she'd known was that she had to get to her husband and children. She shuddered as she remembered the shock of finding out that everyone thought she'd been dead for twenty-two years—including her husband, Buck, who'd remarried. Her six daughters were no longer young, her twins no longer babies. Only the oldest ones even remembered her.

"I did the best I could by you, Sarah. I let Joe and the rest of the world believe you were dead, but once he found out about my deception…" Doc looked away, and she knew she was gazing at a broken man. She didn't want to think what Joe had done to him then or would do to him now if he failed.

"So this is about Joe getting revenge against the world, all because I stopped loving him," Sarah said.

"Not entirely. You don't remember how it was in the beginning. It makes me sad," Doc said. "The Prophecy was this small but bright shining light into the future. I had such hopes for the group. And you—" He smiled at her, as if she were the daughter he'd never had. "You had so much fire in you when you were young. You were determined to change the world. You weren't like Joe. You didn't want to kill a bunch of people for the publicity. You really wanted to make changes. But, Sarah? I think that woman is still in you. I think you still are Red."

Her headache was blinding. She couldn't bear what was going to happen. But nor could she stop it. "You're wrong, Doc. I'm not that woman. I'll never be that woman again, no matter what you do to me."

"I guess we'll see, because I'm going to give you back those memories of who you were. Once you remember it all… Well, who knows?"

She braced herself. Isn't this what she'd wanted for so long? All of the memories back? To be whole again? She told herself she wasn't afraid of remembering Red, the woman they told her had been the true leader of The Prophecy. She was *terrified*.

"Even if you can turn me into Red again, what would be the point? Joe has already orchestrated Armageddon."

He smiled sadly and shrugged as he pulled out the velvet bag, opened it and dropped the pendulum into his palm.

Sarah held her breath. The moment of truth. She knew what Doc was capable of doing. If anyone could turn her into Red again, it was Dr. Ralph Venable.

CHAPTER TWENTY-FIVE

SARAH BLINKED. SHE WAS so tired, all she wanted to do was sleep. She forced her eyes to open. The pale yellow room came into view. For a moment, she wondered where she was as her gaze began to take in the paintings on the wall and she remembered. A guest bedroom in a house somewhere.

She shifted her head, then came wide awake as she heard a moan and looked down.

Dr. Venable lay on the floor in a pool of blood.

Sitting up, Sarah swung her legs over the side of the daybed. The movement left her too dizzy to stand for a moment. She waited for it to pass before she moved to the elderly man on the floor.

"Doc," she said, kneeling next to him.

His eyelids fluttered for a moment before he looked up at her. "Red." His voice came out a hoarse whisper. "He would have ruined everything. I couldn't let him hurt you. He would have never believed you were Red again." His fingers let go of the gun she now saw he'd been holding to grasp her hand. "You—" His voice broke.

"Don't try to talk. I'll find a phone and call for

help." She started to rise, but he gripped her hand more tightly.

"No. Time," he said brokenly. "Take. The. Gun."

Her heart was already threatening to beat out of her chest when she realized what he was saying. In her dazed state at waking up and being shocked to see Doc wounded on the floor, she'd forgotten about Joe.

"Take. The. Gun," he repeated.

She swept up the semiautomatic pistol, checked the clip, flipped off the safety and turned toward the door, surprised to find it standing open.

Rising, she moved slowly toward the door. As she did, she noticed that the laptop computer that had been on the table was gone. She still felt light-headed and had to stop short of the doorway to rest for a moment.

Doc made a sound like a death rattle. She looked back to where he lay. His eyes were open, but the blank darkness she saw there told her he'd passed on to hopefully a better place. She felt a stab of pain heart deep, steadied herself and moved with renewed purpose toward the open doorway.

FRANK WALKED AROUND the small, empty one-story brick building, smiling to himself. It was just the right size. Not too big, not too small. He stepped it off. This area would be Lynette's office. Turning, he walked across the wide room to where he would have his. They would have a small kitchen in the back with a coffeepot. There was already a restroom and plenty of space for storage.

He pulled out his cell phone. "I have something I want to show you," he said when his wife answered the phone. He gave her the address.

She'd sounded surprised, either because he was moving so fast or that he was really going to do this. *They* were really going to do this. "I'll be right there."

He put his phone away and inspected every square inch of the building, inside and out. There were large windows in front of the old dwelling set into the brick walls. That's where the sign would go, he thought, glancing at a spot next to the front door. They wouldn't need a large sign. Anyone who needed their services would be able to find them.

Frank felt the thrill of it move through him. He realized he'd never wanted anything so badly in his life—except for Lynette. That he might never get this building or the rest of the life he had planned made him ache. It would all come down to election night.

He told himself he'd done everything possible to protect the future president and his family, short of locking them all up in the jail for the night. Now he just had to have faith that it would all work out. And yet, he couldn't vanquish that sick feeling at the pit of his stomach that he was wasting his time looking at this building.

"What's this?" Lynette said as she got out of her car in front of the building. She was smiling, clearly knowing exactly what this was.

"I need your advice," he said and pushed open the front door.

She stepped in and stopped, no doubt taking in the wood floor, the brick walls, the loft feeling of the remodeled old building. "Can we afford this?" she whispered as if, like him, she'd already fallen in love with it.

"We can," he said, smiling. "I took a chance and already gave them money down on it. Now it's just a matter of deciding where you'd like your office and how you're going to decorate the place."

She turned to him, tears in her eyes, and then she was in his arms, and he was holding her in the building that, God willing, would be the new Curry Investigations.

SARAH GRIPPED THE GUN, her finger a hairbreadth from the trigger. Some people didn't know if they could kill. She didn't suffer from that question as she peered around the corner of the doorway.

Joe was a few yards down the hallway. From the blood trail he'd left, it appeared that he had tried to crawl away. Now he lay perfectly still.

She moved cautiously toward him, keeping the barrel of the weapon pointed at his back. When she'd returned to Montana after all those years, Buck had insisted she learn to shoot a gun. She'd proven to be an expert marksman, but she knew that was because she'd fired a variety of weapons before she'd met him. That memory had been one that Dr. Venable had taken from her—until now.

Approaching slowly, she nudged his expensive leather shoe, seemingly too expensive for a man Martin believed had been a priest. Or had all that been merely a disguise? Joe didn't react. She kicked harder. Still nothing.

The way he was sprawled, she would have to step past him. That would be the most dangerous part, she thought. Then she saw the laptop tucked under his arm. No, the most dangerous would be when she tried to pull the laptop from under his body—if there was any life left in him.

The house was deathly quiet as she moved closer. She couldn't tell whether or not Joe was breathing. Nor was she going to check for a pulse. She moved closer, shifting the gun into her right hand and stepping alongside him. Pressing the end of the barrel to his temple, she reached for the laptop.

SAWYER TRIED TO stand on his bad leg. A stab of blinding pain shot up his calf into his thigh. With a curse, he fell back into the chair where he'd been sitting.

"You keep walking on it instead of using the crutches, and it is never going to heal," his doctor had told him impatiently. "Stop being a tough guy. Put the leg up, stay off of it, or you're going to end up back in the hospital."

The problem was that he needed to be a tough guy. He needed to be able to walk. Instead, he had no choice but to use the crutches tomorrow night at the Beartooth Fairgrounds. How was he going to watch out for Ainsley when he couldn't move faster than a tortoise?

His cell phone rang. He made a silent wish that it was Ainsley. It was Pete Corran, Kitzie's partner. He almost didn't take it. "Yes?"

"It's me," Kitzie said. "Pete loaned me his phone. Don't hang up. I thought you'd like to know that I just got fairground duty for tomorrow night. I know you're out of commission. I figured you would be worried about Ainsley. I wanted you to know that I'll be there."

"And this is supposed to relieve my mind, given what you've done in the past?"

"That's all behind us."

"Really? How do I know you won't try to get her drunk?"

"Come on, Sawyer. You have to admit it was fun seeing that side of Ainsley. By the way, I'm sorry."

He growled in answer and disconnected, telling himself he was glad Kitzie would be watching out for Ainsley. But there was no way he wasn't going to be there, as well.

JOE WAS HEAVIER than he looked. Sarah was forced to lay the gun down and use both hands to pull the laptop out from under him. It was smeared with blood but didn't look to have been damaged. She wouldn't know until she opened it.

She tucked the laptop under her arm and picked up the gun again. Joe still hadn't moved. She quickly stepped away from him and stopped to listen. No sound came from the house. She still had no idea where she was, but as she headed toward what she assumed was the front of the home, she spotted her SUV parked outside. Past the vehicle were the Crazy Mountains. The landmark told her the general area. She would be able to figure out how to get out of here.

As she pushed open the front door and headed down the steps, her one hope was that Joe had left the keys in the SUV. Otherwise, she would have to go back inside the house and search his body for them. With a sense of urgency already driving her, she didn't want to waste any more time with Joe Landon.

Reaching the SUV, she opened the door, laid the laptop on the passenger seat and felt for the ignition. The keys jangled as her fingers brushed them.

For the first time since she'd opened her eyes, she let herself breathe as she slid behind the wheel. The SUV engine roared to life. Glancing at the house, she half expected to see Joe framed in the doorway with an assault rifle in his hands.

She threw the SUV into Reverse, the image of her windshield exploding on the bullet's impact too vivid in her mind.

Sarah tore off down the road, headed in the direction of Big Timber. All the months of worrying about Red and that part of her memory that had been missing was now gone. She knew exactly who she was and what she was going to do.

CHAPTER TWENTY-SIX

"MRS. HAMILTON IS here to see you, Sheriff," the dispatcher said. Something in her voice warned him. "She says it's urgent. You might want to—"

"Send her back." Frank heard a door open, then the sound of staggering footfalls. He frowned and was getting to his feet to investigate as Sarah Johnson Hamilton appeared in his office doorway.

"Sarah?" Her hair and clothes were in disarray and unless he was mistaken, there was blood on the hem of her dress. There was a bruise on her cheek and blood on her swollen lower lip. But it was the look in her eyes that shocked him the most as she stepped in and closed the door.

Without a word, she moved to his desk and put down what she'd been carrying under her arm. He stared at the blood-smeared laptop computer, then at her. "What is this?"

"It's all there—the series of coordinated deadly attacks The Prophecy has planned for tomorrow night. It will be the most devastating attack in history if you don't stop it."

"How did you—"

"It doesn't matter how I got it. You can stop him."

"Stop whom?"

"Prophecy leader Joe Landon and his plan to kill hundreds—if not thousands—of people across the world on election night." She brushed her hands together as if she had washed them of it. Her palms were dark with dried blood. "It's all in there, where they plan to hit, how many people are involved, everything. If you move fast, you can stop it."

"Sarah, if what you say is on this computer, I have to know where you got it and how you're involved."

Tears welled in her blue eyes. "It's up to you now." She turned as if to walk away.

"I can't let you leave."

Stopping at the door, she turned back to him. "You don't want to arrest me. The wife of the next president of the United States? But more importantly, you don't want to alert The Prophecy by holding me here. If you don't act at once on what is in there, you will regret it the rest of your life. Joe's password is Armageddon. I saw him mouth the letters when he typed it in."

She took a step and staggered. Her hand went to her temple.

"You're hurt," he said, moving to her quickly.

"No. I'm fine. I've never been better." Her gaze came up to his. "Sheriff, you have more important things to do than worry about me. Joe's dead. So is Dr. Venable. After you take care of what's on that computer, I'll tell you where you can find them both."

"I'm going to get one of my deputies to drive you to the hospital."

"No, I drove myself here. I can get home just fine. Don't let me down, Frank. Don't let the country down." With that she pulled away from him, opened the door and staggered down the hallway and out into the fall day.

Frank turned back to the laptop on his desk, a chill moving through him.

BUCK HAD BEEN busy all day. With Sarah in Helena, he hadn't wanted to come home to an empty house. He was furious at her for giving her Secret Service detail the slip. Worse, those men would be reprimanded. He still hadn't been able to reach his wife by phone. He tried not to worry, but after months of being suspicious of Sarah, he couldn't help it. That feeling of doom was heavy in his chest. He felt as if he was now just waiting for the other shoe to drop.

He was surprised to come home to find Sarah's car out front and Ainsley waiting for him. "Where's your mother?" he asked after giving his daughter a hug.

"I don't know. Her car is here, but I haven't seen her. I've been here all day." Ainsley frowned. "She must have parked and then come in the back door. Why would she do that?"

"You must have been in the kitchen when she came in," he said, annoyed that she would be suspicious of Sarah—just like the rest of his daughters.

"She's probably upstairs and didn't even realize you were here. I'll run up and say hello to your mother. Do you need anything?" he asked.

Ainsley shook her head. "No, actually I'm meeting Olivia and the twins. We're all excited about tomorrow night."

"Me, too," he said, pleased that his entire family would be there. "I just hope I win."

"Are we going to have to call you Mr. President?" she joked.

He laughed as he started up the stairs, anxious to see Sarah. He hadn't been able to reach her on all his attempts to call her. He wasn't about to tell Ainsley, but unfortunately there were times that he, too, had suspicions about their mother.

At their bedroom door, he heard the sound of the shower running. He stepped in, closing the door softly behind him. As he neared the bathroom, he was surprised to hear what sounded like…singing. *Sarah was singing?* He hadn't heard her do that for so many years that it made him stop for a moment in surprise.

"Sarah?" he called as he tried the bathroom door. The knob turned in his hand. He stuck his head into the steam-filled room. "Sarah?"

The singing stopped. "You made it home," she said, peeking around the end of the large walk-in shower. "Wanna join me?"

For a moment, she looked so much like the young woman he'd married the first time that he only stared at her. He felt something cold settle in his belly for a second. There was definitely something different about her, but he couldn't put his finger on what it was.

"I changed my hair," she said. "You really can't tell since it's still wet. Sure you don't want a closer look?"

Buck shook off whatever had made him hesitate and smiled as he began to take off his clothes. This was his Sarah. She was back.

THE NEXT MORNING it was all over the news. Homeland Security was taking credit for the huge bust involving a dozen terrorists, thousands of pounds of explosives and what would have been an orchestrated attack from inside the US—as well as around the world—by an anarchist group from the late 1970s.

Sarah watched it on the television only long enough to make sure that the sheriff had managed to make all the necessary arrests. When Buck left to go downstairs to breakfast, she told him she would be there in a few minutes.

She placed the call to the sheriff and told him where she thought the house was that she'd been held in. She'd been too worked up yesterday as she was driving toward town to pay a whole lot of attention to the turns she'd made.

"I'm sure you'll be able to find it," she told Frank.

"Sarah?"

"Yes?" she said and held her breath.

"I kept you out of it."

"Thank you, Frank."

"Don't make me sorry I did."

Disconnecting, she went downstairs to join her husband and found a few of their daughters had stopped by.

"What did you do to your hair?" Kat demanded, sounding less surprised than horrified.

Sarah touched her usually pale blond hair as she glanced toward the mirror on the far wall. She liked the color. It suited her. "It was starting to get gray. Can't have the future president's wife with gray hair," she said with a laugh. "Anyway, I needed a change. You girls change your hair color all the time."

"A change?" Kat repeated.

Her other daughters stepped in quickly to tell her it looked wonderful.

"It becomes you," Olivia said. Harper and Cassidy agreed. Ainsley said it was attractive on her.

"It's...*red*," Kat said, her gaze intent on her mother.

"Just a little," Sarah said. "Now I'm a strawberry blonde," she said, meeting Kat's eyes. "Don't make more of it than it is. Anyway, your father likes it."

NETTIE DID HER best not to think about tonight. She had the day off from the general store, but she still drove into Beartooth to the Branding Iron.

Kate was surprised to see her. "The usual?"

"Make sure it is a big one and center cut," Nettie

said of the homemade cinnamon rolls. She'd always eaten when she was nervous. She'd never been more nervous than she was now.

Kate joined her at the table, bringing the cinnamon roll, two forks and butter. Her waitress, Callie, appeared with two cups and a carafe of hot coffee.

"How are you holding up?" Kate whispered as Callie left them. There were a few tables of residents scattered around the small café. The air smelled of bacon, coffee and cinnamon rolls.

Nettie breathed it in, enjoying the scents, as well as the rattle of dishes and the murmur of voices. She felt at home here and loved her visits with Kate, even though there were several generations between them.

"I'm trying not to think about it, but Frank seems confident that there won't be any trouble," Nettie whispered back. She leaned toward Kate. "But he asked me to stay home."

"That just means he's being cautious."

Nettie nodded as she lathered butter on her side of the roll and cut off a piece with her fork. She took a bite, closing her eyes and enjoying the wonderful flavors. Kate made the best cinnamon rolls of any place Nettie had ever been.

"There is something that gives me hope," she said after a few moments. "He's retiring after the election."

"I thought you were worried that he'd go crazy with nothing to do?"

"I was until he told me that he wants to open

Curry Investigations, and—" she met her friend's gaze "—he wants me to be his partner. He took me to see the building he's buying. It's perfect."

Kate laughed joyously. "That is the best news I've heard. You were made to be an investigator."

Nettie had to smile. When Kate had first come to town, she and Nettie had gotten off on the wrong foot. Mostly because Nettie had known that Kate was hiding something about her past and had been determined to find out what.

Of course, she'd been right. Amazingly, Kate had still become her friend.

"You really don't know what's going to happen tonight?" Kate asked.

Nettie knew she was asking about the pendulum. She'd first heard about pendulums after the doctor's wife had told someone about the tattoo she'd seen on Sarah Johnson Hamilton's posterior. The wife had helped her doctor husband access Sarah's injuries the day Sarah had turned up after twenty-two years. Sarah had stumbled out of the trees right in front Russell Murdock's pickup. He'd rushed her to the closest doctor, a retired physician who lived up the road.

Nettie had been curious about pendulums afterward and ordered one. While it only answered yes and no questions, she'd instantly gotten hooked.

She'd gotten so dependent on it that she'd forced herself to throw it away. "Believe me, I've regretted getting rid of the stupid thing, and yet…it scared me. I decided it was better not to know what was going to happen—if anything. How are the kids?" she asked, changing the subject.

"Good. Jack is great with them, even the twins. I like getting to spend some time down here at the café. I have the best of both worlds since I get to see you. Otherwise, I probably wouldn't have a cinnamon roll." She laughed as she cut herself a piece with her fork.

They both ate and drank to the comforting sounds of the café.

"I'm happy for you, Nettie, though with your new job, you may be too busy to stop by in the mornings," Kate said.

"I will never be that busy." She reached across the table and took Kate's hand. "No matter what happens, we will always be friends."

Nettie glanced at her watch. "I'd better get to work. I'm putting in a few hours at the store." It was just across the street. "It will probably be busy with everyone out voting today."

Kate nodded. "The café, too. That's why I came in. That and to have coffee and a cinnamon roll with you." She smiled, but it quickly faded. "Do me a favor. Do as your husband asks. Stay away from the fairgrounds tonight. It will be televised. You'll be much warmer at home. *Promise*."

SHERIFF FRANK CURRY sent two deputies and the coroner out to find the house Sarah had described to him. He didn't doubt they would discover exactly what she'd said they would. She'd been right about what was on the laptop.

"Where did you get this information?" That had been the question he'd been asked repeatedly.

"From an anonymous source, but I have reason to believe that it is accurate." Given the recent attacks in the world, he hadn't had to spend much time convincing Homeland Security.

Then he had sat back and waited, praying Sarah hadn't duped him and was now on some overseas flight to a foreign country. It hadn't taken long for the news to start coming in as the busts were made. One after another, all of it had been true, including what they'd found in an old barn farther down in the Sweet Grass Valley—enough explosives to blow Beartooth off the map.

Still, Frank couldn't help but question his own judgment in letting Sarah walk away. He felt a chill as he remembered looking into her blue eyes. He'd known exactly what he'd been searching for—Red, the real leader of The Prophecy.

All the time he'd been gazing into her eyes, he'd been reminding himself what it had been like to be young and foolish. Wasn't it possible Sarah had gotten involved in something and found herself in over her head? People could change, couldn't they?

There was no doubt in his mind that Sarah Johnson Hamilton had been the notorious Red. But yesterday she had saved thousands of people's lives.

He'd never really understood what The Prophecy

had hoped to accomplish. Why start a revolution if you didn't know what you were going to do with the country once you overthrew it?

Frank told himself that Sarah had been young and impressionable. Hadn't she proven she no longer believed in any of that when she'd turned over the computer?

When he'd seen her interviewed on television this morning as she and Buck were coming out after voting, she'd looked into the camera and said, "Buck is going to be a great president, and I am going to work hard to be a First Lady that the country can be proud of. Together, we're going to make our country better. I can promise you that."

If the polls were right, she and Buck would be living in the White House soon. Early this morning when she'd called with the directions to the house, he'd wanted to wish her well, but the words had caught in his throat.

Now he walked over to his polling location and cast his vote. He knew Lynette had voted on her way to work her half day at the Beartooth General Store. The four-block walk did him good. It had cleared his head by the time he returned to his office.

Opening his drawer, he pulled out his resignation letter. If Homeland Security, the FBI and the National Guard hadn't missed anything at the Beartooth Fairgrounds, and tonight went off without a hitch, he was done. Either way he was done, he thought with a wry smile.

He looked around his office, a place he'd grown accustomed to for so many years, and felt a lump form in his throat. His eyes burned for a moment, but he blinked the moisture away as he rose. He focused on the future and his next adventure with Lynette by his side, God willing, after tonight.

CHAPTER TWENTY-SEVEN

SARAH TRIED TO relax on the ride to the Beartooth Fairgrounds. They'd all piled into the Suburban being led by FBI agents in another vehicle in front of them and more behind them. She told herself that Joe and The Prophecy were both dead, their legacies now for the history books.

"Am I the only one who is excited?" Cassidy asked as they drove through the dark toward the towering snowcapped Crazies.

There was a general murmur before everyone fell silent again. This was it. The night Buckmaster Hamilton would become the president of the United States. They'd caught enough of the news to know that he was leading across the country.

Even Buck was quiet. He'd insisted on driving himself, rather than have an agent drive them. Sarah reached over and gave his arm a reassuring squeeze. He glanced at her and smiled, then turned back to his driving.

"Bo, are you all right?" Ainsley asked.

"I wish everyone would quit asking me that," Bo snapped. "I'll let you know if I go into labor."

"Your water will probably break up on the stage in front of the world," Kat said.

"Thanks," Bo said with a shake of her head. "I really need that right now."

"It's all going to be all right," Sarah said with more confidence than she felt. Joe had been stopped. The Prophecy had been stopped. And yet, she knew that she wouldn't relax until this night was over.

THE SHERIFF WATCHED the presidential candidate and his family arrive at the fairgrounds and said a prayer. Secret Service and National Guard escorted them to the huge stage that had been built for the event.

Frank had personally inspected every square inch of the venue and kept security tight. People had been streaming in for hours through a metal detector, and any bags inspected. It was cold, so everyone was wearing more clothes than he would have liked, but he was assured that if anyone tried to get in with a weapon, they would be caught.

Just hours before, the whole area had been checked by dogs trained to find bombs. They'd found nothing. He thought of the information that Sarah had turned over to him. Some of the attacks Joe Landon had planned included drones. It was a changing world, one Frank no longer felt safe in. But the National Guard was also prepared for an air strike.

Frank had covered all the bases he could. Now all that was left to do was pray. He was just glad that Lynette had promised to stay home. He wished most of these people had done the same thing—including the future president's daughters and their significant others.

As the family disembarked from the Suburban, he caught a glimpse of Sarah. He tried to tell himself that she wouldn't have turned in the computer if she was the leader of The Prophecy. But she had definitely been involved. Not that he could prove it. He wanted to trust her and yet he might be resigning as sheriff, but he would always think like a lawman.

His cell phone rang. "Sheriff Curry."

"We finally found the house," one of his new deputies told him.

He'd almost forgotten about the house where Sarah had said they would find two bodies, those of Dr. Ralph Venable and a man named Joe Landon, a man believed to have been a co-leader of The Prophecy.

"Unfortunately, there are no bodies here."

"Then you have the wrong house," Frank said, watching Sarah walk with Buck toward the back area of the stage. He repeated the directions Sarah had given him.

"That's where we are. We did find blood that hadn't been cleaned up in a crack in the floorboards. It looks fresh, but someone has recently washed down this place with gallons of bleach."

He gripped the phone, fear turning his bowels to water. "Check the area again and get back to me." As he disconnected, his mind raced. Sarah hadn't told him about the two dead men until the day *after* she'd given him the computer. That left plenty of time to dispose of the bodies—and the evidence.

Frank mentally kicked himself for letting her walk away that day. *But she saved the lives of thousands of people.* And covered up the murder of two? It didn't make any sense, and there was no way he was going to get any answers tonight, he thought, as he watched Buck take Sarah's hand and they came up the wide stairs.

She looked radiant. He frowned; she'd changed her hair, but it only made her more beautiful. All these months waiting for the other shoe to drop… She ushered her daughters toward the shelter that had been built for them at the back of the stage like a mother duck rounding up her ducklings.

This is what the world would see, Frank thought. This all-American family. And maybe that's exactly what it was now. He desperately wanted to believe it was true. The cop in him had too many questions. And even more suspicions.

He reminded himself that he wouldn't be following up on them. Tonight was his last night as sheriff. He had resigned. He wouldn't be the one worrying about what would happen now. Not as sheriff, anyway.

Frank told himself he'd done everything he could as he moved to a spot where he could see the growing crowd. Again he cursed Buck for picking this venue. The only good news was that it was cold enough this

November night that people wouldn't want to stay too long after Buck made his acceptance speech. He would win, just as projected. The election results had been coming in all evening.

Music blared through large speakers set up around the bottom of the stage. A huge American flag moved restlessly in the night breeze. There was an excitement in the air. Buckmaster would be the first Montanan to win a presidential election. It was a big night for the state—just as it was a big night for the Hamiltons.

Sarah and her daughters were tucked away in a warm room at the back of the stage. In a few moments, the results would be announced, and Buck would come out with Sarah. Frank tried to breathe. Everywhere he looked there were agents or National Guard or deputies.

But as he was turning to go back around the grandstand for another security check, he spotted something that made him curse.

Lynette. She'd promised she wouldn't come here tonight, but he should have known she wouldn't be able to stop herself. His wife had to be where the action was. Far be it that she miss something—even if it might be dangerous.

His cell phone chirped. He checked it.

Election results were in. Buckmaster had won by a landslide. The music stopped as the results were announced. The crowd roared.

"Here we go."

AINSLEY WAS FIGHTING tears when she felt a hand on her arm and turned to find Sawyer leaning on his crutches next to her.

"What are you doing here?" she asked in surprise, her words lost in the roar of the crowd.

He motioned for her to follow him, and they stepped outside the room where they'd been cloistered into a pocket of semi-quiet behind the stage.

"Sawyer, you shouldn't be here. Your leg—"

"Is fine. I had to come." He shrugged. "I had to make sure you were all right."

She shook her head and looked away for a moment. "I appreciate everything you did. You saved my life in more ways than you can imagine. But I don't need you to save me anymore."

"Are you going back to law school?"

The question caught her flat-footed. "I don't know yet. I just know I'm not the same woman you met that day in the canyon."

"I liked that woman."

She laughed, tears springing to her eyes. "You seemed to like every incarnation of Ainsley Hamilton."

He smiled. "Yeah, I do."

"I have to get back." But she hesitated. "Maybe when this is over..." She could have kicked herself.

"I'm going to hold you to that," he said, his smile shining in his gray eyes.

It was impulsive. She was merely caught up in the moment with her father about to become president.

Why else would she suddenly step to him, take his face in her hands and kiss him?

He reached for her awkwardly with his crutches under each arm, but she slipped away before he could hold her. Otherwise, she feared she would never want to leave his arms.

She left him there and didn't look back until she reached the door to the room where her family was waiting for her. He was still standing there, leaning on his crutches, his gaze locked on her. The look in his eyes was almost her undoing.

"Where have you been?" Olivia demanded, dragging her into the room. "Come on. Dad is waiting for us."

BUCK TOOK SARAH'S HAND, glanced at his daughters behind them and began the walk out to meet the public. The crowd's roar was deafening. The floor of the stage seemed to vibrate. Overhead a midnight-blue canopy glittered with stars in Montana's big sky. They stood in the shadow of the Crazy Mountains on a November night just miles from Hamilton Ranch. This was home. This would always be home.

Sarah had never felt like this. The cheering seemed to fill her with helium. She doubted her feet touched the stage. Buck gripped her hand as if he was never going to let her go. She smiled over at him, feeling happier than she knew she'd ever been in her life. Happier than she had a right to.

As their six daughters joined them, the cheering

grew even louder. All she could do was smile and wave to the crowd, more grateful than any of them could ever know. Buck turned to her, pulling her close to kiss her quickly on the mouth, before letting her hand go. The crowd loved it. The crowd loved them.

Sarah gave a final wave and left Buck to do his thing as she ushered the girls back toward the warmth of the stage room where they would watch the rest of the ceremony.

Behind them, Buck said, "Fellow Americans. Fellow Montanans!" His voice boomed out over the hundreds of people who had gathered in the cold to celebrate this moment.

Sarah and her daughters had almost reached the other end of the platform when Ainsley stopped, stumbling as if catching her heel. Sarah grabbed her arm to steady her—and saw the ghost from her past as Joe Landon raised the odd-looking weapon. Their gazes met and locked for that split second before she saw him pull the trigger.

SAWYER HAD FELT too trapped at the back of the platform. As hard as it was to get around on the crutches, he knew he had to be down with the crowd. He worked his way along the side of the raised platform that had been built for this event.

The place was crawling with security. That should have made him feel relieved, but he knew Sheriff

Frank Curry too well. Frank wouldn't be worried unless there was good reason to be.

He reached a spot where he could see Ainsley with her family. She was so beautiful. He ran his tongue lightly over his lower lip, remembering the kiss. It gave him hope—just as her last words to him. Once this was over—

Sarah and her daughters had left Buckmaster and were headed back when he saw Ainsley stumble. He saw the expression on her face as she staggered to a stop and felt his heart drop. She was looking down at someone in the crowd. Her mother had grabbed her arm to steady her.

Sawyer pushed his way through the crowd toward the spot where Ainsley was staring as quickly as he could, but it was nearly impossible with the damned crutches. Finally, he dropped one and used the other to force his way through the crowd.

His leg protested the moment he put weight on it, but he ignored the pain. Something was wrong. *Very* wrong.

He was almost to the spot when he saw the man holding what looked like some kind of homemade weapon. He lunged for him, but his bad leg slowed him down. Out of the corner of his eye, he saw Ainsley push her mother aside and dive off the platform toward the man with the gun.

The pop of the gunshot was so faint no one seemed to have heard it as Ainsley crashed into the man, driving him to the ground. Sawyer stumbled and dropped beside her. If only he had been just seconds faster. If only... He had her in his arms.

"She's hit!" he cried, looking around for an agent and seeing Kitzie pushing her way through the crowd toward him. "Get an ambulance! Hurry! Ainsley, can you hear me? Stay with me, sweetheart."

"Sawyer?" Kitzie's voice so close to his ear made him look over at her. She had the man with the gun down. What he saw turned his blood to ice. Under the priest's robes were enough explosives to level everything for a half mile.

He swept Ainsley up into his arms. Her eyes fluttered open. She blinked, but then her lids dropped down again. He began to force his way through the crowd, his leg screaming with each step as he headed for one of the waiting ambulances.

KITZIE TRIED NOT to panic as she stared down at the priest, shocked that the bomb hadn't gone off when Ainsley had taken the man down. She quickly ordered several of the National Guardsmen to move the crowd back. So far, no one seemed to have seen the explosives.

Buckmaster was in the middle of his acceptance speech, most of the crowd unaware of what was going on at the side of the stage.

She quickly tried to assess the situation. There was a lot of blood. At first she'd thought it was Ainsley's, since she'd seen her take the bullet.

But as she looked further, she found that the priest

appeared to have been wounded. Now he lay barely breathing, as if Ainsley had knocked out what little life had been left in him.

But Kitzie didn't take any chances. She removed the weapon from his hand, grabbed both of his wrists at once and rolled him to his side just enough that she could snap on the cuffs behind his back. Now she had to deal with the bomb. The National Guard had moved the crowd back, but short of clearing the fairgrounds and the area for a mile… She knew that would only cause a panic. "I need your help," she said into her phone and gave her location. "Alert the bomb squad."

A few moments later, Pete joined her. He dropped down beside her, frowning. "What—"

She pulled back the priest's robes so he could see enough of the explosives to understand what they were up against.

Pete let out a curse. "We need to clear the area, wait for the bomb squad—"

"What if there isn't time? Not to mention what panic would do to this crowd."

He looked down at the dying priest. "Is there a timer on it?"

She'd had some training. "Not that I could see."

"Then he would have had a detonating device," Pete said. "Why don't you let me—"

"No," she said quickly. "I have it. Just block the crowd with your coat so they don't see what's going on."

She took a steadying breath and very carefully

began to search the man for anything that could be used as a detonating devise. As it turned out, it was a cell phone.

WITH AINSLEY IN his arms, Sawyer made it on his bad leg as far as one of the ambulances parked at the back of the fairgrounds before he collapsed. Two EMTs quickly took Ainsley. A third came back for him.

"No, I need to go back—"

"I'm sorry, but you're going with us," the EMT said when Sawyer attempted to get up and couldn't.

He looked back toward the platform where Buckmaster was winding up his speech to the roar of the crowd. He knew the EMT was right. Anyway, the bomb was in good hands, he told himself, praying it was true as he let himself be loaded into the ambulance.

Two of the EMTs were working on Ainsley.

"Is she going to make it?" he asked.

Neither answered as he heard the ambulance engine roar to life. He reached over to take Ainsley's hand as he laid back and closed his eyes against the pain both in his leg and his heart. He couldn't lose her. Not after everything they'd been through. She had to make it.

CHAPTER TWENTY-EIGHT

"How long has he been here?" Kitzie asked her partner when she reached the hospital room. Sawyer was sound asleep in a chair next to Ainsley's hospital bed.

"He's refused to leave her side," Pete said. "I've brought him food, but he hasn't been hungry. The doctor said he should be in a hospital bed himself, but you know how stubborn he can be."

She nodded. "I know."

"This is the first sleep he's gotten."

They left Sawyer and Ainsley and walked down the hallway to a waiting room. Pete got them each a cup of coffee from the pot in the corner before they sat down.

"How are you doing?" Pete asked.

Kitzie nodded. "Okay."

"You saved the day. It's all over the news."

She'd thought this was the kind of praise that she'd always wanted. Her boss had even shaken her hand and said, "Good job, McCormick. I believe you will be getting a commendation from the president himself once he takes office."

"Not a great way to start your presidency, with

someone trying to kill you at your acceptance speech and instead hitting one of your daughters," Pete said.

"She knew him."

"What? Who?"

Kitzie looked up to meet her partner's eyes. "The First Lady, Sarah Hamilton, she knew the priest." They'd all been surprised to learn that he really had been a priest and wasn't just in a disguise.

"Why would you say that?" Pete asked, looking around to be sure no one could hear them.

"I heard her say his name. Joe."

"Joe? Over that roaring crowd, you heard her say *Joe*?"

"She'd fallen when her daughter had pushed her aside. She was on her hands and knees just inches from me when I reached the priest. I heard her say 'No, oh, no, Joe.' Believe me, she knew him."

Pete shook his head. "If you're suggesting—"

"I'm not suggesting anything," she said quickly. "It was just…odd."

"Yeah, I'd say. You didn't mention this to—"

"You're the only person I've told. Like you said, I might be mistaken." She wasn't, and now they both knew it. If the priest hadn't died, she wondered what story he would have told.

"It is…odd, as you say, since I saw some of the witness statements that were taken. They all said he wasn't pointing the gun at the president elect."

Kitzie shook her head. "He was pointing it at the president's *wife*. If Ainsley hadn't pushed her mother aside and stepped into the line of fire, Sarah would have been killed." She let out a laugh. "Maybe Ainsley and Sawyer do belong together."

"How are you feeling physically?" Pete asked, as if not wanting to get into the Sawyer discussion with her.

"I've been better. Once the ribs have healed, I'll be able to breathe again."

"Well, the boss loves you," Pete said.

Had he not brought Molly Griffin into the bust, Kitzie would have been overjoyed by the news. "Too bad he didn't have more faith in me on the jewelry-heists bust."

"He will next time," Pete said.

Next time. She finished her coffee and stood. "I'm going to go see how Ainsley is doing."

Pete shook his head. "You're really going to wake Nash?"

She waved his question off as she left the waiting room to walk down the hall to Ainsley's room. So much had happened, she was still trying to digest it.

She'd never wanted anything but to be an FBI agent, and yet she hadn't risen in the ranks like she'd thought she would. Or should have. Nor had she received the credit she thought she deserved. Until now. So why didn't it make her happier? Isn't this what she'd always wanted?

As she stepped into the room, Sawyer opened his eyes from where he'd been sleeping beside Ainsley's bed and sat up. He looked like hell, and she felt a deep ache of regret rise from her conscience.

It took him a moment to focus on her. While this probably wasn't the best time—

He motioned for her to leave, that he would follow her out of the room. She watched as he grabbed his crutches and got to his feet, the effort clearly painful to his wounded leg.

"I thought you were supposed to stay off that leg?" she said, breaking the ice as he closed Ainsley's hospital room door behind him.

"And I thought you wouldn't have the nerve to come here," he said.

"Nerve has never been my problem," she said and rushed on before he could stop her. "I'm sorry."

"You already said that when you called using Pete's phone."

"Only because I knew you wouldn't talk to me otherwise."

"I wasn't really in the mood to talk about it then, and I'm still not." He started to turn back to Ainsley's hospital room.

Kitzie touched his arm. "If I could take it all back—"

"But you can't." He swung on her. "You can't just play with people's lives to suit yourself."

"I'll never do anything like that again."

"I wish that was true, for your next former boyfriend's sake. It wasn't even about me. You just don't like to lose. Everything is a contest with you. The minute I told you why I was on that production site, you went after Ainsley when there wasn't even a contest."

She hated hearing the words, worse, the truth of them. "I loved you."

He shook his head. "That's your defense? Love? All's fair in love and war?"

"All right, it wasn't about love. It was about taking something from you since you took something from me."

He stared at her. "You do realize how crazy that sounds, don't you? What did I take from you?"

"My idea of a perfect life. Both of us agents. Both of us working together. I wanted that, and you took it away when you broke up with me. Now nothing seems…right."

"Even though you're an American hero?"

"It wasn't like I *defused* the bomb."

Sawyer looked as if he didn't know what to say for a moment, and then he laughed, surprising her. "Something's missing in your life, right? It isn't me, Kitzie. You and I barely had a relationship. Work was the *only* thing we had in common. Are you so blind that you don't see what is right in front of your face?"

It was her turn to stare in confusion.

"*Pete.* He's been in love with you since his first day." He shook his head again and turned back toward Ainsley's door. "Get a clue, Kitzie. Work will never fill that hole in our lives. I've only recently learned that." With that he reentered the hospital room, leaving her standing out in the hall.

Pete?

AINSLEY OPENED HER eyes and blinked a couple of times before the room came into focus. Hospital room?

She turned her head to find Sawyer sound asleep in the chair next to her. She held her breath, not wanting to wake him. There was a few days' growth of beard on his jawline and dark circles under his eyes. His Stetson balanced on one knee. She watched the slow, steady rise and fall of his chest and listened to his soft breaths, transfixed.

What was he doing here? Everything came back like a movie on fast forward. The last thing she remembered was being in his arms.

He stirred, groaning slightly as he shifted his bad leg. She saw the crutches leaning against the wall and thought of him at the fairgrounds election night. He shouldn't have been there and yet—

He opened his eyes slowly as if he knew when he did that she would be looking at him. His smile was heart-melting. "You're awake," he said quietly. "Do you need anything?"

She shook her head. She had everything she'd ever wanted right here. "How long have you been here?"

"Not long." It wasn't true and she knew it. "I'm just so glad you're going to be all right. Are you in much pain?"

Again, she shook her head. "What happened to the man who—"

"He won't be hurting you again."

"He wasn't trying to hurt me. It was my mother…" She frowned, wondering if she'd remembered it wrong.

"You saved her life."

Ainsley leaned back against the pillow, processing what he'd said and trying to match it to the flashes of memory. "So he's dead?"

He nodded.

"What was his name?" She could tell he didn't want to talk about the shooter. "I need to know."

"Joe Landon, but he had a handful of aliases. One of them was as a priest named John David Williams."

Joe. Oh, no, Joe! That was what her mother had called out. She hadn't imagined it. He was the man she'd seen her mother fighting with all those years ago. Not a stable hand, as she'd said.

"He was the leader of an anarchist group called—"

"The Prophecy."

He looked at her in surprise. "How did you know that?"

She shook her head. "Maybe someone mentioned it here at the hospital." She could tell by his skeptical expression that he doubted that was the case.

He reached for her hand. "Don't worry about any of that. You're safe. Your family is safe. It's all over."

She nodded, not feeling safe this close to Sawyer.

Her heart rate had kicked up, and she felt flushed. "You saved me again. Aren't you getting tired of it?"

"Never! If my leg hadn't betrayed me, I would have saved you a bullet. I'm sorry."

She shook her head, unable not to smile at him. "You were there when I needed you most."

"Actually, you're the one who saved me." His gaze locked with hers. "I didn't know what my life was missing until I met you."

She looked into his eyes and knew she couldn't fight it anymore. She'd fallen for this man. This complicated man with a complicated past, she reminded herself. "I thought I heard Kitzie's voice earlier."

"Kitzie was here. She was worried about you."

"She didn't come to see me. It was you she was looking for. She's certainly determined."

He laughed and shook his head. "She and Pete are an item now. Or at least they will be soon."

"How do you know that?" she asked amused.

"I'm smarter than I look." He smiled, then sobered. "She pulled all those tricks on you to get back at me. I'm sorry about that. But she didn't really think that I would fall in love with you."

Her smile broadened. "But she does now?"

He nodded, smiling. "She knows that I'm crazy about you."

"What about the next damsel you have to rescue?" she asked.

"Only as part of my job." He made a cross over his heart. "Kitzie and I weren't right for each other.

I just realized it before she did. I've never met anyone I wanted to marry before. Now that I have… Ainsley, I want to marry you." He held up his hand to keep her from speaking, even though she was too surprised to say a word. "I want the old Ainsley, the new Ainsley, whatever Ainsley might be around in the future. I want you."

She swallowed. "Sawyer, we hardly know each other."

"That's why we can't waste a minute. We need to start the moment we both get out of this hospital. I love you, Ainsley. So, what do you say?"

She looked into his gray eyes, felt a well of love rise inside her. She'd fought it for so long, afraid of the powerful feelings he'd ignited in her. The new Ainsley was up for the adventure. The old Ainsley?

Her gaze locked with his. A tremor of excitement went through her. What could she say but yes to a life with this cowboy?

CHAPTER TWENTY-NINE

BUCK LOVED THE sound of family in the big ranch house he'd built all those years ago. He looked around the room at his beautiful daughters and felt such a well of pride that tears came to his eyes. That he'd come so close to losing one of them still shook him to his core.

Fortunately, the bullet that had hit Ainsley had missed any vital organs. She'd healed nicely. The fact that she was in love made her glow.

He looked at his other daughters. They'd all found love. Half of them were planning weddings while the other half were now raising their young children—his grandchildren.

"I can't imagine life getting any better," he said as Sarah joined him. He put an arm around her. Now he could admit that he'd been worried about election night. Maybe it was Sheriff Frank Curry's concern that The Prophecy or some other radical group was going to do something violent.

Frank had been right. It wasn't until later that the news was released about the bomb and one of the agents disarming it. Had news of the bomb come

out during his acceptance speech—he didn't want
to think about how many people could have been
injured trying to escape in a panic.

Buck had worried more about his family than he
had himself. And with good reason, as it turned out.
From what he'd been told, the man known as Joe
Landon had been trying to kill Sarah and then blow
them all into the next county. Fortunately, he'd been
stopped—but almost at the cost of Ainsley's life.

"Why Sarah?" Buck had asked those handling
the investigation.

"Joe Landon was a member of The Prophecy."

"So they were still trying to implicate Sarah, even
at the end." Buck had shaken his head. The sheriff
had said nothing.

Now the case was closed. Landon was dead. The
feds believed they had rounded up all of the old, as
well as the new, members of The Prophecy.

Buck breathed a sigh of relief and pulled Sarah
closer. For almost two years he'd struggled to trust
her again. Now, he could finally put those fears to
rest. He just wished it would be as easy to forget
about The Prophecy. Every time he turned around,
that name kept coming up.

Once the Feds began looking into Joe Landon's
crimes, they'd discovered he was responsible for
money that had been hacked from the Sarah Johnson Foundation. Buck had started the foundation to
help small businesses after he'd believed Sarah had
drowned in the river all those years ago. Bo had been

running it since college, but last year a large amount of money had gone missing.

When they'd realized that the accounts had been hacked, they'd never expected to see that money again. But the feds had tracked it to The Prophecy and thought they could get it all back for the foundation.

"A toast," Buck said, raising his glass. "To the Montana Hamiltons!"

Cheers rose and more congratulations. His daughters had thrown this party for them to celebrate their remarriage. Now the talk turned to the inaugural ball and Christmases in the White House.

It did his heart good to see the pleasure on his family's faces. Any doubts he had about being president were quickly forgotten. He could do anything with his family behind him and Sarah at his side. He couldn't wait to take office.

But first he would sweep Sarah away on a much-needed honeymoon. He'd wanted it to be a surprise, but his daughters had encouraged him to tell his wife, so she could take the clothes she would need.

"We aren't going far," Buck had told them. "Only as far as Chico Hot Springs. I've rented a special cabin."

His daughters had rolled their eyes. "A *cabin*?"

"You obviously don't know your mother," he'd said and realized how true that was of all of them. "She is going to love it." At least he hoped so.

"Uh, guys?"

Everyone looked toward Bo. "I think my water just broke."

FORMER SHERIFF FRANK CURRY stood out in front of the building along the main street of Big Timber, Montana, looking at his sign.

"How long are you going to stand here?" Nettie asked as she joined him.

He smiled over at her. "As long as I want."

Laughing, she entered Curry Investigations and put the plant she'd just bought on the corner of her desk next to the name plaque that read "Nettie Curry."

She heard the door behind her open. A gust of winter air rushed in, followed by her husband's footfalls. As she took her place behind her desk, she smiled at the handsome man she'd been in love with since she was a teen.

"We did it," Nettie said.

He nodded. "For better or worse."

"This isn't marriage."

"We'll see what you say after spending a few days in an office with me," he said as he walked over to his desk and sat down. His name plaque read: Frank Curry.

The phone rang. "Curry Investigations," she said into the phone.

FRANK SMILED AND leaned back into his chair. Outside, the winter sun was low in the sky. It had snowed the night before, leaving everything white. Christmas was coming and then a new year. He felt excited, full of anticipation for the future.

He had no idea if this crazy idea of his to be investigators would pan out or not. Maybe they would sit here five days a week, and the phone wouldn't ring again. Maybe within a week they'd be at each other's throats. Or maybe, just maybe, they would have one adventure after another as he hoped.

No matter what happened, he was ready for whatever the future held. He'd thought he would miss the sheriff's office more than he did. His undersheriff had stepped into the position until the election. He wished him well. But that life was behind him now.

"Please, hold the line a moment, and I'll let you speak with our lead investigator," Nettie said into the phone and put the caller on hold.

Her cheeks were flushed, her blue eyes bright and shiny. She smiled over at him and jiggled a little in her new office chair.

"I think we just got our first case," she said excitedly.

He felt a small thrill move through him as he picked up the phone, telling himself that everything was going to be just fine.

SAWYER STARED DOWN at the woman in his bed and lost the last little piece of his heart. "Well?" he asked. "Was it okay?"

Ainsley lay back in the bed and seemed to be trying to catch her breath. "It was…amazing. *You* were amazing. I had no idea what I was missing. But now that I do…"

He laughed softly as he spooned her to him. "Glad you waited?"

"Absolutely."

"I love you," he whispered next to her ear as he pulled her closer. He'd never felt like this before. He couldn't find words to describe it. But with Ainsley in his arms, he felt…complete.

"I love *you*," she said. "Do you realize how long I've waited for this?"

"I do. I hope it was worth the wait."

She laughed. "Are you fishing for more compliments?"

"I just want to be sure I did it right. I was under a lot of pressure, you know," he only half joked.

"Let me say this. I can't wait until we get to do that again."

He laughed and turned her to face him. "Well, my beautiful fiancée, I was only letting you catch your breath," he said. "I could make love to you all day." Then he kissed her.

AINSLEY MELTED INTO him in a heat of bliss. She couldn't believe she'd found true love. She pulled back from the kiss to cup Sawyer's handsome face and look into those gray eyes. That she got to make love with him the rest of their lives was icing on the cake.

They made love again. Sawyer had been so tender, taking her slowly and carefully the first time.

"Love me," she whispered. "Love me like you mean it."

His eyes lit as he let out a low chuckle. "You got it." This time he took her with all the longing and passion she'd seen in those beautiful gray eyes. He filled her, satiating her, and yet making her yearn for more. Just not for a while.

"I'm so happy for Bo and Jace," Ainsley said later to Sawyer after they had taken a break and gone in search of something to eat. Sawyer had moved into her condo on the ranch until his leg was completely healed. Then they were going to look for a house of their own, so they'd have a place to live after the wedding.

"Those two baby girls are so adorable," Sawyer said as he opened a jar of peach jam. "I can't wait until we start our family."

Ainsley grinned at him as she slapped peanut butter on a piece of bread and shoved it over to him for the jam. "Maybe we already have."

SARAH PICKED UP the newspaper, glanced at the headline, and tossed it aside in the large cabin at Chico Hot Springs. She was sick of reading about The Prophecy and was sure Buck was, too. Their soon-to-be son-in-law, Max Malone, had done a series on the anarchist group from its beginning back in the 1970s to its demise the night of the election.

The woman who'd confessed to being Red had died of cancer before her trial. Not that Max or Kat believed Virginia Handley had actually been the notorious Red. Because she'd been dying of cancer, they believed she'd taken a bullet, so to speak, for the real Red.

Max had made a point of telling her what the other members now in prison had said about Red. "They believe the real Red is alive and that she's gotten away with it all. If anything, they are convinced that she will now wreak havoc on the world. Their quotes make them look like lunatics."

"They still believe I'm Red," she'd said to Max after agreeing to meet him at the newspaper to discuss the story before it went to press.

"I'm afraid they aren't the only ones," Max said honestly. He and Kat had been investigating The Prophecy for months now. It was no secret that they believed Sarah was involved up to her eyeballs.

"I know Kat doesn't trust me," Sarah had said. "What about you?"

"The jury is out still," Max had said. "But you know both of us will be watching you."

She'd smiled. "Then I hope I make you both proud."

"Champagne?" Buck said now, drawing her out of her thoughts.

She turned to smile at her husband and take the glass he offered her. "This was a wonderful idea." Outside the cabin she knew there were a half dozen agents guarding them. They were safe—and finally alone. For months there'd been staff and media surrounding them. She and Buck had very little time alone when someone wasn't barging in—especially Buck's campaign manager, Jerrod.

But now Jerrod was in jail, awaiting trial for his involvement with The Prophecy. Buck had been shocked. Sarah knew she shouldn't have been surprised since Joe had been behind it.

But now here they were. Just the two of them. She'd insisted that even the agents keep their distance. "They don't have to be right outside the door, do they?"

Buck had agreed. "I'll have them stay far enough away that you won't even see them. How is that?"

"Perfect," she'd told him. "I just want you alone. Once we get to the White House…"

"This is our time. You can have whatever you want." He looked so handsome and distinguished. She could imagine his photo in the history books and felt a well of pride in this man she'd married.

"I have exactly what I want right here," she said, taking a sip of her champagne before putting down the glass and moving toward him. She slowly began to unbutton his shirt and, slipping it off, let it drop to the floor.

Her fingertips brushed over his flat stomach, his side, his back as she moved around him. She heard Buck chuckle.

"Is there something you want?" he asked as he

put down his glass, his back still to her. He'd told her that he loved it when she initiated.

"There's so much that I want," she said as he turned toward her. "I want you. I want us to make this country the best it can be."

He laughed as he pulled her to him. "With you by my side, that's exactly what we will do."

Sarah smiled. "It's all I've ever wanted. A better world for our children and grandchildren."

Dr. Venable had been right. Red's spark of passion for her country hadn't burned out. While those days of being that woman were behind her, she knew that Buck would lead this country in the best possible way. She couldn't imagine it ending any better.

* * * * *

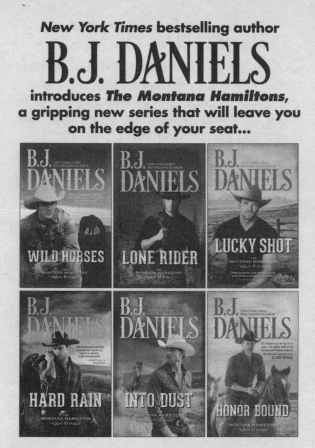

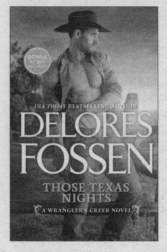

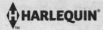

I N T R I G U E

EDGE-OF-YOUR-SEAT INTRIGUE, FEARLESS ROMANCE.

Save $1.00

on the purchase of

CARDWELL CHRISTMAS CRIME SCENE

by *New York Times* bestselling author

B.J. DANIELS,

available November 22, 2016,

or on any other Harlequin® Intrigue book.

Available wherever books are sold, including most bookstores, supermarkets, drugstores and discount stores.

- ✂

Save $1.00

on the purchase of any Harlequin Intrigue book.

Coupon valid until February 28, 2017. Redeemable at participating outlets in the U.S. and Canada only. Not redeemable at Barnes & Noble stores. Limit one coupon per customer

52614242

5 65373 00076 2   (8100)0 12215

REQUEST YOUR
FREE BOOKS!

2 FREE NOVELS
FROM THE ROMANCE COLLECTION,
PLUS 2 FREE GIFTS!

YES! Please send me 2 FREE novels from the Romance Collection and my 2 FREE gifts (gifts are worth about $10). After receiving them, if I don't wish to receive any more books, I can return the shipping statement marked "cancel." If I don't cancel, I will receive 4 brand-new novels every month and be billed just $6.49 per book in the U.S. or $6.99 per book in Canada. That's a savings of at least 18% off the cover price. It's quite a bargain! Shipping and handling is just 50¢ per book in the U.S. and 75¢ per book in Canada.* I understand that accepting the 2 free books and gifts places me under no obligation to buy anything. I can always return a shipment and cancel at any time. Even if I never buy another book, the two free books and gifts are mine to keep forever.

194/394 MDN GH4D

Name	(PLEASE PRINT)	
Address		Apt. #
City	State/Prov.	Zip/Postal Code

Signature (if under 18, a parent or guardian must sign)

Mail to the **Reader Service:**
IN U.S.A.: P.O. Box 1867, Buffalo, NY 14240-1867
IN CANADA: P.O. Box 609, Fort Erie, Ontario L2A 5X3

Want to try 2 free books from another line?
Call 1-800-873-8635 or visit www.ReaderService.com.

*Terms and prices subject to change without notice. Prices do not include applicable taxes. Sales tax applicable in N.Y. Canadian residents will be charged applicable taxes. Offer not valid in Quebec. This offer is limited to one order per household. Not valid for current subscribers to the Romance Collection or the Romance/Suspense Collection. All orders subject to credit approval. Credit or debit balances in a customer's account(s) may be offset by any other outstanding balance owed by or to the customer. Please allow 4 to 6 weeks for delivery. Offer available while quantities last.

Your Privacy—The Reader Service is committed to protecting your privacy. Our Privacy Policy is available online at www.ReaderService.com or upon request from the Reader Service.

We make a portion of our mailing list available to reputable third parties that offer products we believe may interest you. If you prefer that we not exchange your name with third parties, or if you wish to clarify or modify your communication preferences, please visit us at www.ReaderService.com/consumerschoice or write to us at Reader Service Preference Service, P.O. Box 9062, Buffalo, NY 14240-9062. Include your complete name and address.